HAIRCUTS FOR THE DEAD

A Novel

William Walsh

MERCER UNIVERSITY PRESS
Macon, Georgia

MUP/ P732

Published by Mercer University Press
1501 Mercer University Drive
Macon, Georgia 31207

29 28 27 26 25   5 4 3 2 1

Books published by Mercer University Press are printed on acid-free paper that meets the requirements of the American National Standard for Information Sciences—Permanence of Paper for Printed Library Materials.

Printed and bound in the United States.

This book is set in Adobe Caslon and Calibri.

Cover/jacket design by Burt&Burt.

ISBN 978-0-88146-975-2
Cataloging-in-Publication Data is available from the Library of Congress

HAIRCUTS FOR THE DEAD

Those fortunate enough to have read William Walsh's first novel, *Lakewood*, know he is a vital voice in contemporary fiction. Now with *Haircuts for the Dead* we can welcome a story addressing the most important concerns of our time: race, choice in sexual identity, the burdens of the past, and challenges to faith. Walsh portrays the elusive dynamics within families in this era of rapid change, as a story-within-a-story illuminates each. You will be moved by this novel of the search for a home and love, to be found in unexpected places.

—Robert Morgan, author of *Gap Creek*

In Hannah Gardner's search for both a place and a love that feel like home, William Walsh has given us a rollicking tale of a charming heroine healing an injured heart and conquering a small part of a great big world.

—Jessica Handler, author of *The Magnetic Girl*

William Walsh's second novel, *Haircuts for the Dead*, is just as original as its title implies. In it, Hannah writes her "Document of Life," sprinkled with the occasional Bible verse; her mother Lilith is unhappy; her father Darnell is abusive; and her brother Lucas is constantly on the run from Hawkshaw Bales who has impregnated Hannah. And finally, there's Margaret, the loving Black librarian who saves Hannah from it all just before a surprise ending. Indeed, Walsh is one of our most imaginative novelists ever—his every word is arresting—and I, for one, will eagerly read everything he writes.

—Rosemary Daniell, author of *Fatal Flowers: On Sin, Sex & Suicide in the Deep South*

Books by William Walsh

NOVELS

Lakewood

Haircuts for the Dead

POETRY

Fly Fishing in Times Square

Lost in the White Ruins

The Conscience of My Other Being

The Ordinary Life of a Sculptor

Under the Rock Umbrella: Contemporary American Poets from 1951–1977

ESSAYS

David Bottoms: Critical Essays and Interviews

Why I Wrote This Poem

NON-FICTION

Speak So I Shall Know Thee: Interviews with Southern Writers

Flannery O'Connor's Andalusia: Milledgeville and Its Influence on Her Fiction

To David Waehner,

Good friend and confidant,
who has heard every story and idea
and was there at the beginning of this novel.

MERCER UNIVERSITY PRESS

Endowed by

TOM WATSON BROWN
and
THE WATSON-BROWN FOUNDATION, INC.

Acknowledgments

I would like to thank the following people who have supported me in many ways over the years. Emilee Hendrix, an undergrad student, and Tyler Leon, a graduate student, at Reinhardt University, edited the novel as a requirement for their internship, and with a keen eye for grammar and logic, they did a remarkable job offering a critical analysis. Donna Little—thank you for the never-ending friendship you have offered over the years, as well as the tough editorial wisdom that pushed me to make some drastic changes. Without her edits, the novel would have suffered. Clayton Ramsey, a scholar and critic, saw this manuscript at the end and was a good steward who tended to the minute details and kept me from some embarrassing mistakes. To my friend of more than 35 years, Christopher Noel, who saw this novel in its infancy and provided the title—thank you for being my version of Maxwell Perkins. Madison Jones, one of the finest writers of his generation, provided invaluable advice many years ago when the first draft was completed. David Waehner, who for the past 42 years has cut my tangled mess of hair, gave me the idea for this novel one day at *David Salon* while I was in his chair. Our conversation was the impetus for this novel. Big thanks to Marc Jolley and his team for taking a chance on this unconventional story.

“Upon this rock I will build my church;
and the gates of hell shall not prevail against it.”

Matthew 16:18

Contents

Haircuts for the Dead

Chapter 1

The Fishing Trip

When Hannah Gardner was six years old, her father packed up his fishing gear and tossed everything in the back of his 1974 International Travelall, which he had purchased for $500 from a woman whose husband had a heart attack while cheering for Tiger Woods to win the Masters Tournament.

"My husband bought it brand new thirty-three years ago," she said, "and drove it nearly every day until his eyesight started failing last year."

Darnell Gardner bought the Travelall with the money Lilith had been saving for a new crown and to fill three cavities. He left seventeen dollars in her Mason jar high on a shelf in the cupboards.

"You survived this long with those cavities, an' look, a deal like this don't come around often. Waiting a little longer on the dentist ain't gonna make much difference."

"'Cept my teeth are falling out."

"If I don't buy it now, someone else will swoop in," Darnell explained.

For seven months Lilith had to chew on the right side of her mouth.

Darnell didn't care about golf, and normally not an ounce about taking the kids fishing, but he had won a raffle for a fishing derby in Ontario, New York, which was nearly a thousand miles away. The contest was an inserted scratch-off in *Today's Fishing Youth*, a sports magazine that caught his eye on the rack in K-Mart. The cover sported a twelve-year-old boy struggling to lift a fifty-two-pound Muskie he'd snagged on Chautauqua Lake.

The magazine called it "The Fish of 10,000 Casts," but this boy hit it on his third try, and when Darnell saw that cover, he began dreaming. Inside the magazine, he scratched off five squares that won a trip designed to promote fishing among young folks. The fishing derby was for kids, but it took Darnell about ten seconds to hatch a plan to catch a Muskie and give it to one of his kids to win the tournament and the top prize.

It took two days of driving, but Hannah's older brother and sister, Wendell and Greta, and her twin, Lucas, rode with their old man in that beat up Travelall, traveling north for the first time in their lives to Lake Ontario.

"It ain't much, but it's paid for," Darnell reminded his kids. "This here vehicle will run forever if you give it a little TLC. Don't never go into debt except to buy land."

On the account she was feeling puny, Hannah did not go fishing, never left the South, and she stayed home with her pregnant mother, who was set to birth her fifth child.

"I'm taking the kids to New York to this here fishing trip I won," Darnell informed Lilith. "If they catch a big enough fish, they'll win $25,000 and an invite back next year."

"How much is it gonna cost us?" Lilith asked.

"Nothing, except for gas and food. But if you make us enough sandwiches to last, it'll cost next to zero."

"What about a hotel?"

"Most of that's paid for by the fishing people, but I got it all planned out—on the way up, we're camping in a tent instead of paying for a hotel."

"What's that cost?"

"One night up. One night back. Six bucks each night, which ain't bad. It'll give Wendell an opportunity to show what he's learned in Boy Scouts and JROTC."

"We ain't got any money. I mean zero. Nothing," she told him.

"I got a little squirreled away for something like this. Not much."

"How about handing some of it over so I can buy groceries?"

They were gone for six days. Two days up. Two days of fishing. Two days back. Between his children, they caught over fifty bluegill and sun fish, a few channel cats, and loads of perch. Wendell caught a pike that was too small to keep. They never caught anything remotely close to a winner, no trophy fish, no prize money, and no invitation back next year.

When the news of Darnell's fishing trip whispered in Lilith's ears, she didn't complain or discourage him from heading out for New York because when he was a good twelve hours reach away, she had plans to call Myra Leonard, the midwife down the road about a mile. And that's exactly what she did that following Saturday morning.

"I'll come up 'round nine o'clock, me and Grady. It'll be dark by then."

Hannah had not felt good for several days leading up and did not venture forth on the fishing trip of a lifetime, as her daddy called it. Although she wanted to go, her nervous stomach made her ill when she got to thinking about her mother being pregnant and left alone all by herself on the farm. Hannah was protective, even for a six-year-old child, and she liked being by her mother's side. By Saturday, however, she felt better, and things were back to normal around the house, which was quiet for once in her life. At least her daddy wasn't hanging around drinking beer until he passed out or waiting to yell at someone for the slightest misstep, such as leaving the faucet dripping or not going to the driveway for his morning paper.

During the day, her mother played the radio low on an oldies station, and that made Hannah happy because Lilith sang along with the music.

"Sweetie, this is how I lived before I got married, singing and sashaying around."

"Momma, I ain't never getting married."

"Oh, you will."

"Not to no one like Daddy."

The morning was cool, and the doors were open, and a breeze cut through the entire farmhouse, as if Lilith was blowing old ghosts out of the woodwork. The wind was tickling in from the front door and windows and taking everything ugly in their lives right out the back door and into the woods and beyond the tree line and gone forever, or at least until Darnell returned.

That evening, around eight o'clock, Lilith cleared the kitchen table of everything. She moved the fruit bowl and schoolbooks to the hutch so when Myra and Grady arrived everything was ready. She grabbed a pillow from her bed and placed it on the kitchen table. They appeared precisely at nine p.m. when the sun was below the trees and cast a pinkish-purple hue across the pasture and the sky had less than twenty minutes of fading light. They walked the half-mile from their house to Hannah's because they did not want anyone seeing their truck parked at the Gardners' farm. When they walked into the living room, Hannah stared because it was the only time she'd seen a Black person in their house.

After she guided Myra into the kitchen, Lilith climbed upon the large wooden table. She adjusted the pillow under her head and the crook of her neck. Grady stood in the kitchen waiting to help Myra.

"Hannah," Lilith said nervously and out of breath already, "you go sit in the other room and turn on the TV. You can watch anything you like. Turn it up so I can hear, but you gotta stay in there."

Lilith would have preferred that Hannah not be at the house, but she had no other choice. With Darnell gone, it was now or never to take care of this business.

In the kitchen, Myra set her bag down on the counter and pulled out several glass jars of herbs and placed them near the stove. She opened each jar and sniffed them for freshness. She had a large Mason jar of moonshine, which she poured into a sauce pan then mixed in cohosh, cotton root bark, and other spices before stirring the concoction with a wooden spoon.

"Miss Lilith, I'm gonna heat up this hooch with some excitements. It'll be hot but I ain't burning off the fun. You gotta drink it all straight down. It'll make you cork high and bottle deep but we ain't got days to take care of bizness."

When the blend was heated up, Myra filtered it through her scarf into a large coffee mug.

"Sit up," Myra told Lilith. "Hold your nose. This is nasty tasting."

She did, and she drank the hot liquid straight down. It nearly made her vomit. Then she drank round two, which was all she needed to get tanked. When she could barely sit up, Grady leaned her back on the table and placed her head on the pillow.

"We about ready?" he asked Myra.

"I think so."

"When you need to grab something, grab the edge of the table. It'll give you balance and pressure," Grady told Lilith.

From in the living room, Hannah turned down the volume, and when she couldn't hear clearly enough, she walked into the kitchen and stood watching. Myra and Grady were too busy to bother with Hannah and ignored her, if they had even noticed her standing there.

Lilith wore an old night gown that if it was ruined in the procedure would not be missed and could easily be burned or tossed out. When Grady had her head comfortably situated, he pulled the nightgown off Lilith's shoulders and down below her breasts. He began to massage her nipples then pulled down on them to simulate a baby suckling. He'd done this before, many other times to help Myra induce labor. On its own, it wasn't enough, but coupled with the moonshine and spices, and with Myra's other work, this was their plan.

As Grady firmly pulled on Lilith's nipples with his thumb and two fingers, milk dripped and sprayed across her stomach and rolled off her roundness and puddled on the table. While he continued, Myra lifted the daisy-flowered gown up to Lilith's stomach. Myra then began to sweep her index finger around the inside of Lilith's cervix then raised two fingers up and down and in a circular motion over and over to pull the membranes away from the inner cervix.

Hannah sat on the kitchen floor watching from fifteen feet away at what she did not understand except it had to do with her momma's baby. The river stones were cold on the soles of her feet. She grabbed a blanket off her bed and wrapped up in swaddling and continued to watch and listen to her mother's moaning. After an hour, Hannah fell asleep on the cold floor.

Around three in the morning, Hannah was woken by the sound of a baby crying. She jumped up on the kitchen floor and dropped her blanket around her ankles then dashed over to see her baby sister. It was supposed to be another boy.

"What'cha gonna name her, Momma?"

Her mother squeaked out a reply in Hannah's ear.

"Child, step back," Myra said. "There's blood and nastiness you don't ever want to get into."

Myra held the baby in her left arm and brushed the dark strands of hair off the baby's forehead into a wisp that stood up with the gelatin of birth.

"Grady, cover Miss Lilith's ears."

As the baby cried for oxygen in the new world, Myra walked into the kitchen, held the child by her ankles up over her head, up to the height of the cabinets and close to the ceiling, and without hesitation, released the baby. The newborn fell straight down, hitting her head on the stone floor. There was a thunk, then silence.

"Girl, hand me that blanket," she told Hannah.

Hannah gave the blanket to Myra. She placed the baby on the blanket and wrapped her up, folding and folding the blanket until every notion of the baby was covered in a protective cocoon. Myra stood up and handed the bundle to Grady.

"You go do your bizness and I'll get her in bed and this place cleaned up."

"Come with me," Grady told Hannah. "I want you to carry that shovel." He pointed to a small garden shovel near a rucksack.

With a flashlight in hand, Grady set out through the dark woods with Hannah following behind. He showed her how to carry the shovel across her shoulder.

"When it gets sore, switch shoulders," he said.

"Kinda like Jesus?"

"Yeah, something like that."

The Gardner family farm was nearly six hundred acres, and after walking around for thirty minutes and over mounds and up hills and across the creek and then over a flat parcel, Hannah had no idea where they were. For all she knew, they might have been in the next county. But then Grady stopped and set the bundle on the ground. He traded the flashlight for the shovel.

"Aim that light right here," he directed Hannah, and she did. Then he began to dig.

"What's this place?" Hannah asked him.

"Some place you don't want to be. My mammie and pappy live here."

"Where? There ain't no house."

"They live in the ground."

It wasn't a large hole, only one-foot wide by two feet, and no more than three-feet deep when he set the bundle into the hole and filled it back in. He stamped the dirt as flat as he could with his work boots then brushed the ground with a leafy stick and covered the area with leaves and a few rocks. Hannah noticed that the three rocks were each about the size of a football.

When he was assured his job was done, Grady turned toward Hannah and bent down on his right knee. He took the flashlight from her and shined it at his open hand. The light bounced off toward Hannah's face. "You ever tell anyone about this, I'll toss you in there with that baby. You understand?"

Hannah shook her head.

"You best forget this ever happened. You wanna tell someone, tell it to God."

"How come you're putting the baby in the ground?"

"Sometimes child, this is what love looks like."

When Darnell and the kids returned home a few days later from the fishing trip, he looked at Lilith and said, "You sure slimmed down."

"I had the baby. He came early."

"Where's my little Stonewall Jackson Beauregard? Where's he hiding?"

"He was stillborn. I lost him."

"What do you mean, you lost 'im. What'd you do, leave him at the Piggly Wiggly checkout?"

"No. I went into labor while you were fishing. He was stillborn."

"What the hell'd you do with him?"

"I called the county, and they came and got him. They took him away."

"Who came to the house?"

"I don't remember their names. A guy and a woman. It didn't take them but about fifteen minutes to get here but by then the baby had arrived. Just popped out."

"Well, shit-fire, Lilith, I'd think you'd remember the names of the folks who helped you deliver our baby."

"They didn't help with nothing. They arrived after the fact. Besides, I had other things on my mind—not writing down names. Givin' birth is like squeezing out a piano sideways. You ought to try it some time."

"We gonna have a funeral or sumptin?"

"Ain't no money. Those folks said they'd take care of things for us."

"Well, when you're up to it, we can try again."

"Give me about ten years before you start looking sweet at me. Maybe twenty. And for your information, Mr. Big Fisherman, there ain't no way in hell I was naming our baby Stonewall Jackson Beauregard Gardner."

"I was gonna call him Bo."

"Why don't you just name him after the Grand Wizard. All your ideas are nothing more than buffoonery."

The baby girl Darnell believed was a baby boy was never discussed again. However, Hannah could not forget, and every day, she thought about what Mr. Grady told her. She remembered the way the grass smelled and the coolness of the air at three o'clock in the morning, and how for the longest time she was afraid to walk through the woods and pastures, especially at night, for fear the baby might come at her, crawling like a spider monkey in a horror film or something worse. Each Sunday at church, she always said a prayer for her baby sister.

During the past fifteen years, Hannah overcame her fears and set out on many adventures looking for the three rocks Mr. Grady placed on the baby's grave. She wanted to lay flowers on it and talk to her. At times, she took Lucas with her, although he never knew her real intentions. She looked for the graves of Mr. Grady's mother and father, who were sharecroppers on the land for most of their life, and before that, their kinfolk were also sharecroppers, and she heard stories that long ago, their people were slaves. Hannah knew some were buried on the farm, but she never found the graves. As she grew older, she set out late some nights when the sky was clear with just a flashlight and her dog. She looked for that same night smell of grass and air, and there were times when she found it, but never the graves. In the end, she figured Mr. Grady had taken her so far back into the wilderness, they were on someone else's property.

Maybe they'll dig everyone up some day when they build a shopping center out here.

It was a secret Hannah has kept her entire life, and even after Myra and Grady died years apart from one another, she never said a word. Grady died first when Hannah was in the fifth grade, and when she was in the tenth grade, Myra died. Hannah thought she'd learn where the baby was buried if Grady and Myra were buried with their family on her farm, but they were not. They were buried in Antioch, at the AME Church they attended.

Not long after Myra was buried, Hannah wondered if they were both in hell together. Perhaps, God forgave them because what they did helped her mother. She had conjured up all sorts of thoughts and ideas over the years, and many times at night, she woke to stare out her bedroom window, deep into the black trees wondering where her baby sister was buried and maybe she almost found the grave or walked by it without recognizing the rocks. That was all she had to go on. She would stare out the window for a few minutes, but the image of the baby crawling out from between two trees scared her.

One day, she asked her history teacher, Mr. Winkleman, if archeologists ever give up looking.

"I mean, years can go by, and they don't find what they've been searching for—don't they just give up?"

"Sometimes they retire or stop searching for the Holy Grail," he told the class. "But often, Hannah, it's because they run out of money—you know, funding for their project. Their resources dry up. Other times, well, they just can't keep searching. Not everything in this world is meant to be discovered."

Chapter 2

Original Sin is Just a Trick on Idiots

Hannah Gardner, at twenty-one years old, had grown to be one who sought the truth in all things. She was a pursuer of answers, a yearner, and as she searched, she believed the answers she found in the real world contradicted what she had learned growing up on her family farm and in her Baptist church. She did not care what the truth was, just as long as it was the actual truth, which she knew she could handle.

Just give it to me straight, she thought.

Her religious conviction ended one Sunday after services during an argument with the preacher's wife as they stood outside the church doors, under a portico.

"When I look at such a beautiful baby you have in your stroller, I cannot imagine the validity of Original Sin," she said.

"Hannah, that's blasphemy," Laney replied.

"How can it be their fault for being born?" Hannah asked. "What kind of God would condemn a baby to Hell for being born?"

"A true and just God," Laney said. She moved the stroller back and forth like a cradle on wheels and shook her head in disbelief of what she heard.

"There ain't no justice in being born just to be condemned."

"It's so your soul can be redeemed," Laney insisted.

"Why bother at all? Just be redeemed from the get-go. Why do we have to be redeemed? Can't a person be ready for Heaven simply because God loves them?"

"Why do you gotta be like this, always questioning the Word of God?" Laney scowled.

"Why does God want us to be redeemed? Can't He just get over it? If we never sinned, there wouldn't be a need for redemption. It ain't that complicated."

"Look, I'm not gonna argue about this," Laney growled.

"Ain't He supposed to embrace us unconditionally?" Hannah asked.

"Not with that kind of attitude."

"It ain't nothing but jealousy, and that's a fallacy, and if God has a fallacy, then He cannot be perfect, and, if He's not perfect, He can't be God and save my soul and the soul of everyone else. And for that matter, I think the Virgin Birth is a lot of hooey."

"Hannah Gardner, that's blasphemy," Preacher Towns said.

The congregation stood in the doorway drinking lemonade and watching to see if the sun would break through the clouds, but most bent an ear to hear their disagreement.

"Where do you hear such garbage?" he asked her.

"Around," she replied.

"The Virgin Birth gives us the Lord," Preacher Towns said.

"Did you know that hundreds of ancient cultures had the Virgin Birth long before Christians stole it for their own use?"

"Where'd you hear this nonsense?" Preacher Towns asked.

"I read a book about myths."

"That's exactly right. All of that's myth. It's some non-believer's made-up gobbledygook trying to pull you into the devil's den."

"The man who wrote that particular book is named Joseph Campbell."

"I don't care who he is."

"You can check it out at the library," she told him.

"Original Sin is a gift from God so that when we die, He can forgive you and allow you to enter His Kingdom," the preacher said shaking his finger at Hannah, which irritated her because she didn't like being scolded.

"Can't He forgive us now, or better, when we were born?"

"No, it must be earned," the preacher told her.

"Like I said, why bother? Why can't we just be redeemed and be done with it?"

"God needs to forgive your sins in order to open the gates to Heaven."

"My point is this—why can't He allow me to walk up and be welcomed with open arms unconditionally?"

"It doesn't work that way," Preacher Towns said. "We need Original Sin to ensure our redemption."

"Didn't God give us the power to question Him?" Hannah asked.

"No, He did not," he said. "Not in that manner."

Laney shook her head in disbelief at Hannah's blasphemous comments. She looked at her husband before reaching out to hug Hannah for she recognized how lost she was. But Hannah pushed Laney's arm away and shrugged her shoulder in the opposite direction.

"Your momma and daddy did not raise you to think like this," Preacher Towns said.

"You see this?" Hannah removed a newspaper article from her small purse and held it up to Laney, then to her husband.

"A woman in Detroit cut off her husband's privates. She caught him in bed with her sister. Her sister, of all people!"

The preacher looked at the article and read the headline then the opening paragraph before handing it back to Hannah.

"What's that got to do with Original Sin?" Laney asked.

"When something like this happens, what's there for a person to believe in? Why not just sleep with his own momma?"

"Hannah, I don't know where you get this stuff, but you ought to give more reverence to the Word of God and have faith in all He has planned for you," the preacher said.

"Original Sin is nothing more than a trick on idiots—like yourself. You just want someone to control your life. If Original Sin never existed, no one would be compelled to ever believe in anything. No one would go to church, and no one would give a dime in the tithes."

"Hannah, would you like to attend Tuesday morning prayer for women?" Laney asked her.

"No thank you. I'm pretty much over this stuff. Let me tell you what I would've planned for this man if I'd caught him sleeping with my sister."

She waved the newspaper article out in front of herself.

"I'd wait until he's asleep, then tie his feet and legs together with a mile of rope, strap the rope to the back of the car and drag him right out of the house and down the street. What do you think would go through a man's mind as he flopped out of bed and began banging into the walls and doorjambs, reaching out, grabbing onto the leg of a coffee table? That's the kind of message God should send to a man who sleeps with his wife's sister."

That pretty much ended Hannah's association with the Sundown Victory Baptist Church. She had not said anything to her mother or father regarding her recent wonderments about God and the church and Original Sin but figured word got around to her daddy at least because he called and left her a message, "I heard you pissed off the preacher yesterday. You got something on your mind?"

§

Since I was a little girl, I knew my momma and daddy would get divorced because of the nasty ways Daddy treated her. He could say the meanest things in the world. One minute he'd be laughing and telling a funny story and walking with you through the high grass, pointing out pretty things like flowers and telling you wonderful facts about the different sounds frogs make and why spiders let their prey get tired in the web before pouncing on them. The next minute he was hell-bent for leather.

"Who cooked this crap?"

"You used to be rather fine-looking in your day, but now your caboose sags like a ten-pound bag of potatoes."

"For having a tenth-grade education, you sure are stupid."

The tongue is a small thing, but what enormous damage it can do.—James 3:5

First thing, Momma graduated from high school in Somerset, KY. She has more schooling than Daddy. She at least graduated from high school. There will be many more things that I'll set the record straight on. That's just one.

There were occasions when Daddy was nice to Momma, but they were scattered like good deeds in Hell. She would just stand there and take his abuse, yelling in her face like a drill sergeant, telling her that she couldn't cook, and dinner stank, and that she needed to do something with herself, fix up her ugly puss. She would stand in front of the window at the kitchen sink and cry while washing dishes, her tears falling into the suds. When they were living with us, Poppa Raymond and Memaw never said a word, just let Daddy be, maybe out of fear of being homeless or worried he'd move their bed to the dog pen or an old folks' home.

I should mention that for a time, Poppa Raymond and Memaw lived with us for a few years, from when I was in the seventh grade until tenth. Then, they up and decided to live in a small cabin in French Creek, which Daddy said was an ancient Cherokee word for smelly trailer park.

I would hug Momma and say, "Things won't always be this way." I would help her dry the dishes. At night, Daddy sat in front of his little black and white TV, drinking a few beers, and yelling out, "How about making me some popcorn?" Momma or one of us kids would do it, but he was never satisfied. Never a "Thank you, Lilith." It was always, "There's too much salt on this. There's not enough salt. You know I like a lot of butter. Get me another beer. The G-D dog's in the house." Momma would go into the bedroom and lay down. I would curl up with her and listen to her heart beating, and I knew one day while we were curled up, it would stop being broken about once an hour, 24/7.

Momma had surgery once, a double by-pass to repair her malfunctioning heart. When the doctors said she needed surgery, Daddy got a job for three months working nights at The Butler Did It Cleaners. He cleaned offices five nights a week because they had health insurance for the whole family. The day after Momma's surgery, Daddy quit. I will say this, when Momma was in bed recuperating, Daddy was not as mean as before, and he kept the TV turned down low. He and Lucas also hooked it up in the bedroom so Momma could watch in bed. At Rent-A-Center, he rented a color TV for her. Lucas and Daddy somehow stole the satellite signal.

You husbands must love your wives and never treat them harshly.—Colossians 3:19

There were evenings when our whole family sat on the front porch or on the flat rock by the pond, and Daddy'd strum the guitar that Aunt Mavis bought him before he went into the Army. When I was just a little girl, no more than three or four, I remember the porch being newly painted white and smelling fresh and feeling sort of sticky to the touch even though it was thoroughly dry. Momma sat in a rocking chair snapping beans or knitting, and Daddy would ask her to name a song, and if he knew it, he'd play it. If not, he said, "Name another one, Darling."

Back then, the road in front of our house was an oily mixture of gravel and sand. When the county road crew of prisoners came by one year, Lucas and I sat out by the road in the middle of the summer, watching the prison gang drop down a layer of hot tar and cinders. We became friends with them, and each one of those men knew us by name, and we knew their names by the end of the day. My favorite was a short Black guy named Andy. He was funny and kept getting yelled at by the guard. We brought them water and crackers to eat. Not one of them was cross with us, and for three days we followed the crew down the road until they were finished.

There were times when Momma and Daddy hated each other and were after each other like fire eating up dry grass, and by the time they got divorced, the road was paved like a real city street with asphalt. It was hate. They hated each other. They hated everything about the other person.

There was no more burning your bare feet in the summer when you walked on bubbling tar and no more mineral spirits at night to clean the tar from your heel. When they laid down the asphalt, it was just a few men in a big asphalt-laying machine the size of a combine. Few people travel on Old Damascus Road these days. It's just an old country road that leads to a past no one cares about.

And a broken-down farm.

When my family sat on the front porch, we would hear the cars from way far off, long before we saw them, sounding like geese flying by. But once the asphalt was laid down, the cars slunk around like a wild cat, and you wouldn't hear a car or truck until it was almost in the front yard, just a sort of whine coming off the road, unless one didn't have a muffler.

Daddy would tell some corny jokes like, "What do you call a deer with no eyes? I have no i-dear."

I always knew the evening was coming to an end when Daddy played Amazing Grace, plucking each string on his guitar so the notes vibrated like an angel crying, and they were spaced a second apart.

"Alright, you kids," Momma would say, "it's time for bed. Give your daddy a kiss good night, brush your teeth, go pee, and don't make me come in there with a wooden spoon and spank you."

It was days and nights like that when I felt secure and warm and thought that maybe we had a normal family and my momma and daddy loved each other and that if the world was different, they'd be different, too, and we would have nice things, and I wouldn't have to wear the same pair of blue jeans to school three days in a row then trade with Lucas and wear his jeans. We did that until I was about thirteen and grew taller than him.

I always knew if I ever had any money, I was going to buy some nice clothes and never wear the same clothes twice in the same week.

Right now, I'm lying on my back on our porch, shining my

phone light to the porch ceiling, looking at the rusted hooks that once held our porch swing. The hooks used to be black. I watched the entire series of The Queen's Gambit with Margaret, and it would be a Godsend if like Beth Harmon's chess pieces moving on the ceiling, a map would appear on the porch ceiling showing me the directions to the baby's grave.

Throughout our childhood, when we weren't swimming in the pond, Lucas and I were riding our bicycles to town and looking in trashcans and dumpsters for soda bottles. I never liked getting into the big dumpsters, but if I saw a bottle, Lucas would climb in for me so long as I split the money.

One day while riding our bicycles, Lucas and I went by the back of Kroger where the deliveries were made and noticed that they put the soda bottles back there. We carried as many of those bottles as we could into the store and redeemed enough money to go to McDonald's for a Happy Meal, but then on our third attempt, we got caught. The manager made us haul grocery carts up from the parking lot for two hours, but then he gave us each a Moon Pie and a soda for our hard work. I had an Orange Crush. Lucas had a root beer.

"When you two get older, I'll give you a real job, and you can make some money. Young man, you can stock shelves, and as for you, young lady, you can work as a cashier. If I ever see you stealing from me again, I'll call the sheriff."

On most evenings, like this one, the sun would cast a soft glow down over the farm that stretched across the pond. Daddy's great-grandfather, Poppa Charles, who I never met, raised his dairy cows after the Civil War, and he dug that pond with some of his workers. The way Daddy claims, you'd have thought our kin drew up the plans to whack Lincoln in Ford's Theatre.

Somewhere along the way, they sold off the cattle and switched to raising dogs 'cause the women and children could handle dogs if the men were off fighting a war. They raised any kind of dog they could sell, but mainly hunting dogs 'cause they sold higher. The different dogs were kept in separate runs to keep from mix-breeding, but when Daddy was a boy, a tornado came through and hit the town and our farm, blowing down fences, gates, trees, and road signs. It didn't hit the house or barn, but a slew of trees was uprooted to give them enough firewood for ten years. Three dogs were killed, and Poppa Raymond never found his old mule. There was a rumor that a mule ended up in someone's swimming pool in town, but no one in Daddy's family laid claim.

"We didn't tell anyone we were missing a mule," Daddy said. "Folks surely would charge to haul away your dead mule from their swimming pool."

It's late. I need to go home. My hand hurts from writing. I wish I could open the front door and go to my room and just be in my house. That's all I want in life this evening.

§

From the back of the Susan Kendal Memorial Library, in a wood cubicle, Hannah flipped through the yellow pages of her tablet. She'd been writing for several weeks, and now, on the first page of her tablet, she wrote a title across the top: DOCUMENT OF LIFE.

Finally, she thought. *I got a title for this thing.*

This is what she was looking for while sitting on a hard wooden chair with angles of sun casting through the blinds and across the desk—an idea, a guiding vision to organize what she wanted to write. Hannah was excited about her prospects for a Document of Life, which sounded like something important, like a person's medical records.

"You got a wandering eye," Hannah wrote on a yellow tablet, "watch how far I can wander out of your life. I'll be as sneaky as a rat walking on a towline down by the wharf."

The Eleventh Commandment should be: Thou shalt
have permission to kill your man if he's cheating on
you or treating you like a caged dog.

The week Hannah became a hairstylist, when she was nineteen, and knowing she was likely to meet a lot of men who needed a haircut, her mother sat on the front porch in a rocking chair giving Hannah some advice. "If your husband has a wandering eye, poke it out. Set him straight. He gets one chance to change. If he has a wandering of desire, then break the man in two pieces. Otherwise, you'll forever live with what has already been lived by scores of women before you. Men don't change. Men are dogs. Dump him. Find someone new. If he slaps you, hit him with a baseball bat. If he hits you with a baseball bat, run 'im over with a Mack truck. I give you this advice because no one gave it to me."

It was nearly four o'clock, just about the time when the head librarian leaves for the day. Ilene was a woman so uptight that if she were a clock, every spring would snap. Hannah didn't like Ilene too much because each time someone asked her a question, she reacted like it was an inconvenience and the person was ignorant not to already know the answer or where to find it. Hannah avoided asking Ilene anything. She always asked Margaret instead, because Ilene made her feel stupid.

Hannah thought, *Ilene's the stupid one! Margaret's nice to everyone.*

Ilene was always barking orders: "Margaret, are those books shelved yet? Margaret, do we have any pencils? Margaret, is my butt screwed on tight enough?"

Hannah once asked Margaret if she thought Ilene looked like a bulldog with her under-bite jutting out. Margaret got to laughing so hard, Ilene hobbled out from her desk to stop the cheerfulness. That was a rare event for Ilene, as she usually stayed behind the desk. She only rose when it was necessary to bark out orders because of her prosthetic leg. Ilene had lost her left leg when her former, and now dead, boyfriend, Gary Carlson, crashed his motorcycle into the back of a semi-truck nine years ago. Ilene and Gary were riding his Harley down I-400 from Dahlonega when the traffic slammed to a halt and the motorcycle rammed sideways into the back of a semi. Ilene bounced twenty feet away into traffic, where cars and trucks slammed on their brakes to avoid hitting her. She sat up and saw her left leg in the middle of the road, with her tennis shoe still attached.

"What's my leg doing over there?" she asked herself, seeing her severed leg before looking down at her shorts to see her left knee gushing blood. Then she passed out.

Her boyfriend Gary didn't die in that accident. He died while hiking in the Tombigbee National Forest, alone, when a piece of candy lodged in his throat, and he choked. He'd been dead about two hours when hikers found him.

Hannah called Ilene "Elvis," as in "Has Elvis left the building?" If she was gone, Margaret replied, "Elvis has left the building," or "Still singing the blues."

While waiting for Ilene to leave, Hannah stood in the entranceway of the library reading the pin-ups on the bulletin board. One caught her eye.

Needed: Experienced Stylist to give Haircuts to the Dead
Contact: Mr. Guy Fox, Grattan's Funeral Home
$65 per haircut for women
$45 per haircut for men

Hannah pulled the note off the board so no one else would see it and get the job before her. Hannah stepped outside the library, called the number, and spoke to a woman who stated that Mr. Fox was not in, but he would be back tomorrow.

"Sometimes you can cut all of them on one day. It depends on when people die."

"Do I have to touch dead people?"

"You can wear gloves, like a surgeon."

The idea gave Hannah the creeps, but the money was too good not to consider.

Who would complain if I did a terrible job? Hannah thought.

"Don't worry. We'll help you until you're comfortable. Then, you'll be knocking them out without thinking about it. Our other stylist moved to Seattle."

"When would I need to cut hair?"

"It's almost always at night, after regular hours, but it depends on each family's wishes and when the funeral's scheduled."

"I work during the day."

"All you have to do is make certain the haircut's finished before the viewing. We sometimes deviate from that if a person must be buried the next day. But, as a general rule, you'll have a few days."

As soon as Ilene left the building, Hannah asked Margaret if she could type her *Document of Life* on the MacBook in the back office. The computers in the library had a thirty-minute limit for research, and there were already two high school kids using them and others on the sign-up sheet. Hannah didn't want to wait that long since she had a lot of material and knew she needed a few days of computer time to type up all the pages from her tablet. It was against the rules for Hannah to use the office Mac, but Margaret didn't see any harm since Elvis was gone for the day.

For weeks, Hannah had been writing notes. She had over thirty pages of hand-written notes she wanted to type and save on a thumb drive, and now that she had a title, it gave her writing a real purpose and motivated her.

"I don't want to lose my notes," she told Margaret.

Although she had talked to Margaret about living on a farm, Hannah had not yet taken her over. She was embarrassed she'd look like a redneck for having grown up killing hogs, weeding the garden, and picking apples off the ground to make cider. Hannah dreaded the day when she'd have to introduce Margaret to anyone in her family.

Hannah's life was divided between Antioch, Hebron, and Sundown, and she preferred to keep Margaret out of Sundown, because of its history of beating Black people if they are in town after dark. Even if those were rumors or a soiled history of bygone days, the worry stuck in the back of her mind.

"Where'd your family move to after they sold the farm?" Margaret asked Hannah.

"Lucas moved to California with his friends, Greg and Johnny, to strike it rich panning for gold. Lucas read that only about ten percent of the gold was taken out of the ground in California during the gold rush."

"I've read about that, too," Margaret replied.

Hannah and her mother knew Lucas was too restless to work at O'Connell's Worm Farm and Cricket Hatchery in the outskirts of Hebron, and he managed to hold that job for six months before he and his friends hatched a plan to pan for gold.

"My momma said they shot themselves out of a cannon, like redneck beatniks. Momma and I were in the kitchen baking a blueberry pie from the wild blueberries I'd found in a field nearby, talking about how nice it would be for Lucas to strike it rich. She said she always liked the idea of panning for gold and finding a nugget the size of a basketball. Lucas and his friends didn't give two shakes of a thought about it and then Lucas lasted less than a year before coming back to Georgia."

"What about everyone else?" Margaret asked.

"Greta's in Hollywood. Wendell's in the Army over in the Middle East or Europe. Daddy lives in Hebron, and Momma lives on Lake Lanier. Once the farm was sold, we scattered to the winds."

Over the months they had been friends, Hannah had many wonderful conversations with Margaret about life, going back to school, working hard, saving money, and not going into debt, and many of their talks were so personal in nature, it made Hannah feel as though she had a best friend, so much so that she told Margaret some of the rotten things her father had said or done to everyone in her family.

"When I was twelve, we drove to Kentucky for a wedding on my momma's side of the family, a cousin. Well, there was this wishing well where everyone tossed in cash or a Hallmark card with money in it. Patty and Sherman had been living together so they didn't need nothing like a toaster or an electric cutting knife for the Thanksgiving turkey, just cash 'cause Patty was five months preggo. During the nuptials, my daddy slipped out to use the toilet. Funny, all that money disappeared. Some folks accused him, but he denied it. I can't say for certain, but I think he stole the loot. When we returned home, he bought a new backhoe and paid cash. With that new equipment, he did odd jobs and was paid under the table. That ain't all—six months later, Momma's Aunt DeeDee died and when we went up for that, she had requested they play 'What a Friend We Have in Jesus' during her funeral. Daddy got involved in what was none of his business and told the funeral director that under no circumstance was she to play that song or 'Amazing Grace,' which was the other song Aunt DeeDee wanted. About half-way home when we were in the Smokey Mountains, Daddy just started laughing and said he got the woman to play 'Another One Bites the Dust' and 'Ding Dong the Witch Is Dead.' He paid her a hundred bucks but since they were instrumental versions, no one got too upset. A little bit. It could have been worse, I suppose."

"No way. Who has the balls to do that?"

"My old man. Word filtered down that she got fired, and of course, no one was talking to our family. 'That'll show the old bag,' he told us. See, that's why I ain't never introduced you to no one in my family."

Chapter 3

BMF is the Name, Farming is My Game

When he was back living in Georgia, Hannah visited her twin brother, Lucas, about once every two weeks just to check up on him, but never invited Margaret to go along and see his forty-two-year-old worn-down heap of a mobile home with window cracks repaired with duct tape, indoor plumbing that functioned with the consistency of a British sports car, and threadbare carpet, which was worn down to the particleboard. Lucas nailed down any spot that was buckling up or splitting with stolen road signs: Stop, Yield, Do Not Enter, and a 70 m.p.h. speed limit sign, which was in front of his bedroom door "for obvious reasons," Lucas said.

Prior to moving in, no one had lived in his trailer for eight years. There was no electricity, so he, Johnny, and Greg tapped into the power line and hooked up for free. All Lucas needed was enough power to run the television, the electric water heater, and an occasional light. He didn't use much electricity, so it went undetected. With no way to dispose of the water they used, the boys stole PVC pipes from a construction site and rigged the pipes to move the water from the toilet, bath, kitchen sink, and washing machine to a ditch they cut out near the dirt road.

"Just like the Romans," Lucas told her.

Every few weeks, a good gulley-washer took everything out to the Yellow River.

When they set out for the gold mountains of California, they left all their things in the trailer.

"Ain't none of it worth hauling out west," Greg said.

A year later, when Lucas returned, it was unoccupied, so he moved back in, and except for the dust, he found everything looking as if he'd never left. Lucas was told by a local man in California that the easy gold was all gone.

"All the hard gold is still in the ground," the man said. "Back in forty-nine, they took what was simple. Sure, there's still gold there, but it's deep in the ground. If you want it, you'd better start digging, boys."

Lucas had no patience for prospecting.

I got something you can search for. There's more than gold at our farm—there's a history of rottenness no one wants dug up.

Two years ago, Hannah dropped her yearbook in the bathtub and ruined it, and now she wanted to borrow Lucas's senior yearbook to show Margaret, but when she arrived at his trailer, he wasn't home. While rifling through his junk looking for her yearbook, a car pulled up. As the car came to a stop, a Bible verse entered her mind. She grabbed a small piece of paper from her purse.

When your endurance is fully developed, you will be strong in character and ready for anything.—James 1:4

Hannah stepped outside onto the porch to see a gold Lexus parked on the gravel driveway with a Black man sitting behind the wheel. She noticed the personalized plate in front, *BMF*, in glittered letters. He kept the car running and walked up to Hannah standing on the porch hovering a few feet over the man. He was dressed in casual clothes, as if on his way to play golf, which was a clean-cut look she liked to see on men. Hannah wore plaid shorts, a white top, and carried a small, red purse on a spaghetti strap that matched her shorts.

"How you doing today?" he asked.

Hannah did not answer.

"You know the guy who lives here?" the man asked.

"He's my brother."

"You live here?"

"No."

"Your brother owes me ten thousand dollars, and I'm here to collect."

"Lucas doesn't have ten dollars to his name, let alone ten thousand. Take a look around. See that beat-up Oldsmobile? That's all he owns, an' it doesn't run. He's got some lawn mower parts. See all those washing machines and dryers?"

She pointed to a field of high grass behind the trailer, where about one hundred white boxes were shielded by the tall wheat-colored straw. "Those are his, too. Take all you need."

"Sorry, Missy, he lost it playing pool. I need to make my house payment."

"You beat Lucas at pool?"

"No. A friend of mine did, but your brother won't pay him, so my friend sold the debt to me, and now Lucas owes me."

"As I said, look around, take whatever you want. You can have anything you like."

"You got a name?"

"What kind of question's that?" she asked. "You ever meet a person who didn't have a name?"

"My apologies. You're right. What's your name?"

"What's it to you?" Hannah replied.

"Aren't you the spunky one with a quick tongue?"

"I haven't said anything to give offense."

"You're not friendly like other folks," he said, smiling.

"What's friendly got to do with anything? You're not my friend—"

"—Nor your enemy."

"Time will tell."

"I hope to be friends," he told her.

"That's a lie. You don't know me from Adam's housecat."

"Why would I want enemies?"

"Hold out your hands," Hannah said as she held her hands out, palms up. "Wish in one and spit in the other. Let's see which fills up first."

"Ain't you the little pistol?" he said.

"I haven't said a word you don't deserve."

"You don't even know me yet, and you're acting as though I'm a bad person."

"Apparently, my brother's in some sort of situation with you. BMF, I know what that means."

The man laughed, then explained that he wasn't interested in Lucas's money so much as hiring her brother to work off his debt.

"You a drug dealer?"

"What makes you ask that?"

He placed his foot on the bottom of the stairs and smiled again.

"Most people I know don't go around collecting money and have that license plate."

"Because I'm Black?"

"No, it's not that. You're not going to church with that license plate."

He laughed.

"BMF stands for Bales Micro Farms," he said.

"I bet that's a lie."

"No, it's one of my companies. Bales is my name."

"For your information, my name is Hannah," she quipped.

"Bales," he replied. "Hawkshaw Bales. My friends call me Hawk."

He held out his hand to shake hers, but she did not reciprocate.

"Well, Mr. Bales, you stay right there. I don't like your license plate and I don't like you. It's blasphemous."

"Me or the car?" he asked her.

"Both, most likely."

She would not shake his hand, but gave him a stink-eye, thinking, *Bond. James Bond. I drive a gold Lexus with machine guns and an ejector seat. How do you like your Malt Liquor? Shaken, not stirred, of course.*

"Whatever they call you, I'll call you anything but that."

He laughed again.

Even though Hannah thought the man might be a bad dude, he was well-groomed. Whoever cut his hair did a good job. He was tall, about 6'2", and weighed about two hundred pounds, maybe a little more, and he looked athletic. His face was smooth shaven, like a fine piece of marble, and he had a gentle smile that reminded Hannah of Denzel Washington. For a few minutes, he stood at the bottom of the steps talking to her about his recent travels to Central America, where he spent three weeks exploring the ruins on a camping expedition.

"That's all quite interesting," she said, "but it doesn't matter to me one way or the other."

"I suppose not," he replied. "Here's my card. I'll leave one here for your brother. I need to collect my money, but if he doesn't have it, and I understand if he doesn't, I have a lot of work that needs to be done on my farms."

His card read: Bales Industries, Inc.

It had his telephone number and nothing else.

She expected his business card to read: *Hawkshaw Bales: Pool Player. Drug Lord. Bad Mother Fucker.*

"What kind of jobs?" she asked.

"Depends. I have a variety of interests, and I always need people in the warehouse. I won't know until I speak with him and determine what he's good at. I like to match a person to their talents."

"Lucas is good at lots of things."

"Where's he at?"

Bales lifted his foot from the bottom of the stairs and stood straight up. Hannah backed up and held onto the wooden 2x4 that kept the canopy roof up.

"I shouldn't say."

"That's probably a good idea. You don't know me yet. Besides, you seem to be a smart woman who cannot be taken advantage of. Not easily, at least."

"I should say you're right about that. For starters, I don't trust you one bit."

"No offense taken. If you hear from your brother, have him call me. It would be unnecessary to send over any of my other employees to do a job that I can do."

"That sounds like a threat to me."

"No, a threat would be more like—if your brother doesn't pay me, he might get hurt. That's a threat. But, of course, I'm not saying that. That's just an example."

Hannah stared at him, half trying to figure out why she disliked him and why Hawkshaw Bales was so intriguing. Maybe it was the fact that he seemed like a tough guy and could get things done, while looking like Mr. Hollywood. Hannah had never known a person like that.

"Where do you live?" he asked her.

"None of your beeswax."

As Bales stepped up toward her, Hannah thought he was going to hit her, which is what her daddy always did when she smarted off. Instead, he grabbed her purse. She tugged on the strapped, but he yanked once and popped it out of her grip.

"You give that back right this instance."

"Hold on."

He flipped open the purse to find her driver's license.

"Venable Street, that's just down the road a bit. You're at that old, run-down complex."

"What if I am?"

"Nothing. Apartment B-17."

"Hey, you'd be good to forget that information. Don't be showing up at my door. There won't be nothing but trouble waiting for you."

"I can imagine."

When Bales pulled out her phone, Hannah stepped toward him to take it from him. He held his left hand up to stop her. "Just wait, Sweetie. This'll take only a second."

He dialed his telephone number on her phone. His phone rang.

"You give that back right now before I call the police."

He looked at the number that came up on his phone.

"Here." He handed the phone and purse back to her, but he did not release it. She yanked it from him, but he still did not let go.

"Who do you think you are doing whatever you please?"

"Now you have my number, and I have yours."

"I don't want your number. Besides, it's on your business card, and if I wanted to call you, which I don't, it's printed right there."

With all her strength, she snapped the purse away from him in a huff. He released it from his grip, and she jumped back away from him and wrapped the strap around her wrist several times, in the event he thought about swiping it again or if she might need to swat him in the head.

"All better now?" he asked.

"You need to skedaddle on out of here before I call the police."

"Did you know, somewhere around your apartment complex was Bales Plantation before the Civil War? That's a fact. My granny used to say that's where my last name came from."

"I wouldn't know. I wasn't around back then. I ought to call the police, then you'd be in a heap of trouble."

"What're you gonna say to them?"

"That you stole my purse."

"And, yet, you have it with you."

"I'll say you threatened my brother and me."

"Venable Street. The Venable brothers owned a lot of land on the Yellow River and held KKK meetings there. Did you know that?"

"What's that to me? I don't know them."

"Just saying. You're living on a street named for people who hate

Black folks."

"Like I said, I don't know them. It's just a street name. It could have been named Elm Street for all I care."

"But it isn't Elm Street. It's Venable Street," Bales told Hannah.

"A lot of people hate other folks for a lot of reasons. That's not me."

"I'm just saying."

"Yeah, of course, you're just saying. What's it to me?" she asked.

"You seem like a nice woman. If there's ever anything I can do for you, Hannah, give me a call. I have your number, so maybe I'll call you."

"Don't bother, Mr. Pushy. Besides, you'll just lecture me about street names."

Bales chuckled, and as he walked away, said, "You sure don't like anyone telling you what to do."

"Who would?"

She looked at his business card again as he walked away.

"And another thing, your license plate isn't very godly."

Then he was gone. Once Bales had driven away and Hannah could no longer see any dust from the driveway, she went back inside Lucas's trailer. She tossed the business card on the counter, then found her yearbook underneath the TV. Lucas was using it as a shim to balance the old Zenith portable.

She read Lucas's senior quote: *Ninety percent of things in life take care of themselves by showing up on time. The other thirty percent is just good manners.*

Hannah did not like to name the guilty party, but she paid one of the students on the yearbook staff twenty dollars to add Lucas to the senior class, thinking it might motivate him to return to school or earn his G.E.D. Lucas was Photoshopped into a tuxedo using his tenth-grade photo, which was before he had grown a goatee and mustache. By the time the yearbooks were printed, it was too late to remove Lucas.

Then, she read her quote, "I hear Jerusalem bells a-ringing / Roman cavalry choirs are singing / Be my mirror, my sword and shield" – Coldplay.

"Look here, Hannah," Lucas said. "Not only did I get my mug-shot in the yearbook, some dork mailed it to me for free."

Of course, that caused another ruckus when they mailed an invoice to Lucas for $39.95, plus shipping.

He wrote back on the invoice, "I ain't never paying 4 this. I did not odor a yearbook. Never got 1 in the male. I don't even go to school at your school. I will be go-in to school at Harvard next spring. See you on the flippitty-flop." He never heard from them again.

Chapter 4

Throw Me into the Lake of Fire

"Sin rules the world while forgiveness rakes the leaves."

Hannah spoke these words aloud to herself, then scribbled them on her yellow legal tablet, as she sat on the large, flat farm rock and wondered where these words came from—maybe a poem or the Bible—she wasn't certain. They simply popped into her head without cause.

The rock was about the size of an oriental rug in someone's fancy living room, or in *Southern Living*, the type of rug that never graced her farmhouse. It was situated on the edge of their pond, and she loved to stretch out on it and think about her life, especially the words she just wrote down, even if she wasn't certain what they meant. They were the first words she'd written all day, and, therefore, seemed important. She'd sat for two hours by the edge of the pond at her family's old farm, having a picnic by herself—Kentucky Fried Chicken and a Diet Coke. She'd ordered the Famous Bowl with extra gravy, but they didn't include the gravy. She wanted more to dip her potato wedges in.

For more than a year, when everyone was in some state of COVID quarantine, she had been cutting back on eating fast food, trying the best she could to eat 1800 calories or less per day. Once a month, she allowed herself to hit the drive-thru and order anything she wanted. She was proud of herself for having done a good job adhering to her goal long after COVID was pretty much a thing of the past.

When Hannah needed a break from the world and COVID and staying away from everyone, she drove to the farm and spent time alone on the rock. She hated wearing a mask. She enjoyed sitting outside in the sun, away from the craziness of the news and the talking heads changing their stories on the hour and instilling some new fear in the world. A few times, she went for a long walk in search of what she remembered from that night.

Adam and Eve never worried about their diet. God always provided. They never worried about COVID either. For that matter, I don't think Eve ever lied to Adam about her baby dying.

The other times when she had a picnic on the old family farm, she made a cucumber or PB&J sandwich and cut up fruits and vegetables. She always brought two bottles of water and Himalayan salt to cleanse her system. Over the past year, she'd lost nearly twenty pounds and had kept it off. She'd thought about starting a Mediterranean diet but hadn't yet. She also liked to go for walks around her apartment complex but thought people who wore a mask while outside were idiots walking alone wearing a mask, as if they were going to infect themselves.

Forgiveness raking the leaves, she thought, *must mean that things take effort. It's a hard job to forgive people. I could never have been Jesus, that's for sure. People are too stupid. I don't know how Jesus forgives that much stupidity.*

She liked to spend her time sitting on the flat rock, thinking and writing in her journal, as well as staring at the barn's reflection across the calm water. She spread out a durable wool blanket and a votive candle, but the breeze of the early afternoon blew it out each time she lit it. Today was one of the first warm days of spring and few words came to her, but that did not matter too much to Hannah, as she enjoyed the quiet of the farm. There was no one around, and she had few cares or worries, and she simply abandoned responsibility and daydreamed of what life on the farm would be like if her family was together and not pissed off at each other and scattered to the winds. Rarely did any cars drive down the road and pass the farm, and if they did, they'd never see Hannah sitting on the rock, and she never worried about anyone finding her baby sister. With

Grady and Myra dead, only the angels know the secret location.

As she stared into the water, she thought about the number of dreams that had drowned over the years on the farm, most before they were more than an idea, pocket charms, wonderments, some fanciful notion that a person might aspire to something more than slopping pigs or shoveling horse manure.

None of the animals ate each other in God's paradise, but who cleaned up after them? Certainly, Eve didn't shovel manure. I doubt she even had a shovel.

§

It was the 15th, the Ides of March, and Hannah scratched letters on yellow paper in felt-tip. Lately, she'd been dreaming of buying back the family farm, even though she didn't want to work the land. Perhaps she'd hire some people to help out.

I could pay people a good wage to prune the apple trees and mow the fields. I could sell the hay to cattle farmers and the apples to a cider mill. Anything to make money off the farm.

It was a pipe dream. First of all, the farm wasn't for sale, and second, Hannah didn't have a pot to piss in. Selling the farm was an honest business deal between her parents and the airport authority, but she always felt they'd been taken advantage of, if just by virtue of the fact that someone else now owned what was once theirs. It did not seem fair and still did not sit right in her mind even though the transaction was lucrative for her parents.

"Anything more than five dollars is business," Hannah's father said to her and the rest of the family from time to time. "Get it in writing."

After the farm was sold in 2019 and the deal was signed, a check arrived that afternoon to their farmhouse by special courier, along with a cordial letter stating that they had ninety days to vacate the property.

"Three months, that's plenty of time," her momma said. "All

that's left here are ghosts and memories. I ain't taking those with."

Hannah stood up and tossed a stone into the pond, shattering the surface, which rippled like melted glass and wavered the barn's reflection. She wrote a Bible verse down on her tablet, scratching it in green ink, then drawing a few stars next to the verse to emphasize its importance.

Wash me clean from my guilt. Purify me from my sin. For I recognize my shameful deeds—they haunt me day and night.—Psalm 51:2-3

She wasn't looking for an epiphany to explain her situation now five years later, just a sign from God to give her direction.

"Momma, don't you worry about Black folks being hurt?"

"Sweetie, don't worry about living in Sundown," her mother said. "Ain't no Black person been hurt in a hundred years in Sundown. Folks are more civilized now. Folks get along."

"That's not what Lucas told me."

"He's just trying to get your dander up."

"I'm just worried about Margaret. She's Black if you haven't noticed, an' there are people out there who have a problem with that. I'm worried about her safety."

"Don't be. Folks like that are like a kite without air."

"I just worry about her."

"Don't. She ain't nobody to worry about."

Hannah liked working at The Cute Curl as a hair stylist but could not imagine doing the same thing for twenty-two years like her boss, Wendy. She was constantly praying for a sign, for God to shine His steady light in front of her path. "There needs to be something more," she whispered.

She began to write:

I suspect if people read this Document of Life in one hundred years, they may not want to be preached at, so I'll limit my Bible verses to a smattering. I have stopped believing in the church. Completely. I haven't been to church in three years. Writing this down in pen scares me, because the Wrath of God may appear as a lightning bolt and strike me off this rock. God's still on my books because things live inside you. If I had memorized Shakespeare all my life, I'd spit him on these pages instead.

The farm had been in Hannah's family since before the Civil War. The best her mother was able to remember, they acquired it around 1840. In the five years since the land was sold to the Georgia Regional Airport Authority, it had changed hands so often that Hannah no longer knew who owned it but thought it now belonged to a housing developer. Within a year of the sale, the airport authority realized they'd made a mistake and didn't have enough acreage for a new airport, which required twelve thousand. Even with two other large tracts of land on the outskirts of Hebron, a neighboring town, it did not add up to twelve thousand. The airport was to be settled at the convergence of the tri-county that included sections of Sundown, but once the airport authority realized they had 8,200 acres and needed four thousand more, they began selling off chunks of the rezoned land for a profit. After this, Hannah's farm was sold to be developed into a golf course with condos, a gated community, and businesses buffered by thick groves of trees. It never saw the light of day.

Hannah's twin brother, Lucas, stayed up to date on most of the property details, but even he lost track at times. During the years after the sale, the golf course was never developed, and no one had done anything more than erect a few *No Trespassing* signs on the property and a gate in front of the driveway to her house. Because the farmhouse and barn were still standing, she had hopes of one day buying back all the land, five hundred and seventy-three acres. To Hannah, the most egregious thing erected on the property was the large metal gate closing off their driveway. It looked like a guardrail on a winding mountain road. Hannah also disliked the plywood sheets boarding up the windows and doors to keep folks out. It looked like a crypt with overgrown vines, bushes, and high grass, as if someone sealed off some great plague still lingering inside the house.

God will judge us for everything we do, including every secret thing, whether good or bad.—Ecclesiastes 12:14

She tore the page from the notepad, folded the paper into a square, and slid it into the back pocket of her jeans.

When the check arrived back in 2019, Hannah's father did not cash it right away. He placed it in a small, gold frame that had once housed a picture of Hannah's Memaw, and then he carted the check around to everyone he knew to show off, down to Dalton's Bar, the pool hall, Garmend's Auto Shop, the barber shop, Sonic, and to anyone he knew who normally wouldn't give him the time of day, just to say, "Look at me. I'm on Easy Street, and you can kiss my rich, fat ass!" He even showed it to the cashier at Kroger when he bought a Baby Ruth candy bar.

"If it was real, you wouldn't be showing it off to folks," she said.

"It's real, Sweetheart. You can bet the rent on that."

He wanted the local newspaper to write a personal profile on him, but all they printed was each tract of land sold to the airport authority, not once mentioning Darnell Gardner by name.

He showed it to his old boss and a few other managers at K-Mart, where he once worked for three days before getting fired for refusing to clean the bathrooms.

"You hired me to sell fishin' gear an' talk to people about fishin' an' huntin', not to clean bathrooms. You want them bathrooms cleaned, get yourself some crippled nigger." They fired him right there on the spot.

"Big deal, you sold your property," his former boss said when Darnell showed him the check for $3,745,000 in the picture frame.

"Taxes are gonna eat you alive. Plus, you still need to buy a new place."

"Want to see what Easy Street looks like? It looks just like this right here," Darnell said, holding the frame over his head like an Olympic medal. "Think about that while you're sittin' on the crapper."

"You know, land in your area's selling for twenty thousand per acre. More, in a few places. You got taken. Can you spell 'swindled'?"

"Want to hear about a blue light special. They're closing this place down by the end of the year," Darnell smugly told his old boss.

"No kidding, Nostradamus. I've known that for over a year. We're the close-out center for the southeast."

Darnell bolted out of K-Mart like he was looting the place with a flat screen TV stuffed under his arm. He squealed his tires in the parking lot as he left. At the QuikTrip, after rubbing off a dozen $20-scratch-offs, he sat in his car with the calculator app open on his phone, figuring out how much he should have been paid. When he realized that he'd been paid a little more than $5,500 per acre, he realized his old boss was right.

For weeks after the check arrived, life on the farm was reasonably happy and everyone was cordial to each other. Lilith never said a word to Darnell or the children about the money. She went about her business as usual, not even worried about the newfound wealth. She knew Darnell would never share it.

Darnell sat watching TV and held onto the framed check, sometimes staring at it like it might be a prank. Most of the time, he just waited for the phone to ring with someone congratulating him.

"Yes, sir. My ship certainly has come in."

Hannah's family packed up all their belongings and tossed away anything they didn't want or donated it to charity. The Salvation Army and Goodwill stopped by three times to haul things away. The barn was the heftiest job. When Hannah's father looked inside, he shook his head and closed the door, wanting nothing to do with whatever remained. Initially, he thought about having a huge yard sale, but there was too much to wrap his arms around. He never had much motivation for hard work, but if he had, he lost it in the barn when he looked inside and saw years and years of old junk to sort through. He knew it would take months to organize everything. He called an auctioneer, and they struck a deal—$5,000 cash for everything in the barn. Two days later, the auctioneer and six men cleared it out. It was worth five times that amount but not worth the trouble for her father to sell that old junk or rifle through it. Hannah's mother, Lilith, never saw a penny of that cash.

On the day that Hannah's parents went to the bank to deposit the farm check, seeing how the thrill of showing it around town had worn off, her mother refused to sign the back of the check. She asked the branch manager to open a new account in her name.

"Lilith, you sign that goddamned check right now and put it in our account or I'm going to knock you into next week."

"See, this is what I've put up with for twenty-eight years."

The manager had to close his door when Lilith told Darnell she was leaving him, since he was causing such a disturbance.

"How you getting' home? You gonna walk?"

"I'm leaving for good."

"Where you gonna go?"

"I'm leaving, and if you think you're getting any of the money, signing these papers is the only way that's going to happen."

Right there in the manager's office, Lilith handed him an envelope with a thick heft to it.

"What the hell is this?"

"Divorce papers," she said, quivering.

Darnell raised his hand to hit her but did not. If he had, Lilith was prepared to press charges. The manager called the security officer over to settle Darnell down, but even he had to call the local police. The security guard was within a squirrel's hair of hauling him off when the deputy sheriff, Albert Lovell, showed up, and Darnell came to his senses.

"You had to call that asshole. It'll take a lot more than Al-bert to take me in."

"Having lady problems?" Lovell asked. "Can't be money problems. I've heard from twenty people that you been flashing that check all over town. I'm surprised you ain't been jacked or started building a house on the moon."

Having Lovell at the bank settled Darnell down, but he wasn't happy when the manager deposited half the money in Lilith's account and the other half in Darnell's, $1,535,250 each.

"This ain't over," Darnell said, directing his finger at her over and over as if he was hitting the same letter on a keyboard.

"Lilith," the bank manager said, "You'll have to pay about forty to fifty percent in taxes on this money if you don't buy a new house or reinvest it. We can help you manage the money. You'll have between $750,000 and $900,000 after taxes but that has to last your entire life. It's your retirement. Don't think of it as play money. You need to plan for the future."

"Retirement? What the hell's she gonna retire from? She ain't never done nothing but clean house and she's not good at that," Darnell barked.

The security officer, at the request of the manager, gave Lilith a ride home. Officer Lovell volunteered to accompany them. Without money over the years, she was always too scared to leave. She didn't have any resources and couldn't support her children, but now, all that was different. She packed her clothes, a few bags, the family Bible, and grabbed a box of family photographs and a big box of school artwork her children created throughout the years. Since the first day that selling the farm became an option, she planned her escape and had all her stuff packed under her bed or in a back closet ready to go. She had even sorted through all the family photos and had separated Darnell's family from hers. She wasn't taking anything resembling him with her. This was not how she envisioned running away, but it was good enough.

When Hannah and Lucas heard the yelling and screaming outside their house, it didn't seem out of the ordinary, but when their mother started packing and talking about their father nearly getting tossed in jail, they perked up. Instead of returning home rich and happy, their mother had a crazed look in her eyes, as if she was running from the hounds. Their father and Albert Lovell stood in the driveway with the security guard. Hannah followed her mother from room to room as she gathered her belongings and pulled things from the closet and out from under the bed. She'd never seen her mother so determined and thought she might never see her again.

"Now that we're rich, we're going out to celebrate," her father yelled when Lilith brought some boxes out to the security officer's car, trying to entice her to stay. "Good times are on the horizon! I'll buy a steak dinner for anyone who walks on two feet."

"For anyone who wants bullshit promises all their life," Lilith interrupted.

"Why do you have to rain on my parade? We're going to LongHorn Steakhouse. We're going to live like kings, with people waiting on us and saying, 'Yes, sir' and 'No, sir.' We're gonna be treated like royalty."

Darnell turned to the security guard, "Did you think this went well at the bank? I thought it did."

Hannah's father could not convince Greta, her older sister, to return home from California for her share of the money, which everyone knew was nothing. Her father wasn't sharing. Their older brother, Wendell, was in the military, and your old man striking it rich like Jed Clampett isn't reason enough for time off in the Army. Her daddy's expectations were flying high, but when he was put in his place by her mother in front of an important man like the bank manager, and then Albert Lovell, he could not tolerate it.

"Hannah. Lucas," their mother said, "You're old enough to make this decision, but if you're coming with me, pack your clothes. I'll give you fifteen minutes. I'm leaving the Devil's Paradise for uncharted territories."

Lucas said he was staying on the farm, but Hannah ran to her room and packed everything she could fit into two suitcases, knowing she could always return for the rest of her stuff. Her mother could never come back, not without a beating waiting for her.

Hannah and Lucas were weeks from starting the eleventh grade and had just turned sixteen when their house was divided down the middle by loyalties.

Hannah and her mother walked out of the farmhouse and to the security officer's car, turned around, and looked one last time at their old life before driving off. That was the last time Hannah's mother set foot on the farm, and as Hannah looked at the house and as the car pulled away, she swore the white paint faded to gray and began to peel the second the tires hit pavement.

"This is what it would have been like if Eve had been the only person banished from Eden," Lilith said. "Can't you imagine how different the world would be if Eve had been on her own from the get-go?"

As they were heading down Highway 19, Lilith asked the security officer to drive her to a nice hotel. He suggested the DoubleTree in Antioch near the highway and the Target.

"That'll work."

She took several deep breaths, closed her eyes, and sat on her hands to keep them from shaking. It was a good ten minutes before she said another word. She stared out the window at Stone Mountain, watching little specks of people walk up the granite trails.

"That's my old life, and maybe my heart is full of bruises too deep to heal, but I got to try. Before me is new territory, a new life, an' there isn't a damn thing I want from my old life 'cept my children. Everything else is just stuff. Maybe you can talk to Lucas and

Greta about moving in with me once I get settled in a new place. When Wendell visits, he can stay with us. Nature shows you that all things die and rot, no matter what it is. Remember this: nothing lasts."

During the drive, Lilith asked the security officer if he would burn the farm down to the ground for five hundred dollars. They laughed, but Hannah knew her mother was serious.

Chapter 5

Your Church Ain't My Church

When Hannah was nine, her brothers noticed bubbles popping up from under the water of the pond. It looked like bubbling mud in Yellowstone, except there was no mud. When she, Lucas, and their mother walked down to the pond, Lilith could smell methane gas. The bubbles grew until there seemed to be fumes spewing out of the water. Lilith called Darnell on his phone and told him to come take a look at the pond. Darnell had been helping his friend, Skip Coen, install a new kitchen for Skip's mother when they stopped by to see what the fuss was about.

"You kids stay here," Darnell said, pointing to the front porch.

He and Skip walked down to the pond, where they smelled methane gas. They wondered why, without warning, methane would bubble up from under the pond.

"Maybe you got oil underground," Skip said. "Or natural gas."

"You think?"

"It's possible. If so, it's worth a lot of money."

"I'll take care of this." Darnell pulled out his lighter.

"Should you call the county?"

"What for?"

"Safety."

"Naw, I got this."

"I wouldn't do that if I were you," Skip said. "You might set the world on fire."

"What do you know? You ever live on a farm? No, you live in a condo."

When Darnell struck the lighter, there was about a two-second delay until the pond caught fire and the explosion knocked both men backward into the high grass and rattled the barn and windows of the house. When they stood up, flames tickled over the pond's surface, like the eternal flame in Arlington Cemetery. The flames in the center of the pond burned for three days. At night, the children sat on the rock or on the porch, watching a continuous never-ending flow of bubbles and flames dancing back and forth above the water's surface.

"It's a miracle," Darnell proclaimed. "Just like ascending into the afterlife while still alive."

On the fourth night, Hannah, Lucas, and a few kids from their middle school, camped out in sleeping bags on the rock. They had a hotdog and marshmallow roasting party when Wendell hauled the grill to the edge of the pond and cooked for everyone. It was one of the few times Hannah had any girlfriends stay the night. Four girls and three boys, all in the seventh grade, slept in sleeping bags under the stars that evening, told ghost stories, and drank too much soda. No one fell asleep until after three o'clock.

The next morning, the flames were gone. None of the kids had much sleep and were groggy as Wendell cooked bacon and eggs over the grill. Everyone helped clean up, returned the grill to the back porch, and by ten o'clock had been picked up by their parents.

Over the next four years, the bubbles never returned, and Hannah never had another sleep over, and during the summer between tenth and eleventh grade, the deal to sell the farm was underway.

After moving out, Hannah and her mother lived at the DoubleTree Hotel for a week until they rented an apartment at the Summit Creek Preserve in Antioch. Sitting at the pool one day near the end of summer, Lilith told Hannah that she was proud of herself, because she had been secretly consulting with a lawyer during her marriage to Darnell.

"Your daddy never knew what I was up to. I'd been planning to divorce him for years. I just didn't know we'd end up selling the farm. What I wanted to do was steal away in the middle of the night, take the car, and drive so far away the angels couldn't find me. But as soon as talk about selling the farm came up, I knew I was leaving and taking you kids. I wish it'd happened ten years ago. I was always the apple that fell from the tree and tried rolling away, but every time I got down the road, someone threw me back up the hill to the tree trunk."

One morning after they moved into their furnished apartment, Lilith woke up with the idea of walking three times a day to get back in shape and change her life.

"I'm on a new exercise plan called *Someone New is Going to See Me Naked*" she laughed, which made Hannah laugh, too.

They had been gone less than three weeks when Darnell tried convincing them to come back, mostly by calling their phone and yelling. Instead of walking in the front door and declaring, "Honey, I'm home!"—Lilith filed papers for a restraining order. Albert Lovell had the pleasure of returning to the farm to serve him.

"Got yourself a little trouble with the ladies, don't you, Darnell?"

"What's it to you, Albert? You been divorced twice."

"I'm just having a good day. I'm here to inform you that if you get within one hundred feet of Lilith, I get to arrest you. Remember all the times in high school when you and Charlie Vabord beat me up an' squished my lunch? I just want you to know the pleasure I'll have cuffing you if you step out of line. Plant that in your garden."

"You'd better bring some help."

"I'll keep that in mind. By the way, now that you're getting divorced, you mind if I ask Lilith out to dinner? I promise not to bang her on our first date. The way I figure, she ain't never had a real man."

Darnell stared at him, scraping his fingernails across a callus on his right palm. Lovell had his hand on his blackjack, hoping Darnell would do something stupid.

At Dickens High School, Hannah sat with Lucas in the lunchroom. Some days, she rode the bus with him back to the farm. She never allowed her father to drive her home to the apartment. Instead, she called Uber.

"What's your momma saying about me?"

"Nothing much," she replied.

"Anything nice?"

"Mostly, she doesn't talk about you. She said she's moving on, somewhere that's sunny where flowers always bloom and God's gentle hand is the only thing brushing her cheek."

"She said that?" Darnell asked.

"Sumthin' to that effect."

"Good. I hope she stays gone."

"She's got a new phone," Hannah told him.

"I know. The other one stopped working. So what? I got a new one, too. A pre-paid phone. I can toss this in the pond and not have a care."

Going to school and seeing Lucas didn't last long. He dropped out after six weeks.

"I feel like I'm wasting my time in class. All I do is dream about working a job where at the end of the day, I got a pocket full of cash."

He never studied for any of his classes, and what he read at home wasn't a book his teacher assigned. He was not invested in anything except designing a plan for his escape into the real working world.

"Lucas, that's a huge mistake," Hannah told him.

But Lucas would not listen. He said he felt like a wild stallion in a corral, and out there in the world, the open plains were waiting for him to run free.

"What if Momma and Daddy got back together? Would you go back to school, at least night school to get your diploma?"

"I doubt it. Besides, they're never getting back together."

Hannah imagined that her whole family would be together again, and Greta and Wendell would come home, too. However, her mother would have nothing to do with it. Lilith knew that Darnell wanted to spend her share of the money.

Eight months after their divorce was finalized, Lilith met Ronnie Lee Dawkins, a carpenter living in Hall County. They met in line at Lowe's when Lilith was purchasing a do-it-yourself bookshelf. Ronnie was standing in front of her as they waited for the line to move.

"Them there shelves are tricky to put together. You ever done that before?"

"No," Lilith answered.

"I'd be more than happy to assemble them for you. I'll do it gratis. That's French for free."

Ronnie volunteered to help her, and after he checked out, he waited for her. He bought Lilith lunch at Waffle House, then followed her back to her apartment, where he assembled the bookshelves in about an hour. He even used wood glue to add extra stability to the joints. After the shelves were completed, Ronnie Lee made a move to kiss Lilith, and she let him. By the time Hannah came home from school, he was long gone, and Lilith's linens were in the washing machine, and her bed was as fresh as a spring morning.

Without saying a word about it, Lilith dated Ronnie Lee all the way through Hannah's high school graduation. Once the cat was out of the bag, Lilith told Hannah she was moving to Lake Lanier with Ronnie Lee. She sat Hannah down one Sunday and told her about Ronnie Lee and how it was time she moved on. Hannah was welcome to live with her at the lake, but it was perfectly fine if she wanted to strike out on her own. Hannah agreed and said she'd like her own place.

"You can stay here in this apartment. I'll help you out for the first year. After that, you got to pay your own bills. I'll pay your rent and utilities, but if you want cable TV, you have to pay for that yourself. Lucas has been talking about renting a trailer out a ways. Maybe you can move in with him, or he can move in here, in the other bedroom. I'll talk to him about going back and getting his diploma. Besides, it's been long enough. How come he's still living on the farm?"

"Lucas an' Daddy are refusing to leave. There's a lawsuit. The developers ripped Daddy off. That's what Lucas said. Besides, no one's pushing them to get out."

"If your daddy gets more money, you let me know. I get half."

Hannah wanted to be with her mother, but she also wanted to live with her father and Lucas on the farm or wherever they ended up. She was certain she did not want to live in the same house with Ronnie Lee Dawkins and his brother, Eddie Lee.

Lilith moved to the Laurel Ridge area of Lake Lanier, and with help from Ronnie Lee and Eddie Lee, Lilith opened up a restaurant-bar down near the Laurel Ridge boat ramp: *The Diamond Eye*. Lilith invested her money in the eyesore, but with hard work and sweat equity, she and Ronnie Lee cleaned it up and began cooking meals. Soon, it became a respectable restaurant for boaters and fishermen looking for a steak or blackened grouper at the end of the day.

"Beer therapy," Lilith called it. "It's less expensive than a shrink."

Hannah's father, on the other hand, was finally forced off the farm. He bought a small three-bedroom house under foreclosure in Hebron on Bushton Court. The rest of his money, after taxes, was gambled away playing poker, as he believed he was going to Las Vegas to compete in the World Championship of Poker. During the slow trickling away of his money, he traveled to Biloxi, Tunica, and Cherokee, being Mr. Highroller and King of All Things Important, playing poker and living it up. He was everyone's friend until the money dried up.

... evil people squander their money on
sin.—Proverbs 10:16

After Hannah's father was forced off the farm, he demanded more money from the buyers, even though the deal had been final for more than two years. By then, the property had changed hands three times, and the current owners wouldn't give in to his demands. A write-up in the local newspaper said the owners considered allowing Darnell to live on the farm indefinitely, but the reporter quoted his accusation, saying he had been swindled out of millions.

Allen Lovell showed up at Darnell's new house with a restraining order and countersuit for slander.

"This notice says if you set foot on the farm property, even if you ain't there when I show up, I'll come find you and haul you in. You got that, boy?"

After Darnell bought the Bushton Court house, he ignored the restraining order and raided the farm at night, taking anything he'd left behind. It took time to gather all his things, but each Saturday, he had a garage sale consisting of farmhouse garbage and set up a card table in the carport, ran an extension cable into the house and propped up a TV on a lawn chair, put a Yard Sale sign by the curb, then sat there waiting for people to show up. He took all the old lawn mowers and broke them down to parts. All sorts of people stopped to look for a specific part they needed. His sign read: LAWN MORE PARTS 4 SAIL. He also put an ad on Craigslist and sold parts on eBay. He sat around drinking beer and making money.

§

Today is Monday, my day off from The Cute Curl, but it's three weeks since I last wrote. I'm at the library where Margaret works. She's at the front desk at this moment, checking out books and showing people how to research topics for school. Her boss doesn't come in until two o'clock. There's almost no one in the library, so I'm on the computer in the back typing away.

I never thought about writing anything like a journal until I read a story about a box of papers that a woman in Wyoming found, belonging to another woman who might have been her great, great, great grandmother. But they do not know for certain, since the name of the woman from so long ago was not written on the papers. Nobody has named this woman, but I call her Sarah. Melzena Harvey is the one who found the journal. Sarah wrote it in the 1800s when she moved out west on a wagon train. The editors of the magazine who printed parts of the journal, along with some university super-noggin-experts, believe it was part of the Westward Expansion, but that it was about ten to fifteen years after the initial rush to get out there for land. After all that speculation, they said they did not know with any certainty. All they can go on are the details in her journal, which they believe is 170 to 180 years old. That's where the idea for my Document of Life came from. They've got some college minds studying the journal and making a timeline, trying to pinpoint places along the trail. Some person is even counting how many times Sarah used certain words. They've figured out a few things. These people said, in time, they believe they'll be able to determine her identity. I hope so, but for now, she is Sarah.

Ever since my Memaw died last year, I've been thinking about putting down to paper my family history. Sarah has some good stories. I do too.

Of course, my family history is a sorry tale of rotten people doing and saying rotten things to other rotten people, and just being the worst kind of kin a person can have. The only thing we ain't done is get tossed in jail and put to work on the chain gang. I guess that's one thing to be proud of, but that locomotive is probably barreling down the tracks just as well, waiting to knock you over like bowling pins.

A few weeks ago, while me and Margaret were drinking hot tea in the library break room, she said, "Wasn't it exciting when Sarah talked about the Indians attacking the wagon train and killing one of the men—not her husband? I also liked the parts where people were being nice for the first few days, but then got irritated because of the harsh conditions and the long slow hours. No one shared much of their provisions after the first week."

They caught a guy stealing food from the preacher's wagon.

"Suits him right to get kicked off of the trail," I said.

"I wonder what happened to him out there in the wilderness alone?" Margaret asked me.

"They gave him a choice, either leave and be on your own or be turned over to the sheriff in the next town."

When Memaw died, she was living with Daddy in his new house, which she said she liked, but I know her heart was at the farm. That morning, Daddy went in her room to find her peaceful in the bed with her Bible in her right hand, opened to Corinthians 5:4 – "We want to slip into our new bodies so that these dying bodies will be swallowed up by everlasting life."

Memaw knew it was her time. We buried her next to Poppa Raymond at the Antioch Cemetery. That's when I started thinking about all my relatives I don't know–some I never met–as well as the ones that are dead. When we were at the cemetery, Daddy pointed out a bunch of folks who were our kin. He had a story for each one. I want to write down their stories, maybe not for the entire world to read, but maybe if they're interesting enough. I want to know who folks were and what they looked like. Most are forgotten to time. I want everyone, including me, to be remembered, like Sarah.

The thinking heads at the university believe Sarah began writing her diary around 1851, because she mentioned some riots that sprung up when Maryland slave owners tried capturing their runaway slaves in Pennsylvania. Again, it's speculation. They know with certainty that this was before the Civil War. I have a copy of Sarah's journal here beside me at the library, and I read it all the time. When the notion bubbles up in me, I will type some interesting things Sarah said, like this:

Momma died last spring of fever and two days later John talked about leaving Pennsvania. I fought him on this. It got to be late in summer and we would be hit by snow before we rode south a'least to Luweville in our travels. This year I went to Momma's grave early as the snow blew way and cried when I told her I wouldn't see her gain til Heaven. Next day we were bumping on the trail with forty families amoung us, scarfs over our face and ears to warm us. Heard tell we would have to breathe out the dust, but the ground is froze. There is no dust, just tears and cold and lots of manure. No slosh but that will come. As we have traveled a few families joined along the way, up to 53 now. Most are pleasant folks though the women are more ireful than the men. I reckon they did not want to leave either.

I hope she wasn't sad forever. See, if those thinking heads can figure out who died of fever around 1851 in Pennsylvania and when a wagon train left with forty people, those are clues.

Sarah had four children, and during the trip, the youngest one was killed when the wagon wheel rode over him. They buried him somewhere in Indiana under a chestnut tree near a large pond shaped like a scythe. He was two years old. I hope she put soap in her husband's chili to give him the runs real bad, because being on the bumpy, dusty trail and crapping every third bump would fix him good for putting her through such torture of moving from her home and losing her baby. That type of retribution isn't Christian, but God should make allowances for certain behavior. Revenge has its reward and satisfaction. Maybe I can find that pond using Google Earth. Maybe there's a marker on the grave. If I could find it, those smart people at the university would certainly think I was something of a brainiac.

Sarah is the made-up name I gave her. At times it feels real, but I know that's not her real name.

§

Every few weeks, Hannah visited her old house on the farm. Sometimes she just drove by or stopped and stood in the driveway to stare at what used to be. She liked walking around the property, always ending at the pond for a picnic, where she sat on the flat rock that her father had purchased one day. The deliverymen set it near the pond with a crane, then Darnell, once he knew where he wanted it, pushed it into place with his tractor. Hannah remembered watching him angle the rock when she was a little girl, inching it back and forth into the right spot. Now, after parking her car at the mouth of the driveway, cinders crunching under the tires, Hannah climbed over the gate. It was warm to touch, but not like in the summer, when it was so hot, she had to place an old towel on the gray metal and straddle the gate to keep from burning the insides of her thighs.

Since it was early March, before spring had yet cracked open its husk, the high grass surrounding the property was dry and brittle. A few grasshoppers jumped from stalk to stalk as Hannah cut through the walkway to the pond. For Hannah, the rock was always a place to see the farm in its entirety. It was where she liked to sit with her brothers and sister, watching the fish jump out of the water, talking about school or the future and what their lives held for them. They would steal ears of winter corn from one of the nearby farms, scrape the hard nuggets into a pile, then toss them, one by one, or in handfuls, into the water for the fish to gulp as they broke the surface. When the weather was good, she did her homework on the rock. There were times when she wrote for hours, then rolled each yellow page into a ball and burned them one by one on the rock. It was where she dreamed. Sometimes, she sat there, remembering the sounds of the farm and her family, unlike her current situation where she felt there was an emptiness, except for the high grass swaying back and forth. Over the years, she told no one in her family that she visited the farm to scribble her thoughts and more than a hundred Bible verses on a pad of paper.

"What good are words?" she wrote. "What good is the Bible if this is where I end up?"

As the first warm days of March swept through the trees, Hannah felt that God bestows Grace upon some, but not upon others, like musical or athletic talent.

Grace is all but void in my life.

§

Hannah attended college for one semester at Clarkston Community College. She didn't like it, not right after high school, feeling that four more years was too long to wait to make money, so she quit in the middle of the semester and enrolled in cosmetology classes at The David Whitefish Institute of Hair located in Hebron, just off Main Street on Alabaster Way. This suited her better because it allowed her to quit working as a cashier at QuikTrip and take a job as a shampoo girl at The Cute Curl. She liked working at QT, but checking people out was a fast operation with no time to have a conversation with the customers. It didn't take Hannah any time to realize how to massage a man's head the right way to get a better tip, which was her biggest source of income until she started cutting hair, which, if it was a well-behaved kid, she could knock it out in ten minutes. As she learned what she was doing at school and in hands-on training, the transition to cutting hair was smooth.

"If you can develop a steady client base of a hundred people who'll get their hair cut every four to six weeks, you'll make pretty good money," Wendy told her.

"How long will that take?"

"A few years, but then you're golden."

So far, Hannah had six regular customers. The rest were walk-ins.

"I kind of thought I might meet someone to go to the movies with."

"Don't worry," Wendy said, "you'll meet a guy, and when you do, he'll puff your skirt."

"Yeah, but ninety-nine percent of our clients are women and kids."

"What about Dave Edwards? He's good looking."

"Too old."

"Yeah, but he's got that special something going on."

Hannah agreed.

Every three weeks, Dave Edwards stopped in for a haircut, but she thought of him more like her teacher or a guy who might be friends with her father, if her father had gone to college and wasn't a racist. After he would leave, she found herself remembering everything Edwards told her about himself and the world, that he retired early but still worked buying and selling first edition books and rare coins, and how he had traveled all over the world and the United States.

"I sold my company four years ago," Edwards told her. "Now, all I do is play golf, read, and hunt for dinosaur bones in Montana. My favorite coins are Morgan Silver Dollars."

"That's more exciting than my life."

"I'm over needing excitement. I don't want any drama," he said.

"Not me. That's exactly what I need, some excitement," Hannah told him.

To Hannah, Edwards' life was an adventure, and he was the most interesting person she'd ever met. She always spent extra time shampooing and massaging his hair after cutting it. She even massaged his temples, which put him to sleep a few times. He always tipped her at least ten dollars. Hannah noticed that he did not wear a wedding ring, but she never asked about his situation, thinking perhaps he didn't like women, which was fine and none of her business. He never asked her out. Hannah wondered what she would say if he ever did.

Yeah, I would say yes.

§

While sitting on the flat rock, Hannah thought about women in the 1940s, up until the 1980s, and the limits placed on their lives. What did they do when they had ambitions that did not include suiting a man's needs? She made two columns on her yellow pad and wrote a heading: *Girls Club for Girls Who Want to Accomplish Something in*

Life, Now! The second column, *Stuff I will NO LONGER Tolerate!* She jotted down a few ideas on how to make more money, places she wanted to visit, and careers she might consider beyond giving five-year-old boys haircuts.

She thought about her family and how they had not been in the same room together, vacationed together, or eaten Thanksgiving dinner together in years, and Thanksgiving had always been her favorite holiday. She made a third column, one for things she wanted back in her life.

Hannah got up and walked the circumference of the pond, and a few frogs jumped in. She knew that, where something lived, there was something to eat it, and that meant death, snakes lurking in the high grass, but snakes didn't bother her.

Snakes always know where you are long before you stumble upon them.

Once, her father killed a rattlesnake in the barn. The serpent didn't scare her, either.

I know where the snakes are because I can see them, but where is God?

She wondered why she should be afraid of what won't cross the street to harm her, or why God should be feared.

If God truly loved me, He would have crossed that dusty road long ago to save my soul from the evil waiting in the weeds.

She wrote that down, but then stopped and scratched it out.

Why does God care or not care about anyone on Earth? What does it matter if a person believes or does not believe? Some people find success and happiness while others do not. Some have a lifetime of struggles and hunger. God should do something about it.

This bothered Hannah. Day after day, this conflict absorbed her. When she visited the farm, she looked around at the beauty of what was left and realized that people come and go through another person's life and they come and go in houses and property, like vapor, and the only thing that remains is the land.

This is my Eden. I don't need nothing else.

After walking the circumference of the pond, she lay on the flat rock, while the old hay barn stood on the hillside of the pond and the sun illuminated its side, now faded gray as it rose from the east. She noticed the barn was leaning a few degrees to the left and thought for a second before starting a list on her tablet:

#1 Start my own church for injured hearts, for young girls looking for something beyond a boyfriend or husband.

Chapter 6

The Invisible Gate Around Heaven

Lucas lived four miles from the old family farm in Sundown, and on Hannah's drive back to her apartment, she passed a maze of streets backing up to their farm, a subdivision, Rapture Hall. The streets were cut out and paved when she was nine years old, but no houses were built on the property, which years later was also purchased by the airport authority, and as far as she knew, was owned by whoever owned her farm. Something inside her itched each time she was in the area, and she was prompted to drive down the old, abandoned streets on a desolate plot of land. It was a ghost town of discarded beer bottles, fast food wrappers, old sofas, abandoned appliances, worn-out tires, mattresses, and toilets.

At the end of the farthest cul-de-sac, she stopped her car to look around. She parked for a few minutes and listened to Z-93 and Journey's "Don't Stop Believing."

When she was eleven, she watched two men rape a woman in the back of a pick-up truck in this exact spot. She never told a soul that she witnessed this horrible crime until one night at Charlie's Pizzeria, when she told Margaret, who suggested Hannah put the episode in her *Document of Life*.

§

Right now, I'm in the Susan Kendal Library in Hebron, Georgia. Margaret is allowing me to use the library computer since it's not busy. It's Friday night, a few hours until closing time. Elvis has left the building and is probably home munching on a chew toy.

For a few years, I have found myself less interested in church, which may be an understatement. I have no capacity for the intolerance of religion, or those people in religion who are intolerant. However, Margaret goes to church. She says her church is a good church where people are friendly and don't tell you what to do, what to think, or how to live your life.

"We rejoice in knowing God loves us," Margaret said.

Today, I had a four o'clock appointment with Mr. Fox at Grattan's Funeral Home. He reminds me of a black Albert Einstein with hair that sort of stood up and puffed out from his head, gray and wild. I almost laughed during the meeting when I thought how this man, with such a horrible, messy head of hair, a beehive of messiness, was about to hire me to cut dead people's hair to make them look presentable. He was a little hunched over, like he had been injured in a car accident, but he was so nice and soft-spoken, I wanted to hug him when he gave me the job. He showed me a pair of Tsubame ceramic scissors, which I could never afford. They're at least $1,000. I get to use them starting Thursday, after finishing at the salon. Mr. Fox will show me the ropes. He didn't have anyone for me to practice on today, but give it a few days, he said. He laughed when he told me that. I guess even funeral people have to crack jokes. His wife was there with their children, a boy and two girls, no older than ten. His wife, Karen, looked about thirty-five, much younger than Mr. Fox.

For the record, I no longer live near the old subdivision that backs up to my old farm. That was where I witnessed the rape, and the reason I'm writing about it is because Margaret suggested it (almost insisted). Otherwise, this might go to my grave. I finally feel comfortable enough to write it down.

It's a subdivision of seven streets and cul-de-sacs that were developed in 2006, but after the developer cleared the land and paved the streets, he was arrested for murdering his wife in 1988 in Kansas City. It was in all the newspapers. He was going by a different name, Jerry Something-or-Other, but years after the fact, the police matched DNA evidence in a Codex system, and like a pack of hyenas, they were all over him. My daddy would have said they were on him like stink on a pig. He was sent to prison in Kansas for the rest of his sorry life. I don't know what happened to him after that, just sitting around in prison with time to think.

Since the subdivision backed up to our farm, I would walk through the woods or ride my bicycle, sometimes with Lucas, and I would sit in a large Live Oak tree eating apples to watch the land being bulldozed over. I looked out over the unused streets, not a person around, nothing but quiet. Over the years, like with our farm, there have been all sorts of plans for the property, but nothing came of it.

There were plans to build condos, a park, and a golf course but that also fell to naught. Now, all the blacktop streets are overgrown with weeds and scrub brush. It's called Rapture Hall, but I call it Rape Her Hard. It's all fenced off now, except for the portions people have knocked down. I always figured I'd learn to play golf, ride around in a golf cart, and see my old house, chicken coop, and dog lot. When I visit, I get sad because it's not mine, and I can't go back inside and sleep in my old room or help Momma with dinner.

I kind of thought they might find the old graves. That would be a news story my momma wouldn't want to hear.

One sunny day after church, when I was eleven and not long after Mr. Grady died, I packed myself a little sack lunch and a bottle of juice and walked through the woods to the other side, where the streets of Rapture Hall rested, waiting for houses to be built. I set out to find the graves, but like all other times, did not. From the tree I could see out over the entire layout of the subdivision to Goodman Road. On this day, a white pick-up truck kicked up dust as it wound through the streets and headed my way. At first, I thought about jumping out of the tree and heading home but didn't, because I thought they wouldn't park near me. As they drove closer, I got scared about being there. I thought maybe it was their tree and their property. Maybe they were going to build a house on this land, and I might get in trouble for being in their tree.

They parked the truck at the end of the cul-de-sac about fifteen feet from where I was sitting, high up. When two men popped out of the truck, they walked to the back, opened a red cooler, and grabbed a beer in each hand. The woman, who I thought was about twenty, stepped out of the truck and walked back to sit with the men on the tailgate, where she casually talked to them as though they were good friends. They were nice to her and laughed like they were cutting up in math class.

I remember vividly that she was barefoot and wearing blue cut-off shorts and a white t-shirt with sparkling blue and silver letters that said, "Frankly My Dear, I Don't Give a Damn." They sat for a few minutes on the tailgate. Then, as the woman leaned over to pull another beer out of the cooler, one man reached up and hit her in the jaw with his fist, right against the muscle of her cheek. Her shoulder hit the side of the cooler, and ice and water flew out, and the beer in his hand sprayed all over her shirt and hair. Then, the other man sat behind the woman and held her arms down, while the first man yanked off her shorts and underwear. Half knocked out, she didn't move.

The man yelled, "This is 'cause your old man owes us three hundred bucks. He ain't paying, so this is how it is."

He yanked her shirt up over her face and poured beer over it, so that it shrunk around her mouth. Then he was on her, and he grabbed her boobs. When he was finished, the other man jumped on top of her and took his turn. She just lay there with her face turned away from them, trying to breathe through the wet shirt.

While they were doing this, I thought about climbing down from the tree and running back home, but knew I could never outrun them, and it was too far to my house. I sat in the tree, never so much as moving a twig or breathing or passing air.

"There," said the second man, "that's a little going-away present before you get married. Next time Jimmy tries screwing us, we'll leave you to die. Get dressed. We still want our money."

They tossed their beer cans onto the dirt and weeds and sat on the tailgate while she dressed, and then one man walked over to the tree to pee. The woman pulled up her underwear and shorts. I watched the man pee, the whole time afraid he would look straight up and see me sitting there like a bird or an angel. Then, all three drove off in the truck.

I never saw the men again, but years later in eleventh

grade, as my class was returning from a science fair in Tyrone, we stopped at a Waffle House. I recognized the waitress as being the same woman, except now she was missing a front tooth and was not wearing a wedding ring. Seeing that woman scared me. I've never told anyone what I witnessed that horrible day, but I was so upset, I had to leave the Waffle House. I couldn't sit inside. I just couldn't bear to stay there with my insides hurting so much. I sat in the school bus, slunk down but looking at her outside my window. I looked away if I thought she or anyone else saw me staring.

I wanted to rush inside and scream, "I know what happened!"

I could not move. I was paralyzed. When I watched the woman work, I thought maybe she enjoyed her job, but she looked like at any moment she could break down and cry. It made me feel like crying too, but I didn't know what to do, especially if it wasn't the same woman. Thinking back, I'm certain it was her. Back then, the more I thought about it, the more scared I became. What if the bad guys were eating country ham in the next booth? In the end, my classmates, their parents, and the teachers all boarded the bus and asked how I was feeling. The bus rolled out of the parking lot as I watched her, my cheek pressed against the cold window, and the last thing I saw was the woman handing a bowl of grits to a boy sitting at the counter.

It's closing time. Tonight, Margaret and I are walking to the pharmacy for a Cherry Coke, then going back to my apartment to watch a movie. I will pick back up right here next time. Talking about the rape story wasn't the best story to tell, but I cannot be the judge of these things. I can report what I know to be the truth and nothing else.

When the trumpet sounds, the Christians who have
died will be raised with transformed bodies.
—I Thessalonians 4:16

Note to self: this might be Corinthians 15:52-55.
I don't remember exactly.

§

After the library shut down for the evening, Margaret followed Hannah back to her apartment where they found a business card from Hawkshaw Bales stuck in the doorjamb. Hannah looked at it, then explained to Margaret who he was.

"He'd better not show up," Hannah said, "otherwise, I'll call the cops."

Every few days, Hannah found his business card stuck in her door between the crack in the doorjamb, to let her know that he had been there. It was always when she was not home, as if he had planned to visit while she was away. The last time, he wrote on the card, "Have your brother call me. I may have work for him."

Hannah and Margaret researched Hawkshaw Bales online and found nothing regarding Bales Micro Farms. Since 2005, he'd been indicted thirteen times for various crimes, including assault and transporting drugs. In each case, the charges were dropped for lack of evidence, or his alibi was so air-tight that the district attorney did not dare proceed to trial. Hannah even found an allegation that Bales was behind the Farm Contract for Cash scandal, as the middleman who shuffled cash from donors to county and state politicians to obtain bids and favors. However, no one could prove he received any money or doled it back to officials, but everywhere Hannah looked, his name was associated with the scandal. She found an old video of Bales standing next to his lawyer as the lawyer spoke to the press.

"My client, Mr. Bales, is a local businessman who negotiates for vendor contracts and attends many parties to woo businesses, but he had nothing to do with any Farm Contract for Cash or anything illegal."

Since their first meeting, Bales had also called Hannah on several occasions to ask about Lucas, until she blocked his calls. A few times, he used a different telephone, so she wouldn't know he was calling, but after he started talking, she hung up, then stopped answering any phone number she did not recognize.

She texted his number back: *Listen up, Mr. Pushy, you need to stop bothering me. I got friends in this town who will set you straight if you don't.*

The next day, Lucas's trailer burned to the ground. She was scared for her brother and called him to emphasize the amount of trouble he was in with Bales, but Lucas shook it off.

"Don't worry," he said. "He'll go away and give up looking for me. I'm up here in Fayetteville laying sheetrock. He'll never find me here."

"I thought you were in Alabama."

"I was for a few weeks, but I found a better-paying job in Arkansas."

"He'll track you down by your bills," Hannah told him.

"Naw, I'm living in a hotel with a few guys here, and I pay them cash. Besides, I'm using an alias."

One day, some men showed up at their father's house looking for Lucas, suggesting to Darnell that he pony up the money.

"Ain't seen my boy in over a year, not since he joined the military."

"Where's he stationed?" one man asked.

"Boys, even if I knew where he was stationed, I ain't about to give up my son. But if you find him, watch out, 'cause all he does is train to kill people and do it with a smile on his face, kind'a like me when I was in the Forces. He's out there in the desert somewhere. Good luck."

Darnell knew they wouldn't spend time looking for Lucas in the military, and if they tried finding him, they might find his brother, Wendell, somewhere in Germany or in the desert or the mountains or in a sub or floating down to Earth at night with a parachute on a black op training mission. Darnell figured that if they threatened him, and Wendell didn't kill them, someone in his squad would. As soon as the men left, Darnell called Lucas to give him an earful of fatherly advice about staying in Arkansas for the time being or heading back out to California to prospect for gold. A few days later, Darnell walked outside and found his tires slashed.

You ain't seen nothing, yet, he thought.

Last night I cut my first dead guy's hair. It took two hours. Mr. Fox did not help me one bit, just stood there watching and talking to me, giving me advice. Even with gloves on, I couldn't touch the dead guy for fifteen minutes. Clarence Dixon was ninety-three. He looked rubbery and had an ammonia smell. I wish he had had his shirt on because he was gross. He had a sheet over him, up to his waist, and I got him after he'd been "prepared," as Mr. Fox said. He said I could practice on Clarence since it was going to be a closed casket.

"He doesn't have any family. None. He's the last of the Dixons in this area, I suppose. He was a history professor at the community college for years and years. Never married. Has no kids. He was at Crestview Retirement Center for the last eight years. I was told he was fairly active, right up until he died."

I was glad to hear that. I'll get faster as I become more comfortable. I made $45. Cash. Which I ain't reporting.

Chapter 7

The Dead Usually Don't Complain

Hannah had been busy at The Cute Curl during the week leading up to Mother's Day, which was a pleasant change of pace for her. She had at least four or five extra walk-ins per day, mainly college-age boys. From high school—Mike Dawkins—was home from Virginia Tech to visit his mother in the hospital. They'd been in school together since the seventh grade but never ran in the same circles. He played tuba in the band and was on the soccer team. Hannah played tennis and cheer. She remembered how the girls baked cookies and cheered for the soccer team one year, the morning of Homecoming, when Mike scored a goal. She relived that moment for him, which made Mike smile because he remembered that after the goal, she gave him a cookie and a big hug.

Dave Edwards walked into the salon minutes before lunchtime, which perked Hannah up. He was the one man who regularly had his hair cut. Hannah liked how, when they were talking, he treated her like an equal, like her opinion mattered. It didn't hurt that he was a handsome man whose hair she loved washing, and whose scalp she enjoyed running her fingers over. When she cut his hair, it was like an artist sculpting a masterpiece, but she never felt that she had anything interesting to tell him, only how she knew the exact number of steps it was from her apartment to the mailbox—until one time when she told him about cutting dead people's hair for extra money, how she had been training and learning the technique.

"You don't have to worry about cutting the back of their head 'cause no one's going to see that. Dead people don't complain. Not much."

That made Edwards laugh. It was a line Mr. Fox had told Hannah on her first day. She hadn't used it before, but sort of blurted it out.

She also told Edwards about Lucas's trailer being burned.

"I read about that. They thought it was lightning."

"Could be, but I think it was someone in town."

She told Edwards about Hawkshaw Bales, but said she had no proof of anything. He didn't say much except that she should be careful around Bales.

"If you need anything, let me know," he told her.

Hannah didn't have time to eat lunch with Margaret this week, which she usually did. But one evening, Margaret bought Chinese food for them, and they hung out in the park during Margaret's dinner break. Afterwards, before driving to Grattan's Funeral Home, Hannah drove to CVS for paper towels, light bulbs, and dish soap. When she walked out of CVS, she ran into Hawkshaw Bales, who was with a pretty Black girl that looked to be about fifteen.

"Hey there, Mr. Micro Farm. You out doing God's work today?" Hannah asked.

"Seen your brother?"

"You slashed anyone's tires lately or burned down their trailer?"

"I'm not sure what you're talking about."

"I bet. Who's this?" She looked at the young girl.

"This is my niece, Sandra."

"How long has she been your niece, a few days?"

"Very cute. Sandra, here's twenty bucks. Go inside and get me a Fanta Orange. Get yourself something, too. I'll be there in a minute. I gotta talk business." He handed her the money.

"You didn't offer me anything."

"You want a soda?" Bales asked.

"No," Hannah replied. "It just shows your lack of manners."

"I got other business on my mind."

"You got no business with me," Hannah said.

“I’m a busy man an’ my moods changed.”

“Let’s get something straight, Mister. I’m not my brother’s keeper. If Lucas owes you money, what can I do about it? Deal with him.”

“Maybe your old man has money.”

“He ain’t got no money, so leave him out of this.”

“I might if your brother ponies up.”

“What makes you think other people are responsible for him?”

“They’re not, but I’m making it their business. If your ol’ man won’t pay, I’ll feed your brother to the gators. Now, what father won’t pay up to save his son? Maybe I’ll beat your ol’ man to send a message to your brother and anyone who thinks they can mess with me.”

“I’ve read about you. I know who you are and so do the police.”

Bales laughed. Hannah thought her declaration would scare him. She wondered if this was what Dave Edwards meant when he said to let him know if she needed anything.

“Once my friends break open your ol’ man’s head, your brother’ll do something stupid like rob a bank or a Huddle House to pay me. Believe me, people will do anything to save their kin from harm.”

“Are you threatening me?”

“Maybe I’ll pay a visit to your momma at that sorry excuse for a restaurant.”

“Leave her out of this.”

“That little dump will burn in ten minutes.”

“You leave her alone.”

“It’s all on you. You want this to go away, tell me where your brother is. Ten grand ain’t chicken feed.”

“I don’t have that much. I have about two hundred dollars to last the rest of the month.”

“It sucks to be you. Sweetheart, I don’t want your money, but I’ll tell you what. I’ll make you a deal.”

"Don't call me Sweetheart, and I don't make deals with the devil."

"You will to save Lucas."

Hannah stood outside the CVS and leaned on her car, ready to jump in or run around it or run back into the CVS if Bales tried grabbing her. The warmth of the metal seeped through the fabric of her jeans as she tried to figure how to appease this guy to get him to go away. When Sandra stepped out of the store, Bales told her to go back inside.

"We ain't finished talking."

She huffed and went away again after handing over his Fanta Orange. Hannah hoped that Sandra had shaken it up first.

"Here's my proposal. I'll wipe away all your brother's debt for one little thing."

"What might that be?"

"I get three hours with you."

"I thought you'd say something like that. You want me to sleep with you for three hours. Fat chance."

Bales laughed even harder, then told Hannah he knew she'd say no. He asked her to look at it from a business perspective—he would wipe away all of Lucas's debt, clear the books.

"Not many people get out of a squeeze like this so easily," he said.

He told her it was a one-time offer—three hours to have his way. After that, he'd leave and all of Lucas's debt would be washed away. Otherwise, he would collect the money from Lucas or someone in her family.

"Or we beat the hell out of your brother, and then he still owes the money."

"That's a bullcrap deal."

"What do you want? By the way, I know he's in Arkansas. I got my people working on it right now. Where're you going to wash away ten grand like that? There's not an ounce of shaky pudding in the world worth that much."

"Why are you doing this?"

"Normally, I'd want my money. I can get split tail any time, but not a girl like you. I know your type—you don't give it away to anyone. You're fine looking, and I like your pouty lips. I like that on a white girl. I don't care what happens to your brother—it's that simple. They can kill him as far as I'm concerned. Really, you don't have much of an option."

"No is an option."

"I'm giving you the chance to help your brother. It's no big deal. It's only sex, but ten grand's a big deal."

"I don't have that kind of money."

"Who among us does?" he sympathized with her.

"Maybe I can get it."

"You have one day."

"No, no, no." The bumper pressed hard into her thigh. "One week. I need some time to think on things."

"Fine, I'll give you a week. If we find Lucas before then, the deal's off."

She went round and round with Bales trying to get him to lower the amount of money, but he wouldn't budge. Sandra appeared again from the CVS.

"I'm tired of looking at magazines," she told him. He nodded toward her.

"Make up your mind," Bales said to Hannah.

"No funny business?" she asked.

"A straight deal."

"One hour?" she demanded.

"Three or the money," he replied.

"No. One hour. That's all, but I still got to think about this."

"Okay. One hour," he agreed.

Hannah hesitated for a few seconds, then said, "Don't hold your breath."

Bales turned to Sandra and asked her for the change from his twenty. He held out his left hand.

"There wasn't any," Sandra said, with her hands bolted to her hips.

"What do you mean? You bought two sodas." He held out his hand and thrusted it toward her again.

"There wasn't any change," she repeated.

Hannah had no idea where she would find the money, but she was buying time to warn Lucas or to see if he could get it. Maybe her momma or Ronnie would lend it to him. She didn't want to be beholden to either.

"If I do this, and it's a big 'if,' I never see you again and you never bother me, Lucas, or my family."

Bales agreed.

For all have sinned and fall short of the glory of God.—Romans 3:23

By the time she pulled into the parking lot of the funeral home, Hannah was full-out irritated by Bales' proposal. She was still shaking from his threats and thought about calling Dave Edwards but knew she never would.

People say things like I will help you or give me a call if you need any help, but they don't mean it.

With a few minutes to spare before work, she sat in her car to breathe, with the air conditioner blasting, trying to find a calm demeanor before going into the funeral home. The other night, Mr. Fox told her that the next haircut would be on her own. She was ready, and this was the night.

"This is Edith Hobbs," Mr. Fox said to Hannah as he pulled back the cover. "Most families bring us a photo so you can see how they wore their hair, but the Hobbs family has procrastinated, so you'll have to take an educated guess. If the client's been in an accident or was a cancer patient, I insist on a photo. Edith, here, died of old age."

"Do you want to just give her a wig?"

"I don't think we can even guess what kind it would be, what with her hair looking like ham gravy trickling down."

§

It's now that I can see a few things with clarity, unlike when I stood in the forest of my childhood, always afraid the police were going to storm through the door and arrest my father and kick us off the farm. I always thought someone was going to sue us and take everything we had. It's because there were so many attorney shows on TV that everyone was being sued, and I thought we were next. There was an undercurrent of family secrets that scared me. The rumors I heard always dealt with nefarious people and events that seemed just right for the law and a swarm of attorneys.

§

I've spent the entire week avoiding the subject of Hawkshaw Bales. Today is Saturday. After working all day at the salon, I'm too tired to count the bees in the hive. The library closes in twenty-five minutes. Afterwards, Margaret and I are going down the street for a Greek salad with real Kalamata olives. I mentioned to her that maybe we'd find some cute guys hanging out at the bar next door.

I called Lucas twice this week to ask if he had any money, but all he said was not to let Hawkshaw Bales scare me. I don't dare ask Daddy for the money. Momma said all her money was tied up in the restaurant. If Daddy finds out how serious this has become, he'll shoot Bales, and then Daddy'll go to prison. Momma might be happy with that, but I wouldn't.

Chapter 8

Locks Like Samson's

Last night, after having pizza and a salad at Mario's, and because Margaret did not feel like trying to draw the attention of drunk guys at the bar, she and Hannah sat in the park drinking their sodas and listening to a couple of teenagers with guitars, one with a stand-up bass, one with a violin, and another with a snare drum and cymbal. Several other people stood around listening, too. It was a warm evening with a slight breeze that brought a mild chill to Hannah and Margaret.

When the violinist played a solo on "Norwegian Wood," Hannah told Margaret, "That sounds like a refined sawmill." When the boys took a short break to pass the hat to everyone for a few dollars, Margaret started singing the theme to the *Beverly Hillbillies*. Everyone joined in, clapping, and the skittle band jumped back to their instruments and improvised.

People gave them more money when the bass player passed around his baseball cap while Margaret sang, taking the forefront and hamming it up like Diana Ross. When she finished, the guitar players bowed to her and clapped, which encouraged the spectators to clap louder.

Regardless of how much she enjoyed herself, Hannah had one thing on her mind, Hawkshaw Bales. As much as she tried, she couldn't shake the thought of him. She had two hundred and six dollars to her name, not enough to pay off Lucas's debt. Even though she had not spoken to Bales again, her answer was "No." She wasn't going to sleep with him.

She and Margaret sat in the park for an hour listening to the band before Hannah talked Margaret into walking to the Cart Barn for a beer. Hannah wanted one, but didn't want to pay for it, so she thought they might meet a few guys who would buy their drinks. For more than an hour they sat at a table, but no one approached them.

"This didn't turn out like I thought," Hannah said, as she paid the tab.

Afterwards, Margaret was too tipsy to drive home, so she stayed the night at Hannah's apartment.

"I never drink. That's probably the first beer I've had in three years. Let alone two beers. It hit me hard."

With one bed in the house, they shared sides. Hannah lent Margaret a t-shirt and made certain not to bump into her or cut her with her toenails. In the morning, the two women lay in bed talking for an hour before Hannah drove to San Francisco Café for coffee and bagels. Margaret turned over and went back to sleep.

Later in the morning, they hung out, talking, reading the Sunday paper, and sitting out on the patio off the bedroom. It was a small patio that held a round table and two plastic chairs with no room to turn around. Margaret did not mind, but Hannah was embarrassed by how little she had in the way of furniture, and what she had was poor quality, things she bought at Goodwill or yard sales.

Hannah told Margaret the story of how her sister, Greta, ran away from home and hasn't returned since.

"I've only talked to her on the phone. I've thought about flying out to California but it's expensive."

"When I was fifteen, I ran away from home," Margaret said.

"Because of your father?"

Margaret nodded and sipped her coffee.

When Margaret stretched out her legs on to the wooden railing, Hannah noticed two small circular scars from when Margaret's father had burned her with a cigarette.

He must have been the biggest butthole in the world.

"I might'a bought a gun and shot him," Hannah said.

"After that, I ran away to live with my Aunt Claire until I finished high school. Then, I joined the Army for six years. Once I was out of the Army, I lived with her while I went to Chapel Hill, bought and paid for by the U.S. government. It took a while, but I finished up and earned my undergrad degree. Then, I attended Duke and earned a Master's in library science."

"Rescue the poor and helpless; deliver them from the grasp of evil people," Hannah said.

"That's nice. Did you write that?"

"No, it's from the Bible, Psalm 82:4."

"My aunt said I never had to worry about him ever again. As far as she was concerned, she had no idea where I was and never heard from me. I was her secret."

Margaret's father called Claire numerous times, wanting to know where Margaret was, but her aunt held true and said she hadn't heard from Margaret, except once. Claire knew about her brother's evil streak, so she protected Margaret.

When Claire did not offer more information, Margaret's father said, "if you heard from her what the hell'd she say?"

"Herbert, do not ever talk to me that way. I will not tolerate that language."

"Well, where the hell is she?"

"I haven't seen Margaret in over a year. She stopped by one day on her way out west 'cause she had a job. Once she was settled in, she called me from Portland, Oregon. I don't have her address or phone number, and I haven't heard from her since."

Margaret's father had slammed the phone down. She never heard another word about him until her aunt called a few years later to say he was dead.

"Were you sad?"

"I was, because anytime your father dies, it hurts. It was just something else that happened in my life. I knew he was burning in Hell and that scared me. I thought if I forgave him for what he did, then God would too, and maybe he wouldn't be in Hell. Not in Heaven, but he wouldn't be in Hell any longer. I prayed for his redemption. Day after day, I prayed for God to forgive him for all that he did to me. I hope that helped."

"She must have been a fine aunt."

"She was wonderful, an' saved me from whatever else was going to happen. I don't know why, but she never had children. Years later, I wrote her letters and sent poems I'd written. She always lived in the same house, and that's where home is to me. The last time I was in town, I drove by her old house. It looked nice, and there were some kids playing in the front yard, but the folks living there painted the trim an ugly, bright yellow."

"I wonder why she never had children."

"She never married. She said there was a boy she liked in school, and they courted awhile, but then he went off to college in the East, and when he returned, they went to the movies a few times and she fell in love with him. But then he died in a car accident near Spartanburg when a cement mixer crashed into his car. I don't know why she didn't find someone else."

"I think people years ago fell in love with one person," Hannah said, "and no matter what, that was all they ever wanted, just that one person. I don't think that happens much anymore."

Margaret told Hannah more stories about her life and how she'd never met her mother or anyone on her mother's side of the family. Her father never told her one thing about any of them.

"I don't even know their names, but I guess I could figure it out if I did the research. I've met the kinfolk on my daddy's side, but except for my Aunt Claire, they're trash."

Margaret said there was a poem by Sharon Olds called "Cambridge Elegy" that she used to read about falling in love with someone who ended up dying at a young age. It always made her sad.

§

I was supposed to make a decision weeks ago pertaining to Hawkshaw Bales. I have put him off. He called two days ago and asked what I was gonna do. "I'm still thinking." I called my momma and daddy to see if they've heard from Lucas. They have not. I texted him. Hours later, he texted back:

Werking long hours met a girl kinda nice

on the look out for the bad guys

some people have been asking about me

in town strangers

IM werking for cash under the table

using a different name Johnny Macintosh

I know what yer thinking

sounds stupid maybe so but its werking

I have a little extra money, not much, but I'm saving it for a rainy day. I've now cut eleven dead people's hair. I'm making barely enough money to pay the rent for my apartment and what Wendy charges for my chair. If I could have two more customers per day, things would be so much better. It doesn't have to be a lot to make life easier.

Dave Edwards came in the other day for a shampoo and a cut. He stayed for an hour talking while I took my time with him. While he was lying back in the shampoo chair, he closed his eyes, and I massaged his temples, forehead, and the back of his neck while the peppermint conditioner relaxed him. I wonder if there is another woman in his life who does that for him.

From time-to-time, my daddy regaled us kids with stories about his ancestors owning slaves on the farm. When I was young—and Lucas, too—we thought it was normal for everyone to have had slaves, but by the time I was a teenager, I knew his stories were garbage. Daddy attempted to be humorous and nostalgic for that old life, but I found no humor in it.

"You didn't own slaves," Momma would yell.

“Never said I did. My great-greats way back did. I’ve always treated Black folks kindly.”

“You don’t like any Black folks, and I doubt you’ve ever treated any of them nicely,” she said.

“I do what I can all the time to make this a better world,” Darnell smacked back at her.

“Your kinfolk never lived on this land before or during the Civil War, and they never owned slaves,” Momma told him.

“Then Lilith, that ought’a make you happy. How come you always have to ruin a good story?”

We knew better than to refute Daddy’s sense of historical accuracy, for his backhand was imminent. And he wasn’t going to hit us kids.

“I wasn’t alive back then,” he said, “and didn’t have nothing to do with how folks was treated, but according to my great-granddaddy, who you ain’t never met, we had eight slaves. Back then the aristocracy afforded slaves, so to have eight means we were right off, rich by most accounts. In other words, my kinfolks had a buck or two.”

I don’t know if this is true. I’m hoping it isn’t. Regardless, I was embarrassed he might tell these stories in front of people I know.

I always hoped his stories were lies. Instead of slaves, maybe we had a few people who worked the farm and were paid for a day’s labor, but I never saw any conclusive evidence to prove otherwise. On the other side of the pond, about thirty yards deep in the woods, there are remnants of a few small shacks, not much bigger than an outhouse or a chicken coop.

“That’s right. Those were the n-shacks (I ain’t writing out that word). They’re gone now, but when I was a boy, a couple families lived there. Tress have grown up around them but back in the day, if you sat on the front porch, you could see the pond and much of the farm. Mr. Grady’s family lived there for a few generations. One man, nearly his entire life. I don’t recall his name, but Daddy said everyone called him Clock, because one of his arms was shorter than the other arm. Other folks moved in and out with the seasons. If I recall, one of them shacks burned down, but no one was hurt. After the War of

Northern Aggression, those folks weren't slaves any longer, but they lived and worked here up until the 1910s or 1920s, some up beyond World War II. I know for certain there was a black family living there and working the farm in the 1960s, but they were probably the last ones. After that, some folks just lived in them and paid rent, which was a paltry amount."

"You were not alive during the Civil War," Wendell said.

"No kidding, Sherlock Holmes," Daddy said. "I never told you I was. I'm repeating a historical event that occurred on this land. It's a story handed down to me, and if you'd shut up and listen, I'll hand it down to you."

Daddy paused his story and walked into the kitchen for more sweet tea before resuming. He sat back down in his rocker with a thump, like he was carrying the burden of the world on his shoulders. He grunted.

"I don't recall the names of all those folks living in those old shacks. I used to fish with the old man at the pond or down by the river. Clock had to be ninety years old. No self-respecting person would live there, but if that's all you had, you made do. My kin treated folks with respect, clothed and fed them, too, because if you didn't, they wouldn't be inclined to work hard. Folks would come and go. Live for a while in the shacks, work, and one day up and be gone. Somewhere on the farm there are some graves marked by creek stones. My daddy showed me once when I was young, but I don't recall where they are."

When he said the graves, my ears perked up.

"Daddy, can you show me where they are?"

"I haven't been out there since I was your age, and to be truthful, I just don't remember. In fact, the farm used to be bigger, but parts were sold off and those graves might be on the land we sold. Not by me, but your kin."

"What happened to all that money," Wendell asked.

"Like everything else, someone drank it away, gambled it, or lost it to several years of bad crops or the Depression wiped them out. I don't rightly know. I ain't never seen any of it."

Years ago, me, Lucas, Wendell, and Greta searched for the graves to put flowers on them, but we never found the stones.

Afterwards, we all sided with Momma, thinking that Daddy was lying.

"I think you've created a new history or modified it to such a degree that it's not like anything that happened on this land," Momma told him.

"You're damn lucky you ain't living in a barn back in Screwed-Up, Kentucky with that hillbilly family of yours."

Daddy had a book with the "Last Will and Testament" of Eli Klein, his kin who willed the property to be handed out after he was dead. He kept it in his closet, on a shelf, and wrapped in a plastic waterproof bag. We were not allowed to touch it. Many nights sitting on the porch, Daddy read from the will like it was *The Book of Giants*, the last great document of his family history.

"You kids see, we used to be sumthin' in this here county. Back then people knew and respected us. They damn near bowed when we walked by."

"My family was more refined and enlightened than your side of the family ever was," Momma reminded him. "We put a value on all human life. We fought for the Union against slavery."

"Refined my big fat butt," he yelled out, laughing as he rocked in his chair on the porch. "When I rescued you from the hills of Kentucky, you didn't even have running water in that shack. The first night I slept over, your old man handed me a shotgun to take to the outhouse. I asked if it was for the bears, and he said it was to kill other hillbillies if they come upon me."

"Least we never kept another person in bondage and worked them to death," she yelled.

"No, you had sex with your brothers and daddy."

"We did not! That's a lie! You better tell the children that's a lie."

"Well, she never had sex with her daddy," he laughed because he knew how this angered Momma.

"You're a disgusting human being. You're not even that. You're an animal," she yelled before stomping off into the house.

"Well, it's late and your momma is pretty well peeved at

me for talking about owning slaves, so you children ought to go to bed."

There's nothing I can do about my ancestors, not much except sort my inheritance, rid myself of the depraved.

Chapter 9

Smile, You're on Candid Heartbreak

By the end of May, Hannah decided to ignore Hawkshaw Bales. He was old news to her and buried deep.

On her day off, she drove to her father's house for a box of family photographs to use in a scrapbook she was making for her mother's birthday. His house was smaller than their farmhouse but kept it clean and orderly. A visit didn't go by when he didn't insist Hannah should move in to save money.

"I won't charge you any rent, so whatever you're paying right now, you can sock it away or buy silver and gold."

Her father had been living in this house since being "forcibly removed" from the farm by the Airport Authority, as he declared. "It's like having some Yankee pointing a Spencer rifle at my chest."

He paid cash for the house, but the rest of the money was gone from playing poker and slots in Biloxi, and scratch-off tickets from the filling station down the street. He blew through ninety-five percent of the farm money. Now, he only played the lottery—five dollars on Tuesday and Friday. He insisted he broke even, but she didn't believe him.

"I just brewed a fresh pot of coffee," he said as he picked at his teeth with a fork.

"I'll make you a cup if you'll get the photographs," she said.

"Fine, but I'm drinking it black these days. Add a little sugar to cut the bitterness. No cream."

"You know, if you add eggshells to your coffee when you brew it, the bitterness will go away."

"Yeah, I ain't doing that," he yelled back from down the hall.

He walked downstairs to the basement to where he set up an

office, which was nothing more than a card table and an old wooden chair to help his taxes with an office deduction. He returned with a large shoebox, popping open with photos.

"Here, there's a bunch of stuff on your momma's side that she never took, so you'll have to ask who these folks are. I don't need any of this crap, so you keep it or give it to her. Whatever you do, don't toss it out. These might be all that's left of some folks."

Hannah flipped through a handful of pictures while her father sat drinking his coffee.

"I wrote names on the back of the folks I remembered."

Her father walked back to the bathroom with the newspaper and was in there for fifteen minutes, while Hannah checked her email and text messages on her phone, rummaged through the photographs, and fidgeted because she wanted to leave but had a question first. She read the Google news for the day's events, and when he returned, he sat down and placed the newspaper on the table. Hannah noticed that the Sudoku was finished.

"Daddy?" she asked in a soft voice.

"What, Darling?"

She managed the courage to ask, "Have you been married before? I mean, before Momma?"

"What kind of question's that?"

"Years ago, Aunt Mavis said you were married before Momma. She said you got a bunch of other children."

"She was nuts, you know."

Hannah sat quietly.

"Let me tell you something about your aunt. I've known her all my life, but as sweet and good-natured as she was, she did nothing but lie from the day she was born. She made up stuff just to see how long it'd take to make the rounds back to her, just to see how wild it got. You don't know this, but when Kennedy was killed, she drove to Dallas and tried pretending that she was in Delay Plaza when it happened and then a few days later tried convincing the police she was having an affair with Lee Harvey Oswald. She wasn't the only person to climb out of the woodwork like that, but that shows you where her head was."

The following Sunday, Hannah drove up north to her mother's house on the banks of Lake Lanier for a box of family photographs, but Lilith forgot Hannah was coming over and was not home when she arrived. Lilith lived with Ronnie Lee in a house built in the 1960s that was restored a few years ago. It was built after the river was dammed up in 1956 and sat about fifty yards from where the road was swallowed up by the lake. Lilith bought it from a couple going through a divorce. The old blacktop road looked like a strip of taffy slipping under the lake, then resurfacing a mile away on the other side. Between the two ends of the road lay the old town of Oarsville, under eighty feet of water.

"Some nights," Lilith said to Hannah once, "I'll sit out here with a cup of coffee and listen to the voices of the dead people still buried deep down there."

"Momma, it's creepy when you say that stuff."

"I don't hear voices or nothing like that. We sold the farm so the airport-people could plow the history of our land under ground, and now here I am, looking over a lake with all the streets, houses, businesses, and farms down below just festering, rotting, history being denied by one hundred feet of water. Let me tell you something, Sweetie, you cannot bury the past. It haunts you. Hell, dead people are just six feet away."

"Unless you're under all this water. Then they're one hundred and six feet away," Hannah said.

Hannah wanted to bring up her baby sister to her mother, but she could not on this day. She was too tired to dig that deep into the ground. Over the past fifteen years, she mentioned something about it twice—one time Lilith simply ignored her, while on the second occasion, Lilith told Hannah, "If you don't stop with these crazy stories, I'll take you to Milledgeville and hand you over to the nut house. There are a thousand people in there with stories just as crazy. Don't never mention that shit again or you'll be rooming with Sybil."

She told Hannah how, back in the late 1980s, during a drought, folks could see the Lanier Speedway grandstands and other buildings along the lake, old cars, sunken boats, tree stumps, and a few skeletons.

"This was before I moved here, but you can look it up on the Google."

"Is that true?"

"Sure is. There are all sorts of stories. There's a woman down the road a bit, Jean Edington, who has a scrapbook of photos and newspaper articles. I met her at a Memorial Day parade when we sat next to each other and got to talking. She knows all the stories."

On this particular Sunday, Hannah's mother was not home when she arrived. Eddie Lee Dawkins, Ronnie Lee's brother, answered the door.

That's about right, leave the dog home when you go out.

She thought they should have put him in a cage so he couldn't run loose. Eddie Lee sort of came with the furniture when her mother and Ronnie Lee became an item. Hannah liked Ronnie Lee quite a lot because he treated her mother with respect, holding open the door for her, wiping off her soda cup at the restaurant if the waitress spilled some Coke down the side, talking nice and never raising his voice or a hand to strike her, and asking for her opinion and listening to what she said. Hannah couldn't recall her father opening a door for Lilith, except maybe once when she was loaded down with groceries.

"Here, Lilith, that's a pretty heavy load. Let me hold the door open for you while you carry those grocery bags inside."

Hannah arrived at ten o'clock while Eddie Lee was in the kitchen making a ketchup sandwich. When he opened the carport door, he had a streak of ketchup on the side of his face. He looked like he had not bathed in a month.

"Your momma ain't home. She's at the Diamond Eye with Ronnie. They said something about supplies coming in or maybe going fishing off the dock," he said with a mouthful of food. "Come on in."

"You want a ketchup sandwich? They're real easy to make."

"For breakfast?"

"I've had worse. How about a relish sandwich? Takes about the same time to make."

"Just relish?"

"And bread. A hamburger bun."

"No, thanks. I came to pick up some photographs. Did she leave anything for me?"

Eddie Lee limped over to the front hall closet to retrieve a cardboard box of photographs.

"What's wrong with your leg?" she asked.

"Which one? I got issues with both."

"The left one. You're walking like Keyser Söze."

"Is he a rapper?"

He walked like he was dragging a log. He set the box on the table. Hannah noticed how nasty the box was, as if he'd been storing oily car parts in it.

Eddie Lee made another sandwich, and while his back was to her, he said, "Your momma said you might show up. You can go see her at the restaurant if you like."

"I don't have time today. Do you ever go swimming in the lake, you know, over them bodies buried underneath the water?"

"Sometimes. It's not too bad if you don't think about it. This is a nice place. I rent the back bedroom. It's quiet. The only time I know Ronnie and your momma are home is when we eat dinner or when they're fooling around. Your momma makes a lot of noise."

"Come on, you don't need to say that."

"It's the truth."

"I don't care. I don't want to hear that. All I asked about was swimming in the lake."

"My room's real nice. Want to see it?" he asked Hannah, who declined. "I think they dug up all the people in the cemeteries, moved'em some place."

"What about the bodies no one knows about?" she asked.

"I wouldn't know about that. Maybe they'll float to the surface someday."

Eddie Lee sat down at the kitchen table with his relish sandwich and grape Kool-Aid then took a large bite out of the hamburger bun. He brushed his greasy hair out of his eyes with the hand that held his sandwich and left a streak of green relish on his forehead, just above his eyebrow. Hannah started to tell him but stopped herself.

She flipped through several photographs while Eddie Lee poured another glass of Kool-Aid and kept talking about the restaurant. She nodded and mumbled a few replies.

"After I eat my sandwich, you want to help me clean up 'round here? I can use the help."

"I have an appointment," she lied. "I'm working on my family history, researching who I am. Maybe there's some famous people who are kin."

"You writing a book or something?"

"Hadn't thought about it, but you never know."

"How long's it take to write a book, a week or two?" Eddie Lee asked.

She shrugged her shoulders.

"I bought a boat with the money I been making at The Diamond Eye."

"A jon boat?"

"Bigger than that. It's a thirty-eight-foot cruiser, a Sea Breeze. It's real nice."

"You make that kind of money at the restaurant?"

"No," Eddie Lee groaned, "I got a settlement from a car accident, which is why my leg's screwed up. It ain't brand new. It's twenty years old but in good shape. I named her *My Dixie Wreck*. You can come take a ride any time you want. I'll take you out on the lake, and you can stare down to the bottom at all the dead people. I'll take you fishin'. Anything we catch, we sell to the restaurant—fish, not dead people."

"I got that."

"I go out on Tuesday and Wednesday to sleep out on the water and catch fish and bring them back on Thursday. That's one reason business is so good on the weekends. I'm the local bass master. I catch about a thousand bucks worth of fish each week. It ain't legal, but I ain't never been caught."

When Hannah opened the carport door to leave, Eddie Lee stood up and asked if she wanted to give a hug to her brother-in-law.

"You ain't my brother-in-law."

"We're close enough to be something."

"You can give Ronnie Lee a hug," she told him.

"But MY DIXIE WRECK," he yelled before laughing as she walked toward her car.

§

I have been poor all my life, dirt-poor. No-pot-to-piss-in-poor! The land was of value—Daddy owned that, and now that's gone. Not just poor all our life, but all the way back to granddaddy three and four times back, all the way back to the Civil War. My entire family has been poor, like it's a curse on the family name. Memaw told us that we were rich folks long before the Civil War, but the Yankees killed our spirit along with everything else. Then, the Great Depression wiped out the rest. The Yankees took not only our possessions, but our future. Rich folks had slaves. Daddy used to read from his great, great, great granddaddy's will and how he bequeathed land and slaves to the oldest son, which sucked for everyone else in the family who got squat. Momma used to get pissed off at Daddy for acting like owning slaves was a badge of honor. She made certain us kids understood that her side of the family fought for the Union Army and was against slavery.

"Look who won," she always said. "The good guys."

Daddy once said that the big mistake our kinfolks made was buying a whole slew of slaves from other slave owners during the Civil War, dirt cheap. When the war was over, all the money was gone in slaves, and then they didn't own anything except misery.

"They invested in evil," Momma yelled. "Serves 'em right."

"Look who's paying the price now," my sister, Greta said.

It was an argument no one was ever going to win in my family, because when we ganged up on Daddy, he blamed Momma and smacked her. After a while, we knew whatever confrontation he had with us, it was Momma who was in line for a beating.

"If having misery in our life is the price to pay for being honorable people, so be it," Momma said about five seconds before daddy smacked her across the face.

"Everyone suffers. That's why we go to church, to relieve our suffering at the altar."

After the Civil War, no one except the former slaves remembered how to do half the stuff on a farm, and my greats couldn't farm the land without their help, and so the farm went to pot. I wonder what life would have been like if our kinfolk had made better decisions about operating a farm and treating people right.

Love covers a multitude of sins.—I Peter 4:8

Now I understand why Greta ran away. Right after Easter when I was fourteen, she ran away from home, just up and left. Greta worked at Kroger as a cashier and was waiting for Mr. Right to stroll down the checkout line, but that was a pipe dream. Instead, it was always some stubble-faced PBR-drinking loser in a wife-beater asking what time she got off work.

"I'm running away to Iowa City," she told me. "I read about this place where people go to become writers, misfits like me who have all sorts of ideas in their head and need a way to express themselves. These folks will show you how to write movies."

She also worked part-time at the Hope Unity Fellowship Church of Albion, but about a week after Greta ran off, the preacher and his wife showed up at our door. While they were vacationing in Florida, she stole a bunch of money. Pastor Houser stopped by the farm to get his money back, and when he pulled up in the driveway, I thought he was there to say Greta was dead in the middle of Nebraska, face down in a muddy ditch. He couldn't call the police since the money she stole was money he'd been skimming from the tithes every Sunday. Easter, like Christmas, was the high-tide of tithing. Each year, he netted an extra twenty thousand that cruised down Via Dolorosa Lane right into his safe. He said that Greta stole nine thousand dollars in cash, plus a bag full of quarters. I know she stole the money because she said so.

"He's a crook. He skims ten to twenty percent each week. His cash is in a safe in his office. Well, I found the combination."

Greta is movie-star beautiful, with long brown hair flowing, even on windless days. At dinner, she used to talk about a route she could take to Alaska or how she could work her way across the country at the Waffle Houses from here to Santa Fe, just traveling the country.

At nighttime, in the quiet of our bedroom, we'd sit on the floor looking at a map and chart a course and measure the miles from one place to another.

"I'm going tomorrow," Greta would say. "I'm gonna follow the North Star."

"When you get there, will you write so I can come live with you?"

All night I feared I'd wake up the next morning to find Greta gone, maybe a letter or note on her pillow. But she never left. She was always there in the morning, sitting at the breakfast table as if the idea had never been discussed. Except one morning. Greta left in the middle of the night without saying goodbye to anyone. Stealing the preacher's money was her way to be independent.

Iowa City didn't pan out, so she rode the bus to Los Angeles to work in the film industry, answering movie stars' fan mail.

"People mail cash all the time for some star's charity, but I pocketed it. It's my bonus."

I think she called home to say she ain't dead, Momma always wanted to know what movie stars Greta had met. I know she lied: Demi Moore, Jessica Simpson, Burt Reynolds, Kenny Rogers, the Kardashians.

"I've never met anyone except once when I stood behind Joaquin Phoenix at McDonald's. He was ordering a dozen Big Macs to go. Bigshot movie stars hire people like me so they can stay a million miles away from their fans. Most folks write asking for something, mainly money. Sometimes, prayers, but those go unanswered."

"Don't you say a prayer for them?" Hannah asked.

"Hell, no."

When Greta ran away, she left a note on my nightstand: "Going to Colorado—Led Zeppelin—with an aching in my heart." I knew that was a lie to throw off Daddy's bloodhound nose.

The last time we spoke, I asked if she was coming home.

"It's like eating opossum, it takes something mighty fine to get the gamey taste out of your mouth."

I read some pages in the diary Sarah wrote. Did women in the 1800s ever do anything wild in their lives besides letting their husbands uproot the family from the land of their ancestors? I imagine Sarah did not have much choice in the matter, not with the way life was back then, women being essentially property of the man. Sarah mentioned that she had always dreamed of traveling back to Ireland, to County Cork, to where her ancestors came from. Did she and her husband ever jump in the pond or creek naked? I'll bet they didn't because back then they would have been stoned to death.

I was sad for her because I knew what her life was like from morning through the night. For the benefit of anyone reading this in 100 years, Sarah made a lot of spelling errors. I did not correct them. I know that "ffather" was a simple mistake by her and that she was smarter than that, but bumping along on the trail, who's got time to fix stuff? Sometimes she spells a word correctly—other times, she misspells the same word. I ain't fussing, just stating fact about her parsing.

> The day before we left on the trail, I was busy packing goods I'd need. Keeping the children out of things was troublesum itself always undoing those things that I carefully packed in flour sacks. The children kept getting into things I packed and placed on the buckboard. They were just being children. I fussed at them but finally took a switch to shoo them away. After time, most was strone together with no matter as to why. By nightfall it looked as though the r'coons had rifled through our belongings. I left b'hind most of my clothes, gave away what I couldnot sell. I brung my momma's wedding dress that I wore and her brocho that was sposed to be buried with her. John said it was stupid to bury valuables with the dead. We might barter with those. I packed a few books. John was gone most of the day saying farewells to his friends and sum people I don't like much, but who he has known a lifetime and I had visitors throughout the day. That was nice but held me up. The women folk brought food for the journey, jars of preserves a cured ham wrapped in muslin. I was grateful. John did not come home until late last night and he had been drinking all day so riding out of Meadville, he threw up a good half dozen times. I was fit with him. The chilen should not see such a thing of their father. I thought perhaps he would be ill enough to call off this adventure and return home but no he kept right on tellin me to bring him sum water. When he leaned over to puke I almost pushed him over and turned the horses 'round. I wish now I had. We have dust today flying thicker'n locust and smoke. A body has to walk thirty feet off the trail for a good swallow of air.

There you have it. They were from Meadville, Pennsylvania. Those university thinking heads need to do nothing more than research folks in Meadville to see who lived there back in the day. Someone will figure out who Sarah was.

Chapter 10

Digging Graves with a Broken Spoon

Hannah and Margaret sat on Margaret's sofa at her apartment, looking through the box of photographs and watching reruns of *The Office*. It was a plush, brown leather sofa that eased around Hannah when she sunk into it. They'd already cooked dinner and cleaned up the kitchen. The dishwasher hummed in soft silence—unlike Hannah's dishwasher at her apartment, which rattled like a battalion of tanks rolling through Berlin.

Hannah called her mother at that moment, and when she dialed her phone, she put her mother on speaker so Margaret could hear. Hannah wanted to know the truth about her grandfather and his association with Bobby Cherry.

"Sit here and be quiet. Don't say a word," she said to Margaret.

Margaret nodded.

"I didn't know your granddaddy when he was young, only in his later years, so maybe he was wild," her mother said. "We all got a streak. I'm not sure you should hold that against a man if he changed to do good. Even so, that doesn't excuse a person's behavior."

"She said granddaddy drove the get-away car for Bobby Cherry."

"Who the hell's Bobby Cherry?"

"He and some other men bombed the church in Birmingham in 1963 that killed four Black girls."

"I wouldn't put much stock in anything Mavis said," Lilith told Hannah. "Besides, your granddaddy never had a driver's license. I know that for certain. I'm not sure he ever learned to drive. In fact, he saddled up his horse and rode into town. Otherwise, Memaw used to drive him everywhere."

“I got a photograph of him with those men.”

“Unless the getaway car was a buckboard and a team of horses, Mavis has the facts all wrong. Look, I don’t know what to tell you, Sweetheart. Anything’s possible, but not this time. Your grandaddy wouldn’t even drive a tractor. He was nearly Amish in his ways.”

“This is a serious issue. This is history bubbling up like methane gas. If it’s true, Lord knows what people would say,” Hannah complained.

“I say you let sleeping dogs alone. You don’t know this, but they tried putting Mavis in the nut house. She was committed twice. Back in the Eighties, she escaped and hired a lawyer to keep folks out of her affairs. All the way back, the wives in that family got tossed in the nut house. They did it with your great-granddaddy’s first wife, too. They stuck her in Milledgeville, got a doctor to say she was crazy, and she stayed there close to sixty years. By the time she died, I suppose she was crazy. How do you think this family got the farm?”

“I thought his wife jumped off the Black River Bridge.”

“No, that was his second wife, Nell,” Lilith affirmed. “His first wife, Martha, owned that land you been living on all your life. It belonged to her side of the family. When your great-granddaddy married her, he waited three years, then stuck her in the nut house and took over the farm. He forged a suicide note where she was going to jump off Stone Mountain. It became his property, every speck of grass, squirrel, and stone. He got the court to declare her wacko and paid off a few doctors to agree with him. About two weeks later, he got a divorce and the land. She lost everything to him and lived the rest of her life in Milledgeville in one of those nut houses. They got about fifty of ’em. He got married again to Nell, his second wife, but she couldn’t stand being married to him and jumped off that damn bridge. Her whole name was Nellie Parks—look’er up. That’s why I always kept my eyes wide open for that train barreling down the tracks.”

"I didn't realize that."

"The bridge was big news back in those days, what with a Civil War battle having been fought nearby. It was open two months when she hitched a ride out to West Mississippi and jumped seventy feet off the bridge. The water ain't but two feet deep so it killed her instantly. I think she landed on her head and broke her neck. Hardly matters. Dead is dead. Your daddy drove me over there once years ago to show me the bridge. It's a pretty bridge."

"What about the photo?"

"Maybe they knew each other. So what? How's that got anything to do with you?"

After they concluded their conversation, Hannah and Margaret continued looking through the photos for a while then watched a movie.

"Let's watch *The Big Lebowski*," Margaret suggested.

"That's fine. I wonder if my daddy was married before like my aunt said."

"That's easy enough to research," Margaret told her. "We can go to the courthouse and look it up, especially if he ain't never lived anywhere else. He would have divorced in the county where he lived."

"You ought to include those photos in the scrapbook for your mother, making them the centerpiece," Margaret said, which made Hannah laugh.

Later, Hannah jotted down on her yellow pad some thoughts: *I am an imperfect woman. We are just a bunch of misfits.* She almost wrote, "I am an important woman," but she felt nothing could be less truthful.

§

Both Margaret and Hannah had Monday off from work, so they drove to the DeKalb County courthouse to research divorce records.

"It's possible they were divorced in the woman's county," Margaret suggested, "but we need to begin somewhere."

"Where'd you learn to do all this research?"

"In college, doing research papers. I learned how to find anything you need at the library. Information is power, baby! I always thought I'd make a great private investigator."

It took Margaret about fifteen seconds to find a record in the court computers with Hannah's father's name.

"Look here! Melanie Lynn Carlisle versus Robert Darnell Gardner in 1982."

She brought the information up to the clerk.

"Can we see these records?" Hannah asked.

"Those aren't here anymore. They've been archived for years. I can get them, but it'll take a week," she informed the two women. "You'll have to order them."

"Okay, we'll do that and come back next week."

"Hold on one second," the clerk said.

The clerk walked to the back area of the office, then returned to tell Margaret and Hannah that Andre, the man in charge of the archives and sending and retrieving documents, was leaving for the archive building in an hour and that he'd be back after lunchtime, around two o'clock.

"If you can come back, give me your number, I'll call you when the file's in. If he can find it. Old things get misplaced all the time. What's so important that happened back in 1982?"

"Just birth and divorce record information," Margaret replied.

"I'm researching my family genealogy," Hannah added.

During lunch at *The Mint Julep*, a restaurant a few blocks from the courthouse, Hannah told Margaret of the time when Lucas had a great idea for a business that her father funded. Lucas bought one hundred old Laundromat washers and dryers from a guy for fifteen hundred dollars, just fifteen dollars each. None of them worked, but Lucas knew he could fix at least half of them with the parts from the other machines and sell them for a huge profit, at least one hundred bucks a pair on Craigslist. When the machines were delivered, truckload after truckload, the men pulled up and dumped the washers and dryers in the backyard, next to his trailer.

"The trailer ain't there no more. It burned to the ground not long ago," she said.

It wasn't even Lucas's property, just a place he was renting with a bunch of other guys. On paper, it sounded like a good idea, but after Lucas took the first washer apart and couldn't get it working, he never tried again.

"All them washers and dryers, a hundred, are still in his backyard, hidden in the high grass. They ain't nothing but a wildlife refuge now for raccoons, snakes, rats, and spiders."

Without slowing down from eating and talking with her mouth full of food, Hannah asked Margaret, "Did your daddy believe in God?"

"I'm not sure. He never took me to church, and I don't remember him talking about God. He always worked on Sunday, so I stayed home alone. Sometimes, I watched church on TV. That's how I kinda learned about praying, but I think I was always praying to God even if I didn't know it was Him or who He was. I always thought of God as my real father."

"My momma and daddy took us four kids to a fundamentalist church for a while, but even when I was a kid, I knew they were wrong. They think the Earth is a few thousand years old. Not Momma, but Daddy does. There's no way that's true. The Earth is definitely millions, if not billions, of years old."

"It could even be that a *life seed* fell to Earth from an asteroid," Margaret said, "and everything grew from that."

Hannah embraced that idea. When Hannah asked, Margaret said she had never been baptized.

"I'm going to dream up some way to baptize you so when the time comes many years from now, you can ascend to Heaven and not be stuck in Purgatory."

"I didn't think Baptists believed in Purgatory," Margaret said.

"They don't, and neither do I, but why take a chance?"

§

Yesterday, Margaret and I dug up the past like treasure hunters, finding gold six feet under. My daddy was married like Aunt Mavis said, but it was annulled. He has a son by Melanie Carlisle, who sued him in Dekalb County in 1984 for child support, even though the records said 1982. There were five pages of documents, but two of them were handwritten by Melanie. Margaret took pictures of everything with her phone. I can't type any more. Got to go to the funeral home to cut hair.

Since a dull ax requires great strength, sharpen the blade. That's the value of wisdom; it helps you succeed.—Ecclesiastes 10:10

§

After working at The Cute Curl and typing at the library, Hannah worked at the funeral home for about two hours. She gave a haircut to a young woman she went to high school with, Shelly Attenberg, who was a senior when Hannah was a freshman. At first, her name did not register with Hannah, but when she saw her high school graduation picture, which she used as a model for her hair, she had to stop and sit down for a few minutes. Shelly was the first person from high school that Hannah knew who died. Mr. Fox walked in and found Hannah sitting and asked her if anything was wrong.

"I know this girl. Shelly. We went to school together."

"The best thing to do is honor her by doing your best work," he said.

"Do you know how she died?"

Mr. Fox knew the answer, as he had the death certificate.

"Was it an accident?"

"No," he replied. He did not provide any details, having left it at that.

Hannah took her time that evening, paying special attention to her work, trying as hard as she could to give Shelly a simple, yet elegant haircut. She turned on the radio and listened to soft, relaxing music as she talked to Shelly, telling her that everything was going to be fine, and if they had been closer in age, they might have been good friends in school, but now she was there to help her. They had been on the cheer squad together for one year before Shelly graduated. Hannah was surprised at how beautiful Shelly was, even in death, lying there in peace. It reminded her of the photos she'd seen of Marilyn Monroe under a gossamer veil. Shelly looked so alive, as if she were sleeping. When Hannah stepped back, she thought Shelly might sit up and start talking about a new routine they were going to practice to "Don't Bring Me Down."

When Hannah finished styling Shelly's hair and was satisfied she had done a good job, she removed her thin surgical gloves and rolled Shelly's blonde strands between her fingers and thumbs, feeling her hair, as fine as silk, then let it slip from her fingers. Hannah touched Shelly's cheek and forehead.

After work, even though Hannah wasn't in the mood for researching, she sat at Margaret's kitchen table with Margaret's MacBook and searched for Melanie Carlisle and another man, Foster Williams, who was also listed in the documents as a contributor to the break-up of Darnell and Melanie's marriage—all of this in a hand-written letter from Melanie to the judge. Even so, Hannah was tired and felt saddened by Shelly's death, so she lay down on the sofa while Margaret sat at the kitchen table continuing the research. All the personal information in the file was more than forty years old and outdated. When Margaret searched on Bing and 411.com, they did not find any telephone numbers or addresses for anyone in the area named Melanie Carlisle.

"Melanie must have moved away over the years, but I'll guarantee she has a different last name. Maybe she got married again. Or divorced and married three times. That happens all the time."

Hannah listened to Margaret talk, but she did not lift up from the sofa.

When Margaret zoomed into the handwriting, which they both thought looked like chicken scratch, she noticed Melanie's Social Security number.

"That's all we need to trace her. I know a man at a used car dealership who can run the number for a credit check. It's not legal without permission, but he'll do it for me."

In the courthouse file, there was a newspaper article from the *Memphis Press Scimitar* about Foster Williams, who had been murdered around the time Darnell and Melanie were divorced. The article mentioned the deputy sheriff in Coahoma County, Ben Reynolds, who responded to the emergency call the night Williams' body was discovered on the Coldwater Bridge. They looked Reynolds up and learned that he was the sheriff for many years but retired in 2009.

Margaret asked, "You wanna stay the night?"

"No, I'm tired and want to sleep in my own bed."

Not long after, Hannah drove home. She pulled her freshman yearbook from the shelf, and inside, stared at her cheer squad photo. Hannah was on the front row, second to the right, kneeling, while Shelly stood in the back row, middle. That was Hannah's single year on cheer squad, as the following year, she hyperextended a ligament in her left knee and sat out. When her junior year came around, she did not try out.

Hannah decided to attend the viewing and family reception on Thursday night, knowing Margaret would go with her if she asked, but Hannah wasn't certain she wanted anyone with her. It felt too personal to have company.

Wednesday evening, about six-thirty, Margaret made a pot of

decaf coffee, and she and Hannah tracked down Sheriff Reynolds' telephone number. They put him on speakerphone.

"I don't receive many calls about Foster Williams," Reynolds said. "I did years ago—people saying they saw him in Memphis walking along the streets. I dismissed it as hogwash. I mean, I was there. I helped Odis McDougal lift his body out of the car. He had more holes than a colander. Odis was the coroner. He's passed. Once in a while, some curious person will call. The case is still open, so I take the calls, although I end up referring everything over to Dan Rote, the lead investigator with the county. Dan worked with me for twelve years before I retired, but Darling, I have never found one shred of evidence leading to an arrest. Everybody has enemies. Williams had a bunch, but we couldn't find a clue as to who killed him. What sparked your interest in this?"

"I found this article and it kind of piqued my interest since it's never been solved," Hannah replied. "And, apparently, my daddy was his best friend."

"You talking about Darnell Gardner?"

"Yes, sir. That's my daddy."

"How's he doing?"

"Fine. He lives alone. My folks got divorced a few years ago. He walks with a limp 'cause his knee's messed up, but he won't have surgery, so he uses a cane."

"He's a good man. I interviewed him several times because he was a suspect, but I know he wasn't in the State of Mississippi at the time of the murder. He was in Florida at McDill Air Force Base. Everyone was a suspect. Is Melanie Carlisle your momma?"

"No, sir. I never heard of her until yesterday. My daddy married Lilith Tingley."

"Melanie did your daddy wrong. She was married to him and carrying on with Williams when she got caught red-handed. I don't know how your daddy didn't shoot Williams right there, but he didn't. He walked out of the apartment and never returned. I had a slew of suspects, but all of them turned out to be bad leads. I have an idea who did it, but there's no proof—it's just my gut feeling. Your daddy had all the motivation in the world, but he didn't do it. Like I said, he was in Tampa."

Ben Reynolds told the women the entire story. In 1981, Foster Williams, who was from Bishop's Point, Mississippi, not too far from Reynolds' house, was returning home from Fort Benning, Georgia, for a two-week leave. As he was crossing the Coldwater Bridge, a two-lane road in the middle of nowhere, a few miles from his parents' home, he was gunned down. The old bridge was replaced years ago.

"Williams was driving with a friend, Marcus Donaldson, who survived four gunshot wounds and six hours of surgery, told me that as the two men drove over the hill, they saw a set of car lights at the bottom on the bridge. They could not tell the make and model, but thought it was a light blue Chevrolet, or maybe gray."

Donaldson told the police investigators, as they approached the vehicle, a white man was standing near the hood, leaning in as if making a repair. Foster rolled down his window to ask if they needed any help, and that's when someone on the other side of the car stepped out and began firing a 30-30 rifle.

Williams was killed with the first shot when a round hit him under the left eye and blew the back of his head off. In the split second the first shot rang out, Donaldson thought he had been hit, but it was Williams' blood and flesh hitting him in the face. Williams was shot eight more times. Donaldson jumped from the passenger door and was about to leap over the railing and into the river to escape when he was hit twice in the right shoulder, lower right back and buttocks. The force of the second shot spun him around and knocked him over the railing and into the shallow water. He drifted downstream thirty yards before running aground on some silt.

Donaldson was unable to move and lay there praying, figuring he was going to die. He heard more gunshots and the water plunking around him, then a man's voice yelling to get out of there, the hood slamming, the vehicle accelerating, and the fading sound of the engine through the trees.

Margaret wrote on a yellow tablet, *Does your daddy know Donaldson?*

Hannah wrote, *I-D-K.*

"About thirty minutes passed before another car found Foster Williams dead in the driver's seat in his Army uniform. Me and the sheriff were called out to the scene. Donaldson would have died that night had the sheriff not heard him in the river, and they rushed him to the hospital in Memphis, where he remained in intensive care for several weeks. We investigated it for a long time, as did the Army."

§

FYI, if you're reading this 100 years later, I have added a password to my *Document of Life* so no one can ever open it without knowing all about me.

Today is Friday, May 24, 2024, after work. The library is layered in stillness as the last glow of sunlight creeps into the darkest part of the back shelves. I'm sitting alone, curled up in a chair with Margaret's MacBook. Today was Shelly Attenberg's funeral. I did not attend, as I needed to work at The Cute Curl. I attended her visitation service last night with Margaret. It was a somber occasion. I saw two people I knew from high school but no one from my graduating class. We spoke for a few minutes, just pleasantries, and I tried talking to Shelly's mother but never got the chance because she was crying the entire time. I would be grieved, too. I spoke to her father and her older brother, Ray, and wanted to tell him that I did her hair and sang and talked to her, but I kept that secret to myself.

"You did a nice job with her hair," Margaret said, as we stood looking at Shelly in her casket.

Mr. Fox was at the funeral home, shepherding the movement of people like an orchestra conductor. He thanked me for showing up since few people had, saying it's sad when it's a thin crowd. Margaret signed the guest book, ninth on the list. I was tenth. Everyone should have a lot of people at their funeral. I hope the funeral was packed today.

Mr. Fox told me, out in the narthex, that Shelly had been diagnosed with terminal cancer, and instead of going through the treatment that might help, she took things into her own hands.

"She had a ten percent chance if everything went perfect," he said.

I can see how she didn't want to suffer through the radiation treatment or burden her family. I wondered if I could do the same thing.

Chapter 11

When the Devil Deals the Cards

July 1 was Ilene's birthday, Margaret's *bossy-boss*, as Hannah calls her. She took the day off from work at the library to have a four-day weekend with her friend, Toby, in Asheville. That made both Margaret and Hannah happy.

"Ilene won't be back until Wednesday afternoon," Margaret said yesterday. "I'm running the show now, baby!"

Margaret wanted to arrive to work early, so she picked up Hannah, stopped at San Francisco Café for coffee, then zipped to the library a few minutes before eight. In the car, Hannah sang a few Elvis songs, the sad, remorseful tunes like "In the Ghetto" and "I'm So Lonesome I Could Cry."

"If you want, I can style your hair," Hannah told Margaret. "I've only ever cut one Black person before and that was a man. That don't include dead folks. I've cut a lot of dead Black folks. But I'll do a real good job, and I won't charge you a red cent. Free as the breeze."

Margaret laughed and gave Hannah a hug before she hopped out of the car.

June had been a long month as business picked up, both at The Cute Curl and the funeral home. Hannah made more money than she ever had before, an extra four hundred dollars than previous months, which made her feel a little more secure. Most of it was in tips, which Wendy suggested she not report as income.

"Who will know?" Wendy asked. "Keep it in a jar in your closet. Remember, don't ever let your man know where all your money is. My momma gave me that advice."

On that morning, Hannah walked across the street from the

library to The Cute Curl to find a young man standing outside, waiting for the shop to open.

"Do you have a key?" he asked.

"No, but Wendy'll be here in a minute. She must be running late, which never happens. I'll get you out in a jiffy."

Ilene's fortieth birthday. My God, Hannah thought as she cut this young man's hair. *I cannot imagine being forty, not married, no prospects, and looking like a bulldog with a horrible underbite. Toby isn't a prospect, being fifty-two and never married and unlikely to change his nature. Ilene's life must suck, being in a job she maybe likes—maybe doesn't—and no one likes her at work because she's a controlling pain in the butt. She's dedicated her life to handing out books to people and collecting forty-five cent fines. And if she unhooked her prosthetic leg, she'd be hard pressed to hop to the toilet without falling flat on her face.*

Since business was so slow that morning, Wendy left to run a few errands after her two appointments. While Wendy was gone and Hannah was alone at The Cute Curl, Hawkshaw Bales entered the salon.

"What do you want?" she asked.

"A haircut." He sat in her styling chair.

"Fat chance. You came to the wrong establishment, mister. Get out of that chair. That's for clients, not hoodlums."

"Why are you so pissy, Missy?" he said chuckling. "I thought you'd cut my hair, and I'd tell you about your brother."

"What about him?"

"Nothing much. You gonna cut my hair or not?" he said.

"I will never, ever give you a haircut. Never!"

He twirled his chair around twice while Hannah backed away toward the mirror on the other side of the room and grabbed a pair of scissors in the event she needed to stab him.

"I'm a good tipper."

"Be on your guard against all kinds of greed," she replied.

"What's that, a Bible verse?"

"As a matter of fact, it's from the Book of Luke."

"I wouldn't know."

"That's the first truthful thing you've ever said to me."

Bales started laughing again and spun the chair around to face Hannah. He abruptly stopped the chair with is left foot. He knew he was under her skin, having invaded her sanctuary, just like he wanted.

"Do you want me to call the police? They're right across the street."

"Go ahead," he said. "What are you going to say?"

"I want you to leave, and you won't. You're a mobster-jerk who wants to hurt my brother." When she walked over to the door and opened it for him, the sound of a car horn stormed into the salon.

"Well, not anymore."

Hannah released the door and it closed.

"You haven't heard? Oh, yeah, my men found your brother. He got away, but when someone owes you ten grand, you call in favors. It's just a matter of time, Sweetheart."

"Don't call me Sweetheart," she said, grabbing her phone from her back pocket.

"No, don't call the police. I'm leaving, but I'll give you one last chance to help Lucas."

Bales pulled his phone from his pocket and dialed Hannah's. It rang. She looked at it and rejected the call. He laughed.

"How'd you get my new number?"

"I have friends."

"The devil has no friends."

"I have several warehouses, and when they bring your brother back to Hebron, no one will hear him screaming. Then, we'll throw him in Lake Lanier for the gators. If he somehow survives, you'll be feeding him with a straw for the next fifty years."

"To begin with Mr. Who Doesn't Know Shit About Geography, there ain't any gators in Lake Lanier."

"Fine, the Okefenokee."

"Let me see if I can get the money."

"You got no money. You got one choice, an' you know what that is."

Bales stood up and pulled an Atlanta Braves baseball cap from the back of his belt. It was the hat Hannah had bought Lucas a few years ago for his birthday.

"Where'd you get that?"

Bales set it on the seat of the chair. She picked it up and looked at the underside of the cap for Lucas' initials in blue marker.

"Yeah, that's how close I am to having your brother."

Bales, standing in front of the swivel chair, brushed his hands across the front of his shirt and his pants, sweeping away any dust or hair particles. He turned to check his hair in the large mirror behind him, then rubbed his index finger over his teeth and looked at them in the mirror. He walked out of the salon without saying another word to Hannah.

She immediately pulled up Lucas's number on her phone, which wasn't listed under Lucas, but rather, Amos, the Biblical "bearer of all burdens."

"Where are you?"

"I might be heading back to California to pan for gold."

"Really?"

"Or maybe I'm heading back to Hebron or Daytona Beach."

"Hawkshaw Bales is looking for you, and he said they almost caught you."

"Yeah, but I got away. I can't go back to my motel room for my stuff 'cause I'm worried they're waiting for me. One of the guys I room with must have told someone, but I'm not sure which one, so I can't ask any of them for help."

"You be careful."

"Don't worry. I got a gun. I won it in a poker game."

"You need to watch out. Hawkshaw Bales is bad. Google his

name and you'll see."

Hannah feared that Lucas wasn't taking the Bales situation seriously, and each time she said anything, he laughed it off with some joke about how Bales should be looking out for him. That scared Hannah. She texted him a link with Bales' BMF history.

§

On Wednesday, Hannah worked until one o'clock before telling Wendy she wasn't feeling well. With the temperature topping 98, people were staying inside, and business slowed as the afternoon melted on. Hannah did not need Wendy's permission to come and go, since she did not work for her. Renting a chair meant you had to make the rent however you could do that. It was up to Hannah when she wanted to work, but she still felt compelled to honor Wendy as her boss.

Hannah did not go to the library or home. She went to see Hawkshaw Bales and talk about a payment plan, two or three hundred dollars per month.

§

When Hannah pulled into her apartment complex around ten o'clock that night and parked her car in front, Margaret was waiting for her. When Hannah opened her car door, she looked ashen and disheveled.

"You alright?" Margaret asked.

"No. I'm sick."

Hannah pushed the car door open all the way, leaned over, and threw up on the blacktop.

"Where've you been?" Margaret asked.

"Shopping and visiting my mother," she lied.

Hannah threw up three times before Margaret got her to bed. Hannah lay on the bed half-passed out and curled up into a fetal ball.

It took some doing, but Margaret pulled off Hannah's soiled clothes, underwear, and bra, and with a warm washcloth, she wiped away the spittle and mess from Hannah's face and hair. Hannah didn't resist or move much. Instead of remaining in a fetal position, she lay on her back, legs and arms spread open, head turned sideways, sweating like she had the flu. Margaret placed a cold washcloth on Hannah's forehead, wiped the sweat from her body with a dry cloth, and then covered her in a clean bed sheet up to her neck. After a few hours of Hannah lying naked under a sheet, sometimes kicking it off, and with Margaret keeping her company and attending to her, she stopped sweating. It appeared to Margaret that her fever had broken. Margaret pulled clean underwear up over Hannah's knees and around her hips. She sat her up to pull an over-sized t-shirt over her head, then covered her again with another clean sheet, up to her shoulders. It was a white sheet with small daisies.

At four a.m., Hannah woke up. Margaret was sound asleep next to her under the covers. Looking at Margaret, Hannah felt that this was what it would've been like having a best friend in high school, someone sleeping over on a Saturday night to braid hair, paint nails, talk about boys, and make homemade pizza, never worrying about what you talked about because everything was a secret, and no matter what you did, your best friend would always forgive you, and no one in school would ever dare make fun of you because your best friend would always defend you. You and your best friend might even kiss each other once, like Clarissa and Sally in *Mrs. Dalloway*, and no one would know or tell.

A person needs a best friend, Hannah mused.

She walked into the kitchen but did not find anything she wanted to eat. She made a pot of coffee, not because she wanted a cup, but out of habit. As the coffee percolated, she turned the faucet on full blast, as hot as possible, and rinsed her face and mouth. She took off her sweaty t-shirt and tossed it toward the washing machine, not caring where it landed. With a hot hand towel, she gave herself a cat bath in the kitchen sink and washed the sweat from her neck, breasts, and arms. The cool air chilled her and felt good. Then, she sat at the kitchen table, reading the brochures Margaret had left on the counter. It didn't take her any time to know what it meant, including the math notes that stated, "Hannah $400 p/m."

Without pouring herself a cup of coffee, Hannah booted up Margaret's computer and opened her *Document of Life*. She sat staring at the screen for more than fifteen minutes without typing a single letter. She looked in on Margaret to make certain she was still sleeping. She did not know what she wanted to say, but after a while, forced herself to type something.

§

Bottomline: I am not proud of this. I am sick from the thought of what I have done.

Earlier yesterday, Hawkshaw Bales stole my virtues. For almost an hour. I did this to cancel Lucas's debt and save him from being beaten up or killed. The whole time, I kept pretending Bales was a boy in high school I had a crush on. I closed my eyes and pretended Ross McKnight was on top of me. I wouldn't look at Hawkshaw Bales. After he finished, I laid there curled up, while he talked about things, but I wasn't listening. I was waiting for him to leave. I wish I had had a gun because I would have shot him, without regard for prison or the electric chair. I tried pretending it never happened. When my phone alarm went off (I timed him), he was buckling his belt, then he tied his shoelaces before scooting out the hotel door. I sat in the shower with the hot water hitting me, and I don't even know how long I was in there. I fell asleep at one point. This took hours. The thing about a nice hotel, the hot water never runs out. Then, I got dressed and drove home. I have been ill ever since.

I was pure, but now I am filth. He did everything a man can do to a woman. I feel broken. I have another secret I can never tell the world.

Trust in your money and down you go.
—Proverbs 11:28

§

Hannah changed her password then saved her file and backed it up to a memory stick. Once she set the MacBook on the counter, she stripped off her underwear and tossed it in the washing machine, along with her t-shirt, a sweatshirt, a hand towel, and the bed sheets Margaret had piled up. She walked into the bedroom for the clothes she wore yesterday when she looked at Margaret half-tangled in the sheets, naked, and sound asleep. Hannah slid on a pair of clean underwear and tossed on an oversized t-shirt, then slid between the sheets to Margaret's backside and pulled her body close. Hannah was chilled for a split second before Margaret's body warmed her and began to relax her nerves. She had never touched a woman before, not like this, but what she was doing was for comfort and warmth and companionship. She rolled her arm over Margaret and spooned her body. Under the sheets, it was relaxing and safe and warm, and Hannah did well not to touch Margaret's breasts or anywhere else. Within a minute of deep breaths, Hannah was asleep.

Chapter 12

The Canyon of Lost Dreams

When her alarm sounded at six thirty, Hannah reached over several times to hit the snooze button until the radio announcer stated it was Taylor Swift's birthday. Then, he played "Ex's & Oh's," which was not by Taylor Swift. After the song finished, and before the traffic report, the disc jockey corrected himself and reassured the audience the song was by Elle King and it was not Taylor Swift's birthday, but Tom Cruise's. It was seven o'clock when Hannah took a deep, exhausted breath, signifying that she was not ready to roll out of bed. She kept thinking that she needed to be at The Cute Curl by eight o'clock, which seemed too early.

Margaret woke a few minutes after Hannah but stayed in bed for another fifteen minutes. From the kitchen, Hannah heard the rustling. When Margaret walked into the kitchen, Hannah was making a fresh pot of hazelnut coffee, which she bought just for when Margaret hung out. Margaret had put on an old T-shirt Hannah gave her to sleep in, but it was too small and barely covered her rear. Without staring, Hannah watched Margaret's body glide around the living room and kitchen. She looked away but found herself glancing back whenever she felt Margaret wasn't looking.

"Want me to draw a bath for you?" Margaret asked.

"Yeah, that'd be nice."

"Nothing too hot, just warm," Margaret assured her.

While drawing a bubble bath, Margaret lit two candles and turned off the bathroom light. She set the candles on the sink. Hannah brought in two cups of coffee, set them next to the candles. Margaret stepped into the bedroom to leave Hannah alone. She stood there for a second listening for Margaret in the bedroom then removed her underwear and T-shirt before testing the water with her big toe. Margaret dressed then knocked on the door.

"Come in."

Hannah was up to her chin in bubbles when Margaret opened the door. She lowered the toilet seat and sat on the flattop, holding her coffee in both hands and to her chest to feel the warmth. As Hannah lay back in the warm water, she closed her eyes.

"Tell me about the house," Hannah said to Margaret as the warm water seeped around her ears.

"It's called Canterbury Farms, a small subdivision of just twenty-six houses. I found it by accident driving around. The house I really like's on a lot and a half because a small creek cuts between two parcels. It's got a wrap-around porch, dormer windows, double garage, and brick exterior. What I like most—it's secluded. It's on a cul-de-sac and backs up to woods they cannot build on."

Margaret pulled her phone from her pocket and showed Hannah the photo she took.

"Sandy, the saleswoman said that with my job, military record, and the VA loans, I can stop paying rent and own a house instead."

"Doesn't it cost a lot to buy a house?" Hannah asked.

"After paying the principal and insurance, I'm spending $175 less per month than my rent on a thirty-year loan, not to mention gaining huge tax benefits."

"I saw all your math on that tablet in the kitchen."

"Yeah, I was figuring out the numbers. If I buy the house, my monthly note will be $1,407 on a fifteen-year mortgage. If you rented from me and paid $400, you'd save $450 in rent then I can easily make it happen. Otherwise, I'll get a thirty-year mortgage."

§

It was raining hard outside as a huge storm rolled through the south, pushing down from the north and stretching from eastern Texas to the Atlantic Ocean. The bedroom and bathroom windows were open, and a stiff breeze tossed the curtains around. Outside, the dark clouds appeared low enough to touch. For July, there was a deep chill to the morning air, and smoke rose from a fire pit someone was burning way off in the distance and filtered into her apartment. Hannah took a deep breath and smelled the chaw of sweet wood.

This is crazy, Hannah thought. *How can it be this chilly in July? It was hot yesterday*. She did not say anything to Margaret. Instead, she thought about a story her mother told her once about how it snowed in July when she was a girl living in Kentucky. *Strange things happen*, Hannah thought. Her breasts kept floating up through the suds, so she piled bubbles on them to cover them up.

Hannah took a large sip of coffee, closed her eyes again, and wished the world would go away because she didn't want to go to work, didn't want to see anyone, and didn't want anything of her life to be the same. She wanted to open her eyes and be in some other state, maybe deep in the wilderness where your closet neighbor was five miles away. She sunk low into the water until it rose over her ears and muffled all sound. Margaret sat with her, sipping her coffee, smelling the candles and lilting smoke from outside, and watching Hannah at rest.

"We should go over this afternoon at lunchtime if the rain stops."

"Lunchtime? Today's the Fourth of July. The library's closed. So's the salon," Margaret said. Then, both women laughed at Hannah's mistake.

For thirty minutes, Margaret went on with excitement about how they could be roommates, and Hannah could save a ton in rent if she lived with Margaret. When the water cooled, Margaret drained most of it and added more bubbles and warm water. For a few minutes, Hannah lay in the tub naked while the water filled, covered in a thin sheen of bubbles. When it was full again, Margaret shed her clothes on the bathroom floor and stepped into the tub with Hannah.

"Is this okay?" she asked.

Hannah did not reply, and her silence, to Margaret, granted permission.

Hannah watched Margaret as she sat down in the bathtub, even though there was not enough room. She slid her legs to the outside of Hannah's hips. It wasn't the most comfortable position, but the water felt soothing. They lay in the water together, talking for a few minutes. Then, Margaret adjusted Hannah's right foot by bringing it up to her chest, between her breasts, where she massaged it with her fingers and thumbs before washing her foot with a cloth. Hannah did not resist. Margaret ran the washcloth between each toe with the precision of a jeweler, careful not to tickle Hannah's feet. Hannah thought how nice it would be if she had a jacuzzi with enough room to splash around. Hannah asked her several more questions about the house, and Margaret answered what she knew, as she washed the other foot and spoke softly among the glow and scent of vanilla candles and hazelnut coffee.

The water cooled for a second time. Margaret said she needed to wash her hair.

"Me, too," Hannah replied.

They stood in the shower while the tub drained, hot water crashing upon them from the overhead sprayer, and Margaret washed Hannah's hair and then her own. Margaret grabbed a loofah and washed Hannah's body before rinsing her down with the handheld nozzle. Hannah enjoyed being pampered, her body almost limp from a lack of energy, shattered, but feeling the tenderness of Margaret's care. Margaret ran the loofah over her own body and closed her eyes as she rinsed. When she opened her eyes, Hannah was leaning against the shower wall, crying. Margaret hugged her in the shower as the hot water shot across and in between their bodies. Hannah convulsed with sobs as she tried to catch her breath. When the hot water subsided to warm, Hannah stepped out of the shower.

Hannah dried herself with a cotton towel and clothed herself in plaid shorts and an oversized shirt to cover up her body, while Margaret dressed in the clothes she had worn yesterday, thinking that if they drove over to see the new house at one o'clock, she needed to stop at her place to change.

With several hours before the real estate woman would be working, Hannah and Margaret sat on the carpet in the living room, leaned against the sofa and watched *Bridget Jones's Diary*. About halfway through the movie, Margaret paused the TV to go to the bathroom. When she returned, Hannah was laying on the sofa curled up in a fetal ball. Margaret sat down on the floor and leaned against the sofa.

"I'm sorry, Hannah. I shouldn't have gotten in the bathtub."

Hannah did not say a word, just shook her head "no." Hannah's tears rolled down her cheeks to the crevice of her lips, then dripped onto her old, second-hand sofa, turning the fabric dark wherever the tears fell.

"It's not that," Hannah said.

Margaret pulled the hair away from Hannah's face and tucked it behind her ears. Hannah stared at Bridget Jones' wide eyes on the paused TV, as if she couldn't believe what she was seeing and hearing from Colin Firth. But Hannah was gazing far beyond the TV, through the wall and deep into the future.

Hannah then fell asleep for a few hours.

§

When she woke, Hannah rambled on to Margaret with stories about her family, trying to avoid the real issue and how it led to Lucas owing ten thousand dollars to Hawkshaw Bales and how she was trying to keep him out of trouble.

Finally, Margaret yelled at her.

"What the hell are you trying to say? Spit it out!"

Hannah bit down on her lip and pinched her thigh to keep from crying while she told Margaret.

"What did he do? Did he rape you?" Margaret yelled.

"Yes. No. I kind of let him. Really, he made me let him do it."

"What did he do?"

"Everything."

"What's everything mean?"

"He did everything imaginable."

"Did he force you?"

Hannah could not make herself give up the details of how she met Hawkshaw Bales at the Wellington Garden Inn in Buckhead.

Bales had a room and sent her a text with the room number, so she knocked on his door of her own accord. Bales knew that by driving to Buckhead, Hannah was demonstrating a knowable intent. If things went toes up, Bales would play before a jury that Hannah arrived knowing she was going to have sex with him.

"I thought I could talk Bales out of hurting Lucas and take a lesser amount of money or I could make payments," Hannah told Margaret. "I got seven hundred and fifty dollars saved up after putting new brakes on my car last week. But he laughed at me. I mean, he was real nice to me in the hotel room, saying how this was the best thing for Lucas. He had a bottle of wine, but I didn't want none of that. Plus, it looked like cheap wine or something you'd buy at a gas station."

"What'd he make you do?"

"He told me to take off my clothes. So, I did. I stood in front of him naked. Then, he took off his pants and grabbed the back of my hair and pushed me to my knees—"

Hannah stopped herself.

"He was going to hurt Lucas or have someone kill'im. After ten minutes, he pushed me backwards on the bed and then got mean and started saying scary stuff to me."

"What'd he say?"

Hannah could hardly utter a word except to say that Bales was a big guy, heavy, and he lay on top of her and pinned her arms down so she couldn't get up.

"I asked him to be gentle, but then he told me to shut the hell up, that he was gonna break me wide open, but he didn't say it like that."

"Who the hell is this guy? I'm going to kill him!" Margaret yelled.

"He kept saying horrible stuff, telling me how worthless I was. Then, he turned me over on my stomach—"

Hannah paused. She started crying and gasping for air. Margaret held her and stroked her hair for more than an hour as she cried. She rocked Hannah back and forth in her arms.

Margaret walked into the kitchen for a towel, ran warm water over it, and returned to the sofa with a Coke. She wiped the spittle from the corners of Hannah's mouth and gently washed away the tear streaks. When Hannah regained her breath, she took several sips of Coke. Hannah told her everything lasted about an hour.

"It was difficult driving home. I was shaking so much. Maybe it wasn't rape, but it wasn't love."

Margaret screamed a guttural bellow and pounded her hands on the sofa armrest.

"I'm going to kill this guy."

She was ready to call the police, call some old military friends to beat him up, or go over and shoot him herself. Margaret talked for more than an hour about other actions they could take against Bales.

"No, I don't want anyone to know," Hannah said. "Just leave it be. No one can know."

Margaret sat on the sofa and hugged Hannah.

"I understand more than just about anybody in the world. My father raped me almost every day of my life. When he came into the room, I made myself dead. I was nobody. There was nothing I wanted more in the world than to be dead and meet my momma for the first time in Heaven, but that was the wrong way to think. I just wanted to be dead long enough for him to go away."

When someone tells you something like her father raped her when she was a girl, there's nothing you can do but listen. You can't say, "Well, let me tell you how bad my life was."

Hannah's body fell limp into Margaret's arms. Margaret stroked her fingers around Hannah's temples to relax her.

"I wish I had the money to pay Bales but look at this place. I'm so poor I can't afford a bird house," Hannah told Margaret.

"All I had was a bird trailer," she replied.

When Margaret said "bird trailer," she made Hannah laugh. Even though Margaret confessed her deepest secret, Hannah still could not do the same. She feared Grady's hand would reach up out of the ground and grab her ankle and pull her into that little grave.

§

At noon, Margaret walked Hannah back to her bathroom and ran the bath water again. She poured in a couple teaspoons of spearmint bubble bath and made a cup of green tea for both women to calm their nerves.

"Here, this will taste good. Take another bath. Then, we'll go look at the house and do something to make you feel better and take your mind off this, if that's possible."

Hannah agreed with her. She lay in the tub for thirty minutes before she felt too hot. When she stepped out of the tub, Margaret dried Hannah with a thick fluffy cotton towel, which reminded her of when her mother dried her off as a little girl. Margaret reassured Hannah that no one was ever going to bother her or take advantage of her again.

"It's one o'clock," Margaret said. "I told that woman I'd return today. I want you to look at the house, if you feel like it."

"I do. I don't want to stay here alone."

"I promise, I'm going to take care of this Bales fellow. Don't you worry."

Chapter 13

In One Hand I Carry a Bundle of Darkness

The real estate saleswoman unlocked the front door and allowed Margaret and Hannah to tour the house on their own while she drove her golf cart back to the sales office.

"We'd better take off our shoes," Margaret recommended.

It was misty and overcast, and the temperature was seventy-one, which was twenty-four degrees less than the day before. Normally, it would feel great, but such a drop in temperature made it feel cold. Inside the house, it was chilly because the air-conditioning was on. Margaret checked the Thermostat—67°. She turned it off. Then, she and Hannah opened every door and cabinet drawer, turned on the lights, pulled down the stove door, looked in the refrigerator, ran their hands across the carpet, walked from room to room, turned on each faucet and shower, flushed the toilets, and walked down the steps into the basement, then upstairs to the four bedrooms. Three were small to average size, but the master bedroom was large with a sitting room, fireplace, vaulted ceiling, walk-in closet, and a large Jacuzzi bathtub that had enough room for two people.

"Oh my God, Margaret, this is the most beautiful house I've ever seen. Look at this closet. You could park your car in here."

They walked back into the hall where Margaret knelt down and felt the new carpet, beige like beach sand, clean and vibrant. She ran her hands and fingernails all over it, then lay down and stretched her body lengthwise to bury her face in the carpet and smell its cleanliness.

"I can have this room, and you can have the master," Hannah said. "We can use the others for offices."

Margaret stood back up and leaned into the doorjambs. She

took a deep breath and looked right at Hannah.

"I was thinking this room could be both of ours."

"Why would we share? We both get a room."

Margaret walked into the master bathroom, and Hannah followed. Margaret said nothing as she turned on the faucets and the shower.

"Look," Hannah said, referring to the tub, "you can fit two people and four dogs in there."

"You can have a sink," Margaret said pointing to one, "and I get the other."

Margaret turned off the shower and the faucets but left the tub running at full blast. She ran her hand under the thunderous waterfall and motioned for Hannah to try, which she did.

"Wow. I wonder if it's powerful enough to wash away sin?" Hannah asked.

§

The next day, Hannah did not want to go anywhere and called in sick at The Cute Curl.

"If you got COVID, stay home," Wendy said. "You can have stuff delivered to your apartment."

"No. I don't have COVID."

"You can't come to work with COVID and infect all the customers. It'll put me out of business."

"I don't have COVID. If I did, I'd quarantine myself."

Margaret called her several times to get together, but Hannah declined and stayed inside watching TV Land and Nickelodeon all day. She did not get dressed and did not take a shower.

Over the next few days, Margaret was busy filling out paperwork and searching for the documents she needed to go along with the application to buy the house. She and Hannah did not see much of each other. Most days, Hannah was exhausted from standing on her feet cutting hair. She had two people at the funeral home to tend to on Friday—one was a holiday drowning, a middle-aged man, and the other was an older woman who died of natural causes. She cut their hair that night and did a fine job.

That Saturday at The Cute Curl was the most lucrative day she'd ever had, with tips totaling a hundred and eighty-six dollars. She had worked from eight to six without a break and had cut more than twenty people. There was an endless supply of hair clippings in her workstation trash bin. She never took lunch, which made the day go by like a scalded cat running through the house. Without eating, she felt weak. She and Wendy stayed until seven-thirty, cutting the remaining people who were waiting. Wendy had to lock the door to keep more people from entering the salon. At the end of the evening, Hannah was too tired to drive home and too tired to cook. When she vacuumed up the last of the hair on the floor and around the chair, Margaret walked in.

"I'm too tired to go out. All I want to do is crash in front of the TV."

After saying good-bye to Wendy, she and Margaret walked down the street for Chinese take-out, but all Hannah wanted was won ton soup. Margaret suggested they go back to her apartment, but Hannah declined. She wanted to eat her food and go to bed, so Hannah took her soup home. She stayed home on Sunday, slept in, did not answer her phone or step outside her front door.

The Cute Curl was swamped again on Monday, which made Wendy laugh with giddiness at the amount of business she had. It was so busy that Wendy phoned Hannah and asked her to work. Again, they did not have time to take lunch, so Hannah snacked on fruit slices that she bought at Kroger that morning. When the day's work was finished, she jumped in her car and drove off to Lake Lanier to see her mother. Traffic was congested, and the normal forty-minute drive took three minutes shy of two hours, which frustrated the hell out of her. There were four accidents along the way. Margaret called Hannah's phone numerous times, but she never answered. Hannah wanted to be alone in her thoughts and not talk to anyone but her mother. When she arrived at her mother's house, no one was home.

"Duh," Hannah said to herself, "she's at The Diamond Eye."

Hannah was proud of the job her mother had done building her business. It was a nice restaurant, nothing fancy, but it was comfortable, and the food tasted good. It was busy when she arrived, but her mother had small snippets of time to talk because she was working as the hostess and cashier. Ronnie Lee brought out three steak filets and three Walleye filets to Hannah's table.

"Eddie Lee caught two Walleyes yesterday. One was over seven pounds."

Hannah had lost her appetite for most of the past week. She ordered the steak filet and picked the smallest cut on the platter. Eddie Lee cooked it up just right, Pittsburgh-style. Hannah loved the crisp outside and the juices trapped within. She was cautious to tell Eddie Lee that it was one of the best steaks she'd ever had for fear that he'd take it as a marriage proposal or a chance to hook up. When things slowed down, he stepped out from the kitchen and sat at her table, along with her mother.

"How was it?" he asked.

"Tasty and juicy."

"That tater casserole's a special recipe," he told her. "It was my momma's."

"That was good, too."

Hannah finished her meal and talked to her mother for a spell but said nothing about Hawkshaw Bales or Margaret, though that had been her original intent. Her mother was too busy, and Hannah did not want to have an abbreviated talk. Besides, she'd eaten too much, but it was the first meal she'd had all week besides soup, apple slices, and bananas. When her mother asked why she was acting so puny, Hannah lied and said she'd been sick with the flu and had lost some weight but was on the mend.

"Chicken noodle soup, orange juice, and rest. Make sure you get plenty of those," her mother said. "It's not COVID, is it?"

"For Heaven's sake, aren't you over that government scam? It's not COVID. I was just sick."

Hannah thanked her mother and hugged her, then drove home without having said one word to her about what had been most important on her mind. When she was at the intersection of Ridge Road and Clark Street, just as she stopped for the stop sign, she opened her car door and threw up on to the street. She began to sweat. It was late when she returned home, and she had three messages from Margaret on her phone, the last telling her to call no matter what time she got home, but Hannah did not. She slept in her clothes on the sofa. Throughout the night, she threw up several more times.

The hair cutting business proceeded pretty much like each day prior, busy with no time for Hannah to call Margaret or respond to her texts beyond "real busy." She had stopped throwing up, but she was not at all hungry. When she wasn't busy at the library, Margaret called a few old military friends to ask their advice about her options with Bales. All of them said they would think about it and get back to her, which wasn't satisfying because what she wanted was someone to inflict great pain on Bales.

At twelve-thirty, Margaret took a quick lunch break from the library and walked across the street to The Cute Curl. When she entered the salon, Hannah was cutting a woman's hair and had several people waiting. She was too busy to take a break and couldn't talk about anything of a private nature.

"Let's go to San Francisco Café after work and just sit for a while," Hannah said.

Since the Hawkshaw Bales episode, Hannah had withdrawn, curling up at night into herself, pulling away from Margaret and bowing out of staying overnight at Margaret's apartment to play

Cribbage and Scrabble and eat homemade vegetable soup.

Margaret sensed Hannah's withdrawal but didn't know what to say or how to help her out of it, even though she felt she should know better than most.

§

The following Saturday, after work, Hannah hung out with Margaret, but they stayed inside and watched a few shows. Hannah surfed the Internet looking for a gun that would fit her hand. The one she liked best was a Ruger LCP 380. She watched several videos about the gun but did not mention this to Margaret. Other women seemed to like this model handgun, and as one woman said in a video, "I have small hands and haven't grown since I was twelve years old, so I need a smaller pistol."

Hannah was not in the mood to stay at Margaret's apartment, but by the end of the night, she was too tired to drive home, so she stayed over. She wore a T-shirt to bed like always, and Margaret usually wore something similar, but this night Margaret wore a nightie that was sexy as anything Hannah had ever seen. It was sheer white and showed everything, but not crystal clear like a digital computer photo. Hannah was uncomfortable with Margaret being as close to naked as naked gets. She wanted to wear wool pajamas.

When they lay on the bed to watch *You've Got Mail*, Hannah wrapped up in a blanket like a cocoon. She looked over at Margaret laying there on top of the bed in her nightie and wondered if Margaret knew she was beautiful. Hannah fell asleep around the time Meg Ryan's character and Greg Kinnear's character were sitting in the restaurant with the full understanding that they were not in love with each other. Hannah remembered Greg Kinnear asking Meg Ryan if there was someone else in her life, and she answered, "No, no, but there is the dream of someone else."

On Monday, Wendy sent Hannah home, as she was looking pale, but Hannah did not go home and did not answer her phone when Margaret called repeatedly. She drove to her farm and sat on the big rock for a couple of hours to think about what she had done with Hawkshaw Bales. She shaded herself from the sun and heat with an umbrella, then she walked around the farm, crying and talking to God, and asking Him for forgiveness.

Why did such a thing happen to me?

When darkness fell, she sat on the rock until it was pitch. The air cooled to a warm stickiness, and the stars looked like frog eyes shining on the surface of the water. Then, she walked back to the farmhouse and sat on the porch in a rickety, fold-up metal chair, pretending her family was inside watching *The Cosby Show* and that she'd be in her bedroom momentarily, ready to go to sleep.

Holding her phone to light the page, she began to scribble on her yellow pad. For several hours, she just wrote and wrote and when her phone began to die, she sat in her car writing and charging her phone, then back to the porch.

§

I had a dream the other night that people were driving in their cars and walking down the street when they disappeared. Their cars, empty of drivers, swerved off the road into other cars, or off a mountain cliff, or ran over people on the street. Suddenly, dog leashes hit the ground and were being dragged by dogs, looking around, thinking, "That's odd. Where'd Barbara go?" Pilots all over the skies were unexpectedly no longer flying 747s and small planes and news helicopters, and the planes full of people began to veer off course in all directions then plummet to Earth. Some passengers in those planes vanished, too. Just poof! Gone. Buses and trains had no one to stop them, and police officers looked down at handcuffs on the ground, and bicycles were abruptly without a cyclist, and for a few moments, balanced in loneliness, until losing momentum and tipping over. Fishing poles fell to the ground and people having sex were unexpectedly without a lover.

Chapter 14

Shopping Before the Rapture

Margaret's in the other room of the library with a group of schoolchildren, watching a documentary on the moon and how the Earth wouldn't be like it is today without its influence. I'm listening with a selective ear. She has cookies and juice for them. I'm tired today. This is all I will write.

It is Wednesday night, October 23, and it's been months since my last entry, sometime in July.

The library is open late tonight. I have not written in my *Document of Life* since the downward spiral when Margaret and I had a huge argument and stopped being friends. We didn't see each other for three months even though she's just across the street at the library, and we live less than a mile away from each other. Our friendship broke up when I told her to stop bothering me at work all the time. That pretty much did it. It wasn't her fault. It was mine. I just stopped caring about everything. It took all my effort to drag myself into the shower each morning. I have made a lot of money working hard at the funeral home and the salon, but all I did was go to work, cut dead people's hair, go home, maybe eat, maybe not, watch TV, fall asleep on the sofa or floor, go to work in the morning, cut dead people's hair, repeat, repeat, repeat. Even some of the people at The Cute Curl acted dead. I cut a lot of dead people. I mean a lot. One day, they had four people at the funeral home, all old folks. It was an epidemic.

A dead body no longer bothers me. Not much bothers me anymore. When I'm cutting their hair, I talk to them real nice and ask questions about their life.

"Where did you grow up?"

I sing songs to them, whatever's playing on the radio. I hope they can hear me. I ask about their family, their momma and daddy, children, who was their favorite pet. One day I had an infant, a little boy, who was a year old but just up and died.

Crib death, Mr. Fox said. I was so struck with sadness I cried the whole time I was cutting his hair. I went to the funeral, alone. I don't know who came up with the word funeral, but there's no fun in it, that's for damn sure. It may be the saddest day of my life, listening to the baby's momma talk about him. She couldn't finish.

After Margaret and I had a fight, I decided to save all my money to skip town in the pitch of night. Maybe I might still do that. But Margaret and I are friends again. We bumped into each other three days ago at Baro's gas station. I pulled into the left side of the pump, and there she was on the other side. We didn't notice each other for a minute, but then we stood around talking until people wanting gas started honking their horns. I realized then how much I missed her. She suggested we drive over to her apartment because she was packing all her stuff. She's moving into her new house, which took months to close.

"It's not like buying a sofa," she said. "I'm moving this weekend."

I should have written on my yellow pad during this time, but I didn't. All I did was think about stuff to write, ideas, stories, people, Hawkshaw Bales, my momma and daddy, Lucas, and running away to some place where no one could find me, and no one would know me.

§

What happened the most in my life over the past twelve weeks is something that did not happen. I missed two periods in a row. I went to the clinic in Rabbittown because it's free if you live in the county, which I don't, but I lied and filled out everything and used my fake ID that I still had from high school so I could buy beer. Plus, it's the one clinic that takes a reservation. All the other clinics make you show up at seven o'clock in the GD morning and take a number, sitting there with all the low-life pregnant losers, staring at each other and trying to figure out what happened to them. I wanted to stand up and ask, "Has anyone else in here been raped by Hawkshaw Bales?"

It wasn't a shock finding out I was pregnant. I pretty much knew. After the examination, and after the doctor left to attend to the next loser, the receptionist asked if I wanted to make an appointment for a pregnancy termination.

"A what?" I asked.

"An abortion."

I hadn't considered it but then began to run it through my head as a possibility, an easy way out of this situation. It was then I knew why my mother called Myra and Grady.

"What's involved?"

"You schedule an appointment and thirty minutes later you walk out."

I don't remember how long I stood there at the counter thinking about it, considering the option, but then she told me not to wait too long.

"The longer you wait, the more involved the situation becomes."

"What's it cost?"

"Around one thousand dollars."

"I don't have any money."

"Do you have insurance?" she asked.

"No."

"Don't worry. I'll give you the name of a clinic that does it for free if you can't pay."

When I told Margaret everything, she insisted I move into her house.

"We will paint the baby's room, and you can stay there."

She insisted that I go to an OB/GYN, a real doctor, and have proper healthcare.

"I'll pay for it," she told me.

I also told her I went to a psychiatrist three times to talk about Hawkshaw Bales and my messed-up life. The doctor made me realize I was going to be okay but agreed that it was consensual sex, and I could not have him arrested for rape. This was the argument I had with Margaret. She wanted me to press charges against Bales or have friends of hers pound him into the ground. I thought Margaret was going to pay for my abortion, but she refused. She wants me to have the baby, despite the father.

My head doctor told me in our last sessions that she spoke to an attorney friend and a detective she knows. If I went to court on this, both said I would lose. Bales would never be convicted since I went to see him on my own accord, knowing why I was there. In fact, the detective knew for certain that a good defense attorney would show that I was selling my sexual favors, like a prostitute. It didn't mean he wasn't a creep and a horrible person, but he would never be convicted of rape. Margaret's still angry and said she still wants to put a bullet through his noggin.

I'm going to buy Margaret dinner tonight from Mary Lynn's, a health food restaurant in Antioch that opened a few weeks ago. I read a positive review in the local paper about the restaurant and how the owner is from Busti, New York but moved down here because of high taxes, snow up to his earlobes, and fresh vegetables year-round. Busti is not too far from where Sarah was from, maybe fifty miles. Margaret wants a fruit salad, no dressing. Afterwards, we're going back to her apartment to finish packing. I'm sorry for our argument. I feel as if I have lost time in my life.

I haven't read much about Sarah since my fight with Margaret, so I am happy to reunite with her. She has a lot of wisdom.

> It is now twenty years since my brother Robert died of the epidemic that swept through Meadville. Scarlet fever. He was seven. For three days we traveled. Father took Susan and me to Allegheny, near the Genessee River where we stayed with a Seneca man, his wife and children. He was a friend of fathers. Each day we played with the other Indian children, many of them liked to touch our skin and rub it then look at their fingers for the color. We braided hair, made beads, cooked bread in a mud oven and played in the creek. I cot a fish so big it nearly pulled me into the water.
>
> When we came home Robert was buried.
>
> I was thirteen when John and I met at a dance. We

courted a while then I went to housekeeping. For a time I warpt a webb for Mister Lenna at his bisness but he sold it and moved to Jamestown to start a new bisness. He took his wife and children and built a home somewhere on the big lake. He was nice and his wife was polite to me, looking over my shoulder to admire the work I did. Sev'ral times she said I did the best job. She taught me more to read and gave me three books and old clothes to wear. Some needed repairs but I did not mind that at all. The books were my favorite things. The leather fronts are smooth and deep red. When Mr. Shulmak took over the bisness I worked for him three days. He tried to kiss me and brushed my front real hard. I told him no. The next day I had no work. My poppa was angry with me for losing my job.

When reading about Sarah, I feel like I am entering her house. Sometimes, I wonder why the world seems so small when you look out a window or stand on a porch or while riding in a car, and all you can see is what's just over the horizon and nothing beyond, just through that small window, nothing more. When you're on the mountain, you have a window to all the world has to offer.

Growing up, we could have been starving, but on the way home, Daddy'd take his last ten dollars and buy a twelve-pack of PBR and a dozen hot wings so nuclear hot that none of us could eat them, pure-fire-from-Hell-hot, and he'd get loaded up so he wouldn't have to remember we were starving little birds. After yelling at Momma for something he saw on the TV, like the county raising the car tag fee, he'd either pass out or stumble into the backyard and puke next to the dog pen. They loved that, I'm forever certain. It wasn't enough that he barely fed them, or that they had to sleep in the dog pen under a feeble lean-to in the cold and rain, he had to barf on them. It wasn't like he barfed up a steak. It was hot nasty nuclear chicken wings and PBR. I'm sure dogs have stories handed down to them like humans do, and I'll also bet they say stuff like, "I hear this was once a mighty fine place to live, fed twice a day, a running path, fields and woods, bitches day and night. Not like now, we're in the ghetto of dog housing projects."

Do dogs pray for a sunnier day or believe a better life is a possibility?

It is 6:30 in the evening, thirty minutes left for library business, and the sun is casting a long glow down the street and through the window into the library with about an hour of shine left. I worked hard today at The Cute Curl, made good tips. I still ain't telling the government how much.

Sarah had to be sad for a long time after her little boy was run over by the wagon wheel. She never said, so I don't know if she went back to Indiana to visit his grave. I would have been falling all over it, crying, and wanting to die myself.

All Sarah said was:

> Three days ago, near Springfield when folks were celebrating the mild weather, two sisters who are riding together with one man who is not eithers husband or relations got into a fight over which was going to dance with him. Some fes'tiv'tys were at hand and a pig was roasted. Everyone took turns pulling from the pig which was good tasting 'specially the almost burned crispy parts. Several men drank too much to drive themselves to sickness. Some cannot indulge without the devil's excess taking over. A few menfolk had fiddles and so it was a musical time and one young gal sang a song. She has a wonderful voice. The men had to drag the sisters off each other. Ones blouse got torn down the front to her waist and opened for all to see, but the other one was bloody around the eye. I am sure they found comfort in where they ended up that evening. John had too much to drink and came looking for me late. I pushed him off the buckboard and he rolled underneath in the dirt. He stayed there snor'n til morning.

Serves him right. At least they didn't have to deal with COVID and these stupid masks and wiping the world clean with Clorox-wipes and hand-sanitizer and pretending we give a damn about other people to the extent we are trapped in the house. I'm glad that stupid crap is done with. I note this because today, I saw a woman walking her dog—ALONE—and she was wearing a mask. I wanted to ask if it was for her safety or her dog's.

I wish Sarah, and other women for that matter, had more say of their own when dealing with men and making their own decisions. It ain't like they could up and go do what they want. They almost needed permission to fart. I'm sure I'd be in jail if I lived back with Sarah. I couldn't tolerate it. Maybe that's why Lizzie Borden chopped up her daddy and step-momma... she just couldn't take it no longer. Maybe she bought a tube of red lipstick and they said, "Take that back to the store, you whore" and that set her off.

I had to go shopping for some new jeans. I've gained weight. The whole time I was standing in the checkout line, I kept thinking the cashier might disappear in the Rapture, and my new pants would fall to the ground. I paid with cash and counted my change to the exact penny.

Chapter 15

The Black Forest of Doom

Margaret rented a moving truck during the week, to be delivered to her apartment on Saturday while she was at work. The men called her when they were a few minutes away from her apartment. She had to zip out of the library to take possession and sign the papers for the truck, which she would return Monday afternoon.

It took all Saturday evening and Sunday morning for Margaret and Hannah to load up Margaret's things. Then, they drove to Hannah's apartment and took what Margaret did not already have. Hannah left everything she did not need or want or what was worthless, old third- and fourth-hand furniture, cheap pots and dishes, warped bookshelves, and other misfit items no one would want. She left her Goodwill bedroom furniture and thread-bare linens. She took her clothes, nice towels, TV, radio, books, coffee maker, and other personal items. She left everything else, including whatever was still in the refrigerator and pantry, as if she took off in the middle of the night without warning or was swooped up in the Rapture. In which case, leaving behind all her possessions was a glorious thing, she thought. Hannah was already two months behind in her rent, and she did not pay her gas or electric bills during this time. She kept up with her phone and car insurance but nothing else. It wasn't for lack of money. She had lost all motivation to pay her bills. She had promised the apartment manager, Beth Johnson, she would have all the money on Tuesday.

Monday morning, Hannah and Margaret, although sore from all the physical labor, woke by 5:30 and ran out to grab coffee at San Francisco Café, and in a few hours, finished unloading the remaining boxes. They returned the moving truck before noon and saved twenty dollars. They worked hard all day to arrange the furniture and unpack. Margaret had purchased new bedroom furniture, which was delivered by two men who asked both women out on dates after it was delivered.

"Look here, boys," Margaret said. "This gal is three months pregnant. She's decided to have the baby, so which one of you still wants to go out with her with the possibility of taking on the responsibility of another man's child?"

"I think what Margaret is saying is thank you, but we're good."

All week they worked their real jobs, unpacked, ate take-out, and fell asleep before ten o'clock.

On Friday when Hannah answered her telephone, it was Beth Johnson wanting to know when Hannah was going to pay her past due rent.

"I've been trying to contact you for weeks. You owe rent for two months."

"I moved out here to Colorado but don't have a job yet. When I do, I'll send you the money."

"I pulled your file, and you don't work at the QT."

"Not any longer."

"Not in two years."

"Like I said, I'll pay you as soon as I get the money."

"You abandoned the apartment, an' I have to pay to have your junk removed."

When Johnson started yelling, Hannah hung up then blocked her telephone number.

§

One day, out of the blue, when I was ten or eleven, Daddy thought of calling the farm a ranch.

"I like the way that sounds, like we got a thousand acres of cattle or oil wells. A farm is small time, but a ranch sounds like you're somebody."

"Daddy," Lucas said, "we ain't got nothing but land."

"Don't have anything but land," Momma corrected.

"Listen to your momma about proper grammar, but that's not true," Daddy said. "We have all that land out there and that means capital, and capital is power if you have enough."

"No one's farmed this land since before you were born," Momma said. "All this land produces are property taxes and weeds. No more cotton. No more corn, no cattle, not in seventy-five years."

"We got apples," he said. "That's a cash crop."

"Except we have weeds coming out our ears," Momma said as she stood in the kitchen, stirring a bowl of mashed potatoes. "What we need to raise are weed-eating rabbits."

"Shut up, Lilith," he yelled from the other room.

"How much cash can we get for weeds?" she asked him, provokingly.

"Hey, nobody asked for your mouth, Pinhead. You don't know squat about a ranch."

Momma walked to the living room and stood in the doorway, stirring the potatoes.

"I know you're never going to convince a bank that this is a ranch and that they ought to loan you money to raise alpacas."

"Where'd you hear that?"

"Word travels. I know a little bit about what goes on around here. You don't think the other men tell their wives about your stupid ideas? Somehow you think alpacas are service-free, no maintenance. All you got to do is feed and water them, and they will yield fleece. Hell, they might even shear themselves and take the fleece to market."

"Here's an idea. Shut up for once in your life."

It wasn't often that momma talked back because she learned what his backhand tasted like, but sometimes you're willing to go that far when your husband is talking crazy.

"I might just make this ranch profitable by raising alpacas even though you morons won't give me any support. First, I need a name."

"How about the Lazy Boy Ranch," Wendell smarted off.

"Keep it up. Someday you'll be on the street begging like all those other urban outdoorsmen."

"Why don't you nurture the apple trees the way you're supposed to in order to increase their yield?" Momma asked. "That right there will bring in cash. You can't just plant them then expect apples. You have to prune the trees and make certain they're healthy. You act as though all you have to do is sit on the porch then one weekend each year, pick apples. Those trees yield about ten percent of what they should."

"When did you become an expert?"

"I'm not," she replied, "but I'm not so lazy to think there isn't any work to do around here. Apples, a good harvest, take planning and work. You don't do either."

That's when I knew it was coming. Daddy raised up out of his chair and walked to the kitchen. At first, it didn't look as though he was going to slap Momma because all he did was yell at her—–he stood right in front of her face like a drill sergeant. Then, as he turned away, his backhand smacked against her cheek, knocking her up against the refrigerator. He grabbed a few peaches off the counter and walked out the back door.

"Keep walking," I thought. "'cause I'm fixing to light you on fire someday."

You must burn their idols in fire, and do not desire
the silver or gold with which they are made. Do not
take it or it will become a snare to you.
—Deuteronomy 7:25
This is all I can give today.

§

It's been four days since I've been to the library. I've been sick a lot lately. Margaret has scheduled another appointment for me with an OB/GYN.

At work, business has picked up, and I'm thankful for that, but I get tired after a few hours. As soon as I have a break in my schedule, I slip off to the back and lie down on the sofa to take a quick nap. Working extra at the funeral home makes me even more tired. I've saved some money and now have a few thousand in the bank, plus what I keep in my closet in a large glass bottle I bought at a flea market, tips that I haven't reported to the IRS.

§

I knew I was pregnant, and the OB/GYN confirmed it a long time ago. It's the same doctor Margaret goes to. I have to be honest, the first thing I thought of was getting an abortion. I did not even consider having the baby and being a mother.

"No damn way!" Margaret yelled at me. "That ain't happening."

I should have written about this before now, but when you're knocked-up by a drug-dealing micro-farmer, you kind of put it out of your mind with the hopes that it will go away if you don't think about it. Instead of being angry and hateful toward me, Margaret is supportive, but she acts like the father, which is a good thing. I don't smoke. I rarely drink, maybe a beer or glass of wine occasionally. Never liquor. She goes overboard with me eating healthy, which is fine, since most of what she cooks tastes great; however, some of it tastes like dirt sautéed in margarine.

"Well, goddamn, Margaret, I don't want to give birth to Hawkshaw Bales' kid. That man is rotten. What kind of child can you expect?"

"A child that's a gift from God."

"You have the baby then."

"I can't."

Then she started crying because she's unable to have children. I did not know that.

"We can make this work out. We'll raise the baby by ourselves," she assured me.

That's how she is. There are some people, like my daddy, who if I told them, would take me down to the local service station, put me on the car jack and perform the abortion with a new set of air wrenches. Margaret is nothing but all-loving and caring.

§

Margaret just made some Earl Grey tea. She's sitting at the front counter looking out over the library. There are three people here: two high school girls working on term papers and an old man researching the history of Hebron. All else is quiet.

Margaret and I are going to start walking and working out, an easy light routine while I'm preggo. We've decided to run a marathon sometime next year, maybe a half-marathon after the baby is born. Margaret insisted we watch our calories. She cannot have more than 1500 calories, while I can have 2000. She keeps track of all the food we eat. When counting calories, you cut out all the garbage.

Earlier, as I was leaning against the counter, a woman returned a book, *The Feminine Mystique* by Betty Friedan. Margaret called it *The Feminine Mistake.* I've never read it.

"I mean that in the most positive way. It's mis-titled. Women have been forced into making a mistake in the choices they have. They don't look beyond the horizon to see all their possibilities."

§

I want to be remembered. Is there anything wrong with that? There're things I think are important. Sarah's life was important (and is important to me) and it's of consequence to a lot of people.

Carolines birthday is today. We celebrated at breakfast with wheat flapjacks. I bartered for the wheat. She is now five. Charles is eight. Antom four. Samuel he was a handful from the moment he 'rived. The heartbreak he has caused makes me want another baby. I have not allowed John to lay his hand upon me in a while. We celebrated again tonight for Caroline and ate corn flaps around the fire. She was a'lud to lit the fire for the camp. She was excited with dizziness. John gave her his pocketknife for the day and Charles helped her cut shavings to throw into the fire. They had a pile near a foot high.

I am the light of the world. He who follows Me shall not walk in darkness, but have the light of life.
—John 8:12

§

On Saturday nights after work, as a tradition, Margaret and Hannah took a long walk, showered, and headed out to dinner. They both decided that eating out cost too much, so they allowed themselves one splurge at a restaurant per week. Since moving into their house, Margaret and Hannah also started another tradition on Sundays of cooking dinner for an in-home, sit-down meal between three or four o'clock, then staying close to home to relax and spending time together. On those mornings, they enjoyed lying in bed and sleeping late, drinking coffee, and listening to the radio—sometimes soft music, sometimes a preacher. Hannah never saw herself having a roommate. She expected instead to have a boyfriend, date for a few years, and if he was the one, she'd get married and have children. But everything with Margaret had worked out so well—being best friends, learning about life, educating each other, and supporting each other in their careers.

"Why don't you open up your own salon since business is booming," Margaret asked.

"Having a salon in Colorado would be nice."

"I could live there," Margaret replied.

A few songs played in the background and both women sang "Bette Davis Eyes."

"One thing about my daddy," Margaret said, "he liked the symphony. Go figure. Such a brutal man liked Beethoven, Mozart, and Chopin, so I was always listening to music with him. He listened to jazz, blues, and soul, too, but he liked instrumental music, almost elevator music. One time when I was on the school bus, I threw up all over the place. I told my father I didn't feel good, but he made me go to school anyway," Margaret said as they lay in bed.

To look at her, Hannah thought, *you'd never think Margaret had thrown up a day in her life. That's how pretty she is.*

"He didn't get angry with me, but I had to stay home by myself because he had to work. I wasn't but seven. All he said was, don't answer the door or telephone, and if the house catches on fire, put your clothes on and run across the street. Let the place burn."

When Margaret fell back asleep, Hannah pulled the sheets away and looked at Margaret. She liked the smell of her shampoo and leaned over to smell her hair. She also liked how Margaret's body looked like melted chocolate. Hannah ran her finger across a scar, about four inches long, running down the back of Margaret's thigh. It looked like an earthworm. Hannah thought if Margaret wanted to be a model, she could—she just couldn't do swimsuit photos. Everything else would be fine. After a minute, Hannah covered her up and tucked her under the sheets.

At eleven o'clock in the morning, the doorbell rang, waking Hannah from a dream about being in Egypt and at the Pyramids. She turned toward Margaret.

"Stay there. I'll see who it is," Hannah said.

Hannah jumped up and tossed on her clothes that she'd left on the floor from the previous night. She ran into the bathroom and brushed her teeth with a once-over then pulled her hair back in a ponytail. The doorbell rang again. She ran to the door and was surprised to see her mother standing there holding a cake and flowers.

"Momma, what're you doing here?"

"I was in the neighborhood."

Does she know my good news? Hannah thought. *How could she?*

"Your daddy said I'd find you here at Margaret's. Where's she?"

"She's still sleeping, I think. I haven't seen her this morning," she lied.

Hannah closed the door behind her mother, and they walked into the kitchen where Hannah put a kettle of water on the stove for tea. She did not want her mother snooping around and finding Margaret in bed then start making assumptions.

"You want coffee or tea?"

"Tea's fine."

"What kind of cake's that?"

"Fluffy cake. How come you didn't answer your phone?"

"I had it turned off. I slept in a little but then got up to clean my room. You'd be proud—it looks like *Better Homes and Gardens*."

Hannah placed the bouquet of daisies in a vase then set it on the kitchen table.

"I'm gonna have a piece of cake. You want some?"

"No," her mother replied. "I bought too many for the restaurant. I'm sick of it. Is Margaret getting up to say 'hello?'"

"Probably not. She was out late last night, a real night owl. I'll bet I haven't seen her but once this week."

Hannah did not enjoy lying to her mother, but it was the easiest way to maneuver around her meddling.

While the water boiled, Hannah gave her mother a quick tour of the house and her bedroom, which looked as if no one had ever spent the night in it or even walked on the carpet. Not one thing was out of place.

"This sure is a nice house."

"It's Margaret's. I pay rent."

Hannah gave her mother the grand tour of downstairs, the basement, and all the rooms except Margaret's. As they passed her room, Hannah whispered to be quiet so as not to wake her. Once the tour was over, Hannah sat down at the kitchen table and poured two cups of tea.

"Greta called. She's going to be in a soap commercial. Look for it on TV."

As Hannah sat eating a piece of fluffy cake and sipping her tea, she didn't believe for one minute that Greta was in a soap commercial, but her mother went on and on, as if Greta had been anointed by the Academy of Motion Pictures for Best Actress in a tragedy of a runaway racist farm girl who stole a boat load of money from a crooked preacher and disowned her family in search of a new life.

I'd like to thank the Academy.

Hannah and her mother stepped outside onto the back porch where the new chairs and chaise lounge sat, purchased last week at Costco. Hannah sat in a chair while her mother lay in the chaise lounge under the bright morning glow, seeping heavily through branches and leaves of the Bradford pear trees. Together they looked at all the photographs in Hannah's box. Lilith named everyone she could and wrote their names in pencil on the back. She recognized some folks from Darnell's side of the family, not enough to do much good, but she recognized her family's kin.

"Well, you tell Margaret I stopped by to say 'hello.' Maybe one of these days I can finally meet her. Maybe you can stop by the restaurant for dinner sometime."

Once Lilith left, Margaret walked outside onto the patio. The morning air was refreshing, and the sun began to rise high above the stretched-out pine trees swaying in a northeast wind, back and forth a few inches, like they were dancing to a slow waltz. A long way off in some small backyard, a dog was barking.

As Hannah and Margaret sat on the patio, the smell of rain drifted in, as the wind picked up.

"When I was a little girl, I feared God would flood the earth again. I remember standing near the road in front of the house with Lucas, just thinking a tidal wave would rush down our road and sweep us away, wash Old Damascus Road off the face of the Earth. Gone. Everything we knew and loved cleansed of evil. Some days, Lucas and I rode our bikes into town to wave at all the passing cars, yelling for them to slow down because we thought if they crashed, they would start a fire, and the earth would burn. The only way the fire could be extinguished is if God flooded the earth."

Wash yourselves and be clean! Let Me no longer see your evil deeds. Give up your wicked ways.—Isaiah 1:16

That afternoon, Margaret and Hannah prepared spaghetti with sautéed ground turkey. Afterwards, they listened to soft instrumental music, each trying to guess the song by the arrangement. They drank sparkling grape juice, no wine, because the doctor had warned Hannah against it.

"Here, take your vitamins," Margaret told her. "The doctor prescribed these for a reason." The due date was April 2, give or take a week. She had not told anyone, including her mother.

After dinner, they played crazy eights, double solitaire, then a few games of cribbage.

Chapter 16

A Grief that Understands My Heart

Mr. Fox called from the funeral home to say he had three clients who needed haircuts and asked if Hannah would stop by after work. Although she wanted to drive home and sleep, she was kind of looking forward to working with someone who didn't ask a lot of questions.

Mr. Fox was in a talkative mood when Hannah arrived late that afternoon and followed her around as she prepared her things before cutting hair. His humor brought her out of her funk, and by the end, Hannah was talkative. She asked him about cremations, so they walked to a part of the building she'd never seen before. They had cremated a man that day, a few hours beforehand, and Mr. Fox showed Hannah how a body does not burn and turn to ashes without some parts remaining.

"Pelvis bone, skull, and the spine. These don't always burn completely."

Hannah watched as he scraped those pieces into a container. Then he showed her a metal pin.

"See this?" Mr. Fox asked, holding up the metal pin. "This fella had a pin in his leg. Stuff like this doesn't burn up, so we toss it in that canister."

From eight feet away, Mr. Fox tossed the metal pin into the recycling bin, then took the unburned bones and poured them into the bone cruncher.

"This machine crunches the bones up, like seashells. On TV, you see people with actual dust. Ashes. That's a lie. No one wants their old man's spine or pelvis returned to them, so we grind it up to powder so it fits in the urn."

When Hannah returned home later that evening, after giving haircuts to two men and a curl to an older woman, Margaret was standing in the kitchen sautéing mushrooms. Hannah dropped her bag at the door, walked over to the sofa, kicked off her shoes, and plopped down into the pillows. She was exhausted. She closed her eyes and wanted nothing more than to sleep. Her breathing became heavy. She didn't say a word to Margaret, not even when she asked her a question. Margaret turned the burner to low and walked over to sit next to Hannah's feet on the sofa. She lifted Hannah's feet up and began to massage them.

"What did the doctor say?"

"How'd you know I went to the doctor?"

"Wendy told me. When I ran over to the store for a ginger ale, I stopped in for a second, and you were gone."

Hannah said something, but Margaret couldn't understand her garbled talk through the muffle of the pillows. Margaret asked again, but still she did not understand Hannah, who lifted her face off the pillow.

"Just nausea. She gave me something for it. I'm just tired."

> He who sins is of the devil, for the devil has been sinning from the beginning. To this end the Son of God was revealed, that he might destroy the works of the devil.—John 3:8

§

I prayed a lot yesterday. However, it's not the God I prayed to when I was growing up. It may be better than God because it is my own God, maybe one of nature or of the cosmos, but it's not the God of any church. Maybe it's the God for the Church of Injured Hearts.

In one hundred years, I will surely be dead and buried. Hopefully, you're reading this at the beach or in the park or on the patio or in bed with your lover or on a jet that takes you to Mars. At this exact moment, I'm in the library, tucked deep in the back in a cubby-hole study-booth, and I have Margaret's MacBook. If libraries still exist in 100 years, I hope you will visit them. As for this one, once you're inside, turn to your left and walk back to the corner in the deepest part where the two walls join. You will find four cubicles. I'm in the last one. Please sit down where I am now and know that over the span of time we're here together. Connected. Doesn't that sound like something Albert Einstein would say, or maybe Mr. Spock?

I don't want to write about me today except to say that I'm as worried as ever even if Margaret said not to worry. . . we're going to raise the baby together. I don't think she signed up for this and that's what worries me, as well as what people will think.

"Don't worry what anyone says. It's your life," Margaret told me.

But I cannot help it.

Without Margaret, I would be alone. I have flown so far from God even the angels have stopped looking for me.

The eyes of the Lord watch over those who do right,
and his ears are open to their prayers.
—I Peter 3:12

Sarah never mentioned her religion, but I'll bet she was a Christian. I used to believe in God despite the lack of proof, which made it all the more believable, taking the leap of faith that He exists. I'm not sure any longer. From day to day, my opinion changes. These days, I can count on no one else except Margaret. Maybe Sarah was a good friend, like Margaret, except stuck on a dusty trail.

A man on a horse delivered a sack of mail to the wagon master and some people had letters from back home. I did not. Billie, a woman I have become friends with, got an upliften letter from her mother. She is from Titusville. She let me read it. [Billie's momma] When we last talked we were in poor health and the weather was chilled. Now a pleasant reverse has befelled us. The crops are in the ground. Your father could do no more than advise as we watched the hands take over. They did a fine job. Expecting a harvest in mid to late September. Your brother Henry has moved to Lakewood, New York to work at The Sterling Inn. It is a hotel of magnificent luxury. He and Claudia and the children visited two Sundays ago and stayed for several days. We have been invited to stay at the hotel and enjoy the good weather and company of others. We expect to take them up on thar kindness next spring when the crop is planted. We can stay for several weeks with not a worry about the crop. The man with the mail showed the boys where he was shot years ago in the leg with an arrow by Indians. He has a large scar the size of my hand. He said he lost half the muscle. I asked the man if I could send a letter to my sister in Meadville. Yes save it would cost eight cents. John said no. He is right. We do not have any extra money. Late last night I took a short letter to the man and one cent. John did not know of this. The man said he would d'liver my letter to Susan in maybe two months if I allowed him to lay his hands on my breasts. I about cried. I did not tell John of this because he would kill the man and beat me. After much grave pain, I delivered my lotter to him this evening. He assur'd me my letter would arrive. He also tried to touch me low. I halted his efforts. I slunk back to our wagon with tears in my soul. I told Susan to stay in Meadville. Some of the men folks are bothered that we stopped for the day while a young girl from Pittsburgh gave birth. We stopped at the farm of a man and his family and they were ha-spit-a-ble and allowed ever'one on to their land. We about trampled the ground into dust but they did not seem to mind. It was more his idea because his wife seemed dizzy from the excitement. The young girl Emma Ruth and her husband O'Dell now have a baby boy – Bennett - and we are back riding once again. She cannot be feeling well and there are many folks helping her and the baby. I ran up ahead to look in on her and she was sleeping in the buckboard so I did not bother her, speshlee since she was in care for by several other women. It will be a hard journey for them hence forth. We stayed one day at the farm and folks camped on this mans land. His name was Stephen and his wife was Hattie Belle. Once the men had secured their places, they put together their hands and helped Mr. Card with things around his farm. John and Charles went off to chop wood and stack it. Others helped by walking his crop rows and tugging up weeds. In the end so much work was done, Mr. Card was brought to tears when he bid us farewell. He offered work for anyone willing to stay. None took his offer. Westward winds are blow'n through ever'ones hair. Repairs were also made to his barn. All sorts. The men can look at something and know what needs to be done and get right to it. Before you can turn around they have it fixed. Everyone worked well together. It was hard to believe that a few days ago tempers were high and folks upset with even good weather. Nothing could sa-tis-fy them. Being that the baby was born on a Sunday, services were held in a field near a pond full of ducks. Most everyone attended. I had an idea. I write letters for folks for a penny. They tell me what to say and I write it down on a paper up to four pages. After that it is another penny. I have made eleven letters for folks. John said it was a stupid idea and if I made any money, he wanted it. I told him no. I was saving it. He said we will see about all of that. I have hidden the money, twenty-seven cents.

That's a lot from Sarah. I hope I don't get sued by anyone for typing up what she had to say. Sarah might have been one of a few women on the wagon train who could read and write, more so than most men. I think I spell better than Sarah, but I can't kill a chicken and rip its insides out to cook dinner. She did that all the time.

§

On Sunday at ten o'clock, the doorbell rang while Hannah was in the shower. When Margaret opened the door, Hawkshaw Bales was standing there with another man ready to serve papers on Hannah. Margaret had never met Bales, but she remembered him from the videos she and Hannah had found online. Even though he was older now, she recognized him.

Now would be a good time to shoot this asshole, she thought. But Margaret had more restraint and composure than to have a knee-jerk reaction.

The white man with him wore a tartan sport jacket, which had a cheesy used car salesman-look to it. She thought he couldn't have looked much cheaper unless he had worn a gabardine trench coat. Something just didn't suit her when she looked at Bales. It was a look she'd seen from other men before, pleasant but with intentions she sensed were immoral.

"I have a delivery for Hannah Gardner," the man said.

"She's not here."

"I can give it to you since you live here, too."

The man tugged on the screen door handle. It was locked. He indicated that he needed to hand Margaret a large thick envelope with legal papers.

"What's this?"

"Legitimization papers to prove I'm the father of her baby," Bales said.

"Who are you?" she asked, even though she was certain she already knew.

"Hawkshaw Bales."

Margaret looked at both men, noticing Bales' paisley tie and how the other man's left eyelid twitched like an electrical pulse was shooting through it. She thought about what she wanted to say to them but held her tongue. It was difficult, as she wanted to give Bales both barrels full.

"You'd be good to get off my property," Margaret warned him.

"You tell that little girlfriend of yours I intend on taking that baby from her."

"No judge will ever give you custody," Margaret yelled.

"Not permanent custody, but every other weekend and holidays. My momma and sisters want time with their blood."

"I can tell you this, if either of you set foot on my property again, I'll shoot you. As far as I see it, you're threatening me with assault. That's why you're here."

"Whatever you say, Sweet-pea, but Hannah had better respond," Bales said.

"She doesn't live here, so your service is invalid. Tell that to the judge."

"Where's she living?"

"Did you check her apartment?"

"She moved," said the white man.

"Check with her momma or daddy. I don't know where they live, but that's not my problem. We had a falling out months ago, but I heard something about her moving to Colorado. We used to be friends, but no longer."

Bales and the other man looked at each other, because that's what Beth Johnson told them when they tried serving her at the apartment.

"You know you have to serve her personally or serve someone at her residence," Margaret said. "This is my house, and she doesn't live here."

"Can you help us out?" the process server asked.

"Go to hell," she replied.

"Listen here, you little whore," Bales yelled, "I'll make you one of my bitches and you'll be turning blow jobs for five dollars on Memorial Drive if you don't give us her address!"

"You listen up, I've dealt with jerks like you all my life, and you don't scare me. You think you're a tough guy. I dealt with tougher guys in the military, and I'll deal with you the same way. You come at me with threatening words, I'll hit you with a baseball bat. You come at me with a baseball bat, I'll bring a platoon of Marines to your front door. You think I'm kidding, try me."

Margaret slammed the door in their faces and turned the lock. Upstairs, she pulled back the window blinds a half-inch to peek out and watch the men standing in her driveway, talking. She didn't want them looking in her windows or walking around her property and into the backyard, snooping around.

So what if Hannah is over here all the time? They can't prove she lives here, Margaret thought.

The men stood by their car talking. Then, the process server opened the driver's door while Bales walked around to the passenger's side. As the men backed out of the driveway, Bales held his phone out the window and snapped a photo of her house. As he did, Margaret pulled away from the blinds and hid behind the wall. She walked back downstairs and checked the locks on all the doors again, including the garage. Then, she walked upstairs to the bathroom to find Hannah stepping out of the shower.

"What was all that yelling?" Hannah asked.

"Let's get ready. I'll tell you on the way to Home Depot."

As Margaret drove to Home Depot, she kept an eye out for Hawkshaw Bales and his friend but said nothing to Hannah. She turned down a few cul-de-sacs to see if they were being tailed.

Hannah asked, "Why are you driving down here?"

"Just looking at the neighborhood for ideas."

As she drove behind Kroger and came out the backside of the parking lot, Margaret gave Hannah the low-down on Hawkshaw Bales trying to serve her with legitimization papers.

"He can't do that, can he?"

"Only if he serves you." Then Margaret explained everything to her. "If he can't find you, he can't serve you."

Then, she drove to Publix and around the back of the building, but this time, she stopped for three minutes to determine if any other cars were following. When she was confident they were not being followed, they continued to Home Depot where she bought four No Trespassing signs to post on her property, as well as window tint to cover six garage door windows because she did not want Bales or his friend looking in the garage to see Hannah's car parked inside. She also purchased a do-it-yourself RING HD Wi-Fi video doorbell to install and two video monitors—one for upstairs and downstairs. She wanted to see who was standing at her front, back, and side doors. She also told Hannah to have her mail delivered to a post office box.

"When you fill out the paperwork, give'em your apartment address. They won't check to see if you're still living there. You're breaking the law, but no one at the Post Office will ever check. You don't want anything tracking you back to our house. Also, don't use our address for anything, especially official reasons. Use your apartment or your daddy's address."

"I'll use the farm address," she laughed.

Monday morning on the back porch, the mid-October air felt crisp and clean as Hannah sucked it in through her teeth. She and Margaret slunk out of their garage in Margaret's car with Hannah hiding low in her seat until Margaret knew they weren't being followed.

"He'll just serve me at The Cute Curl, won't he?"

"Probably," Margaret replied.

Margaret drove around, in and out of subdivisions, behind the grocery store, behind Lowes, and to the countryside. When they were close to the old farmhouse, Hannah directed Margaret to turn down Sundown-Antioch Road, then Cemetery Lane, and then on to Old Damascus Road. As they approached the farmhouse, Hannah said, "Slow down and stop."

"This is where you grew up?"

"Yeah, that window near the oak tree was my bedroom. Me and Greta, 'til she ran away."

There was no traffic on Old Damascus Road, so Margaret put the car in park and the two women sat looking out the windshield at the farm. Margaret asked a bunch of questions about her childhood and growing up there.

Hannah noticed something odd. Behind the barn, the apple trees were gone.

"Back the car in the driveway," Hannah instructed Margaret.

The last time Hannah walked the property, she hadn't noticed anything like this. They exited the car, and with Margaret's help, Hannah hopped over the gate, followed by Margaret. They walked to the barn down a narrow dirt path, which had been wider, before the farm was sold and nature began to reclaim it. They stood in front of the apple trees, more than fifty, each felled, knocked over like huge stalks of broccoli, yet still with a smidgen if ripe apples. The stumps were two feet high, sawed off at the same height as if a machine had come through. Margaret looked down but saw no tracks from heavy equipment.

"This is freshly cut, no more than three or four days ago, a week at the most," Margaret surmised. She rubbed her fingers across a cut stump.

Hannah was pretty certain she knew what this meant. Some company was about to develop the land, bury her house underground, including the barn and the family history, and sweep it under as far as they could until the past no longer existed or mattered. Hannah walked up to the first tree closet to her. The branches were crushing down onto the tall grass and dirt. She looked at the trunk sticking up and angled high into the air. Hannah rubbed the bark. She ran her hand along several branches then stopped to pull two apples from a branch. She thought she would cry when this day arrived, but she was so angry at the audacity of killing what produced fruit, nourishment, that she was without words. Inside, rage festered. She wanted to hit something. These were the trees of her childhood, trees she had climbed, dreamt from, and where she sought refuge.

Hannah turned around and in a curt voice said, "Let's go."

With an apple in each hand, she walked toward her old house and then to the car. Margaret followed behind her on the narrow dirt path, saying nothing. She also grabbed two large apples off a branch.

§

Down the road from the post office, about a mile and a half on Bushton Court, Hannah's father answered the door. The same man who tried serving papers to Hannah was standing on his front porch with an envelope.

"What'cha got, Bossman?" Darnell asked.

"Here, you're being served on behalf of your daughter, Hannah Gardner."

Darnell opened the screen door and took the envelope from the process server. He looked at the name and address, turning it over several times.

"She ain't here," Darnell replied.

"When's she coming home?" the man asked.

"Don't know. She don't live here. Never has."

"What are you talking about? That little nappy friend of hers told me yesterday she's living with you or her mother."

"Not here," Darnell told the man. "I'm certain she ain't living with Lilith but give it a try. Last I heard she was living in an apartment in Antioch. You know, near the train depot. If ya like, I'll give this to her next time I see her, but it's been more than a month since we've spoken. She's kind of pissed at me."

"Naw, that won't do. You sure she ain't living here?" the man asked.

"I'd know."

"I've been over to the other place already," the process server said. "She moved out a time back."

"Is my little girl in trouble over something?"

"Trouble, no. My client's the father of her baby."

"You got the right gal? Hannah doesn't have a baby."

"Not yet. She's pregnant. Hawkshaw Bales is the father, and these papers prove it."

The man stood on the porch while Darnell read the paperwork. He read the first two pages of the complaint then handed the paperwork back to the man. As soon as the man walked away, Darnell dashed over to his phone.

"Darling, where are you?"

"Running errands."

"A fellow just left here trying to serve you with a lawsuit claiming you're pregnant with some Black fella's baby. Not that I believe much of what he said, but I thought you ought to know 'cause he's heading to your momma's to give her the news."

"It's not true. They got me mixed up with the wrong person," she yelled into the phone.

"Well, your momma's gonna have a cow if that's true."

"It ain't."

"I told this here fella that you were more likely to get knocked up by an angel sent from God than by a Black man."

"Daddy, I don't need you saying crap like that to people." She hung up.

Hannah screamed in the car, which compelled Margaret to slam on the brakes, thinking a car, a deer, or a person was about to get hit.

"Can we move to Mexico or Canada?" she asked Margaret.

Hannah called her mother's phone, but Lilith did not answer. She called her mother's house.

"Hay-low," the machine answered. "If you're calling 'bout the chickens, they're five dollars each or eight dollars if I ring their necks for you."

"Hello, Eddie Lee. Momma. Ron—"

Eddie Lee turned off the answering machine.

"Hooty-who, this here's Eddie Lee."

"This is Hannah—is my momma there?"

"Nope. Them two lovebirds needed a day off from work. She and Ronnie are out on my boat. Barbara's running things during lunch, and I'm running the restaurant for dinner. You want a steak? We open for lunch at eleven, dinner at five. I'm heading over there around two or three o'clock."

"I called her phone, but no one answered."

"I don't know what to tell you except maybe they ain't answering the phone 'cause they're doing the nasty out on the water, tucked deep into a cove somewhere see-clu-did."

"Come on. Don't talk like that about my mother."

"If you come up to The Diamond Eye for dinner I'll apologize personally."

"I need a favor. A man's on his way to deliver a lawsuit against me. He thinks I live there. Do not accept the papers. Tell him I moved to Colorado."

"How come?" he asked.

"Just do it."

"Only if you come up for dinner."

"I can't today, but I promise I will."

"You promise?" Eddie Lee asked.

"Yes, but you also have to tell my momma not to accept the papers and don't believe anything this man has to say. He's a liar. Be careful 'cause he's a real bad guy. Tell 'em I moved to Colorado."

"Why Colorado? Is it the pot laws? I can hook you up."

"That's not it."

"This fella ain't gonna believe you moved to a foreign country."

An hour after their conversation, the doorbell rang and Eddie Lee answered it, wearing a Texas state flag shirt, jeans, cowboy boots, and a Glock 9mm in a holster on his right hip. The process server and Hawkshaw Bales were standing there, acting stiff and official, like they were the law. They had driven up in separate cars, both left running in the driveway.

"I already know what you boys want, and she don't live here. Hell, I don't live here. Hannah's momma owns this place, and my brother's kind of her favorite pole to dance on if you know what I mean."

"Do you know where she's living?" Bales asked.

"I most certainly do. She done moved out of the country to Colorado, and as soon as my passport arrives, I plan to meet up with her. She's my wife."

"Wife?"

"Yep. We fell out for a spell but I won'er back."

"Where in Colorado?"

"Pineapple Springs. I'm waiting on her call for the low down on the hoe down then I'm shipping out to be with her. You need me to take a message to her?"

Eddie Lee made all sorts of hand gestures, like he was a gangster rapper.

The process server looked at Bales with a what-do-you-want-to-do-now look.

"I think you're full of shit," Bales said.

"That's not nice," Eddie Lee whined. "I hadn't said a foul word to you boys. I don't need no talk like that around here. I'm a God-fearing man who goes to church every Wednesday and Sunday."

"You're a liar," Bales said.

"Listen here, Cowboy, that may be so, but I can redeem myself. You and this here other fella, I can tell just by looking at y'all, you're beyond redemption. You have an ill disposition, a quality unlikely to change."

"You ought'a watch your mouth," the process server said.

"Up here on the lake, you'd better be careful after sundown," Eddie Lee said.

"Listen up, Peckerwood, you threatening me?" Bales said.

"Just handing out free advice."

"If I have to come back up here, I'm bringing some friends to teach you a lesson."

"That's real interesting, a man who's looking for a nice girl like Hannah has to act like a tough guy. What'd she do, snip your nuts? She's just a flower blowing in the wind, but she's sure gotten under your skin."

"Better watch yourself, Cracker," the process server warned.

"I heard you're a Bad MoFo. You don't scare me none. Just remember, when you got two objects of equal force that will not budge, the one that's tougher will win. Know where I learned that—Georgia Tech. I did a couple semesters before realizing I liked fishin' better than books. I been in the gutter all my life, an' I seen it and I done it all, and I'll slit a man's throat jus' for looking at me wrong. Going back to prison don't scare me none. Now, get off this property before the sheriff has to bring some body bags over here."

Eddie Lee placed his hand on his pistol and unsnapped the strap.

Chapter 17

When Faith Comes a' Knockin'

It's Friday evening, and today's the first day I've stepped inside the library to type in over two weeks. I've been busy at home looking for a new job. Margaret suggested I quit The Cute Curl, which I did, even though I did not want to and felt bad telling Wendy. Hawkshaw Bales was sure enough going to serve me with papers as soon as the salon opened up. I called Wendy at home and apologized to her.

"I'm moving to Colorado."

I don't think she believed me. I also asked her not to tell anyone anything if they come snooping around, especially Bales and his process server buddy. I told her I would send a check for this month's chair rental. I did not want to cheat her. She's been good to me, like an older sister or an aunt. I also asked her not to tell anyone about me working at the funeral home. I still have that going for me. Sure enough, not long after she opened up, Bales and his buddy handed Wendy an envelope with all the paperwork. As soon as they left, she called me.

"Those men just showed up," Wendy said.

I'm worried about not having a job, but Margaret said she wouldn't charge me for rent or anything.

I've decided not to respond to the legitimization claim from Hawkshaw Bales on the account I was not served according to the letter of the law. Margaret called a friend of hers in Little Rock, an attorney, who said it was not proper service, so I'm off the hook. They left a copy with everyone at any place I have ever lived or worked. When me and Margaret came home, there was a copy on the front steps. Her friend said that once I get served, and I will at some point, I won't have much choice but to answer. For now, Bales cannot touch me.

I rarely leave the house now, and when I do, I sneak out the back door and Margaret picks me up on the backside of the subdivision near Lucille Road. I have to jump the creek and walk through the woods to get there, but it's a nice walk. I called five lawyers—all are between $200 to $450 per hour. They said the same thing—if Hawkshaw Bales is the father, he will have the right to visitation. We've talked about filing rape charges against him, but they said that since I went to his hotel room voluntarily, it's unlikely to hold water. Of course, I knew that. Margaret's been researching his background again, and if we can prove the devil has a criminal history or is dealing drugs or is a mass murderer or has the moral turpitude of an alley cat, then I might be able to keep him away from the baby, maybe keep his family away, too.

"I could move away, change my name," I told Margaret.

"Sooner or later," she said, "a guy like him will track you down."

> If you forgive those who sin against you, your heavenly Father will forgive you. But if you refuse to forgive others, your Father will not forgive your sins.—
> Matthew 6:14-15

I don't even know where to begin with my contempt for such a Bible verse.

You cannot forgive a man like Hawkshaw Bales. Otherwise, he will forever have a boot on your neck, but if I have an abortion, then the Bales problem goes away.

Margaret needed some aspirin so I drove to the pharmacy, and while on my way, I realized God can never be proven. If he could, the mystery would be gone. There would be no faith. People live for the mystery. Believing in God or Jesus is not based on rational thought. It is faith, which is the greatest leap a person can make in this world, the leap of faith that God exists without proof. I believe in God despite a lack of evidence, and by placing my entire soul on the line, I leap forward toward God's grace. I give in to the idea that He may not exist, but I have faith He does. I give everything to that belief. Where has my faith been all these years? Faith is different than religion, especially if it's organized. I love the idea of faith, but I abhor all organized religion.

§

Hannah had turned her phone off hours ago and did not turn it back on until late that night before she went to bed. She was tired and tucked in by nine o'clock, but Margaret was still up in the other room listening to Adele in concert on the TV and reading a book that had been recommended, *Excellent Women*. Hannah had seven text messages and three voice messages from her mother, but she didn't want to talk to her, didn't want to hear from her or anyone. Hannah checked the house alarm and had just placed her head on the pillow when her mother called.

"You'd better answer that. It's not like her to call this many times," Margaret said from the other room. As the phone continued ringing, Margaret walked into the bedroom and lay next to Hannah to listen. Hannah answered the telephone.

"Momma, I'm tired. I'll call you in the morning."

"Eddie Lee says he's your baby daddy."

"Are you serious?"

"He said he was the daddy."

"Oh, holy hell. Do you really think that's true?! Whatever he told you, it's not true. Tell Eddie Lee to stop causing trouble."

"Why's your phone been off all day?"

"It was off because it was off."

On Monday, Hannah snuck around the county with a scarf over her head and sunglasses, trying to shield herself from Bales and the process server. She'd called Wendy at home on Sunday and asked if she would cut her hair before the store opened.

"When are you leaving for Colorado?"

"In two days."

"Meet me at seven. Use the back door but bring me a coffee and two old-fashioned donuts from Maggie's Coffee Shop."

At The Cute Curl, Wendy cut Hannah's hair short, up to her ears and bleached it blonde. Hannah wanted a cropped, trendy look to disguise herself as much as possible.

"I'm tired of being a brunette."

"Okay, but will the carpet match the drapes?" Wendy laughed.

Hannah laughed, as well, then Wendy laughed when Hannah said there was no carpet.

"Girl, what'cha got going on down there?"

Wendy went to work, and Hannah told her the entire truth about Hawkshaw Bales while trying to avoid the legal entanglements.

"When everything blows over, come back any time."

Hannah also wrote her a check for what rental she owed on the chair.

She snuck out the back door after Wendy made certain there was no one waiting for her behind the store. When all looked clear to Wendy, Hannah drove around for a few minutes to see if she was being followed, through the back streets of a neighborhood before driving to the library. She sat in the parking lot and put on some deep red lipstick, sunglasses, and a baseball cap.

At the front desk of the library, Hannah stood in line to check out a book and waited for Margaret to notice her. Margaret walked up to the counter but did not notice it was Hannah.

"Can I help you?" Margaret asked.

"Yes, do you have a book called *How to Completely Disappear and Never Be Found*?"

Margaret looked at Hannah for a second, then looked at Hannah's right hand for the one ring she wore, her grandmother's garnet signet ring. Margaret shrieked then ran around the counter to hug Hannah.

"Oh my God, look at you! From the back with the baseball cap, I thought you were a boy. You look so spunky wearing men's Dockers and tennis shoes, just like Meg Ryan in *You've Got Mail*, just before she meets Tom Hanks."

"Except I'm preggo."

The two women were giddy and laughing so much, Elvis stepped out of her office.

"Look at you," Ilene said. "I didn't recognize you. Take off your hat."

Hannah showed the women her short blonde hair and shrieked again. Both touched it and felt the neckline, brushing their hands up the short stubble of her neck.

"Wendy cut it this morning. She did the color, too."

After talking for a few minutes, the women went back to work, and Hannah sat down in a study cubicle in the back with Margaret's MacBook. Margaret walked back every so often to see Hannah, and on her last visit said, "I just want to eat you up."

§

I'm a blonde and I feel like a new person, with my new short haircut. What a whirlwind this has been. There's so much I want to write. I bet Sarah never forgot one nugget or got anything wrong in her journal. I have been thinking, maybe I'll go back to school and study law. Then, no one will mess with me.

"You haven't been out of school long," Margaret said the other night.

She's right.

"There's nothing to it as long as you commit yourself. For some people, taking a few years off helps them mature."

She makes me want to do things to be a better person. I wouldn't make any money for years, but Margaret said not to worry about money.

Margaret's a Methodist, and I'm thinking of changing to her church. We could join together. She makes me want to love God again. Otherwise, I'm frozen mud.

"Get out of the sanctuary, for you have sinned...."—
II Chronicles 26:18-19

I think Sarah was a Methodist, too.

B'fore we left Meadville I told John we should take two wagons and I could manage one but he did not want this. Instead, he sold our team of horses and the buckboard. I thought we could pack our b'long'ngs and what we did not have use for, other people would buy from us. He said that was a stupid idea because it cost extra money to have a second buckboard and team. Yes, I told him but it could pay for itself. Now I'm being shown to be the smart one in this house. People need everything on the trail. No matter what, some person here needs it. All the things we left behind now belong to whoever moved into our cabin. I told Susan she could have it all. I hope her husband Henry was fast enough to get over to the farm. On the trail people help out one another at times, but it didn't take folks long to r'lize they can charge ought-rageously. I could have done the same, start a store on the buckboard to sell all the things needed. John said to be quiet about such nunsense but he's angry with himself because it was my idea. Things cost three x's what they cost at home like meat and milk. A team of healthy horses is worth a pretty penny. About once a week a horse is shot because of an ankle or other reasons not to be burdened with on the trail. They cut the horses up for meat. The leftovers are scraps for the dogs. Nothing is wasted. I wouldn't but many folks eat horse meat. John brought home a steak he won in a bett'n game. I would not touch the thing. Charles tasted a little speck but spit it out. John laughed. One woman has set the bones out to dry after boiling them all night for soup. She plans to make them brittle in three weeks time of sunning and air. She has several large sacks of dry bones she brung along with her from mainly cow and pig bones. She said maybe there was a deer in there or a goat, maybe a dog. She showed me how she crushes them to a powder to make biscits with milk and butter she had bartered for. I split a biscit with Charles. It wasn't not so bad as I imagined, til I thought 'bout what I was eating. Animal bones. Some folks have goats and cows tied and walking behind their wagon. What a mighty burden it is to pull them along or round them up when they break free. The other day the children run after a luse cow. Finally the men took over and roped him up. Last night Sunday was a beautiful evening.

A few clouds, deep black sky and the stars looking like bull frog eyes when you're out gigging in the creek and the lantern catches them just right when cool air is blowing through the weeds and rustling the trees and you're worried you may be a little too far south of the ridgeline and there might be a mountain cat tracking you while you're looking for frogs and turtles.

I'm outside the library typing on Margaret's MacBook. There is a deep chill in the air that feels good. I'm bundled up in my winter coat, although I don't need it quite yet. It is November 21st, and there is a couple walking down the street having an argument about the man's parents. Somewhere a fire is roaring because I can smell the smoke. Few cars have passed through the streets in the last twenty minutes. I came out here to type and think while Margaret finishes working. Over at the police station, minutes ago, I watched the cops with a guy in handcuffs. I wonder what he did. I was hoping for a struggle, then the cops could get all over him if he got away in the parking lot. If he started running my way, I'd yell to him, "Sanctuary City. This is a holy sanctuary." I would hold open the door for him. When he ran in the library, he would be trapped with his hands cuffed behind his back, and it would be easy pickings for the cops.

If the snake bites before it is charmed, then is there
no profit for the charmer's tongue.
—Ecclesiastes 10:11

This is what I mean. Sarah, even when her writings are sad, makes me feel good for reading about her life. Margaret's a lot like that.

When my mother died the county came to her funeral even in the bitter of winter. For days folks stopped by the farm to console me and Susan and brung food. Preserves worked the best. As grateful as we was to have so much food, it made for much work storing it not to rot. Felton the gravedigger burned a fire over the ground for days to soften the top. He said February is always his hardest month. Most folks store the body in a mossaleeam til spring. Felton studied up through the fourth grade with me before working all the time on the farm.

He stayed awake for days keeping wood on the fire prodding the ground then digging a little, heating up the dirt again for digging. Then more coals in the hole he's dug, fiery coals. A week later, mother was buried on Sunday afternoon after church. Cold but no wind. A blessing. The sun shined and Susan and I took it as a sign mother ascended Heavenly. Afterward John went into town and late night returned after drinking with men I do not approve of. Many have never set foot in church.

Chapter 18

A Bird with One Wing

The following Tuesday, Hannah was up and out of the house before Margaret woke. She left without an explanation. Hannah still had her secrets, and when Margaret inquired, Hannah always said she was visiting her mother.

She stopped by San Francisco Café for a large coffee before walking the footpaths of her farm, one last time, to narrate to her baby what her life used to be like. She brought along her phone to take pictures of everything she knew would soon be gone. She talked and talked to her baby and took more than one hundred photos. Hannah had searched Google for information about developing the property but found none.

The farmhouse looked as though no one had lived there for thirty years. The driveway entrance was boarded up with new 2x4s stretching across from one fence post to the other like a big X. She peered in the windows as though she were window shopping at Saks 5th Avenue, knowing she could never afford anything in the store; therefore, she was not wanted there.

> **God said to Adam, "Because you ate the fruit I told you not to eat, I have placed a curse on the ground. All your life you will struggle to scratch a living from it."—Genesis 3:17**

Returning to her farm on that particular day reminded her of the old lady in *The Trip to Bountiful*, trying to find her way back home, but when she returned, she found nothing but a dilapidated old life that no one wanted any more except in memory. The grass on Hannah's farm was so high, a dog could get lost walking from the mailbox back to the front porch, which Hannah noticed was sagging inward because of wood-rot. The wood planks on the house were bare in most places, with small remnants of white paint scattered throughout, like the odd missing pieces of a jigsaw puzzle. The plywood boards covering the windows were warped and grayed. Painting the house was one thing her father didn't mind doing to keep it fresh and sparkling. He liked repairing it in October or early spring, painting or touching up the house when the weather was cooler. Darnell painted the house every other year. He brought the radio outside and was content with being his own boss, not like when he worked as an animal control specialist for a few months and had a boss always looking over his shoulder. He rid homes of squirrels, raccoons, and the occasional possum. Once, he rounded up fourteen rattlesnakes from a barn. He never understood why animals upset people, as if a squirrel running into the house was chaos, that nature had invaded the serenity of Eden, and now all that remained was bedlam.

"Possums are the most beneficial animal you can have," he told folks.

"Why's that?" they always asked back.

"It's a good luck charm to have a possum. If it were me, I'd feed him and make sure he was happy," he said, but no one believed him. He'd catch a possum, then take it back to his farm and let it go.

Darnell was fired after filling out a recommendation for a family with a rodent problem. They wanted him to rid their house of rats and cockroaches. He didn't do the work because there were too many. Instead, he handed them an estimate with the message: *Clean This Shithole.*

Hannah did not enter the farmhouse. She walked around the property instead, scoping things out, talking to her baby.

"I don't know if you're a boy or girl yet, but as soon as I do, I'll give you a name."

She told her baby what life was like on the farm and where things were at one time and who lived here.

"This used to be a nice place to live, if you can excuse some folks' behavior, but somehow the farm is more dilapidated than ever before. It makes me sad because I wish I could show you a place brimming with vitality. Someday, you and I can walk around here, and I'll tell you all about the good times."

Hannah did not have any worries about snakes, not this time of the year as the chill would keep them underground, or curled away in the barn, or in an old woodpile. She had not noticed before, but the barn roof was cracked open and falling in slightly on the backside. It looked like a hole someone had punched in the drywall. The old hay bales in the loft were exposed and gray, which she knew meant rot.

No animal will eat it now.

It had been years since she'd been inside her house, and from where she stood in the backyard, the dog pens and chicken coop appeared to have survived the best. She thought that a person could use them if they were inclined to do some hard work by breeding animals and cutting down weeds. Her mother's clothesline was still standing with clothespins attached to the dry line. To Hannah, the clothespins looked like children hanging from the monkey bars at school.

Someone would also need to trim the bushes and trees, she thought.

The pond, which her father kept cut down so the cows had easy access to the water, was thick with high grass and weeds and windblown trash. It looked stagnant. The turtles had survived and were lined on the bank like flat rocks, sunning themselves. A bunch of trees had grown in thick clusters in certain spots around the pond. They had not grown too tall, perhaps six or seven feet high, and their trunks were thin.

Other than just lying to folks, why don't they build a golf course on this land? she asked herself. *It would be a wonderful idea.*

She dreamed about her and Margaret learning to play golf, and every day, she'd see the farm and walk the land, and if no one found the graves, she and Margaret could search for them when they hit a wayward shot.

Maybe I can get a job as the cart girl selling sodas, beer, and sandwiches to the golfers. I could ride my baby around on the golf cart and give historical tours.

§

A few days later, around lunchtime, Hannah returned to the farm and parked her car in Rapture Hall, almost in the exact spot where the rapists parked their truck years ago, under the live oak tree. She walked underneath and stood where the one man peed. Hannah looked up to where she had climbed. If he had looked up, he would have had no other choice but to kill her. She realized how close they were to each other—not more than six or seven feet apart. She thought she was forty feet up. What a different perspective she had from the ground.

Hannah walked through the woods. It was not like the other day when the sun shone, but darker and more ominous than she remembered, as though there were more trees now, larger and closer together, squeezed like they were closing in. If someone were hiding behind the trees, she wouldn't see them. She was astounded by how nature claims back the world, but still, there was a dusting of the old trail leading the way to her farm. When she stepped out of the woods and into the clearing, she saw her house, like a vision of heaven on earth. From upon the hill, the house still looked lived in. She sat on the hill for a moment to catch her breath, imagining that her mother was in the kitchen making sandwiches for lunch; her daddy was in the barn tending to the horses; Greta was on the front porch with Wilbur the Pig reading a Hollywood biography; and Wendell and Lucas were sitting on the big rock, fishing. This made her feel good. Through the prism of bad times, there were good memories, like how her father built an oversized rocking horse out of the wood from an oak tree struck by lightning, and then he sold off the rest of the wood and bought Momma a nice Sunday dress. The problem was Darnell never took Lilith anywhere except to church, and Lilith ended up wearing that dress more to funerals than anywhere else. That was the fall when Hannah was eleven, and it always seemed to be the happiest time of her life.

Hannah walked down to the house and circled around to the front. Being pregnant had zapped her energy. Tired and out of breath, she sat on the porch steps, which were sun-warmed but not hot like in the summer. She remembered sitting with her family on the porch listening to stories, and when kinfolk stopped by, they gathered outside, and her mother would serve tall glasses of sweet tea on a tray. It was on this porch where Hannah first stood with a boy and was kissed, Lester Mannin. She and Lucas would crawl under the porch and look through the latticework, pretending to be spies as they watched anything going on in the yard or listened to Lilith's footsteps walking around the kitchen floor. Oftentimes, she and Lucas would call out for their dog, Max, and he would spin around looking for them, sniffing the air, trying to figure out where their voices were coming from, his senses deceived by their trickery. When their grandmother lived with them, she would fall asleep on the porch in a chair, and they'd hear her snore at naptime from under the thin floorboards.

After Hannah caught her breath, she walked around the house again to the barn, to the back where all the apple trees lay dead, cut down and ready for a machine to grind them up and spit out the shards into a huge pile for burning or pulp left to rot. It was then that she realized their apple trees had been producing apples for one hundred years, since her great-great Poppa planted them back in the 1920s. She wasn't sure why she felt compelled to visit today, but somehow the other day did not satisfy her. It used to be that her kin harvested plenty of fruit from those apple trees. Now, the fallen trees had been stripped of their fruit. Each tree had one or two apples remaining. Hannah reached over and pulled a big red apple and bent a branch until the apple snapped off. She shined the apple on her shirt then on her blue jeans before crunching into it. The sweet juicy taste reminded her of sitting in the woods with Lucas, eating so many apples they got sick.

Around the back of the barn, close to where part was falling down, Hannah noticed some boards were loose, maybe pulled apart by a wild animal, she imagined. As she stepped in through the opening in the boards, the strong smell of wet hay and farm animals still lingered years later. She could smell the horses in the stables, pungent but sweet and wonderful, nonetheless. All her father's farm equipment and tools were gone, sold off years ago in the auction or in his yard sale. There were some old, rusted milk cans, farming magazines, and candy wrappers that were new—someone had been inside eating a Snickers. She looked up toward the hayloft, but the ladder looked frail. They used to climb up in the loft and jump onto the hay bales and hay piles until Greta broke her arm by landing on the clay floor. That put an end to their horsing around.

When Hannah walked out of the barn, she returned to her favorite spot on the farm, the flat rock. She lay down on the rock, shielded by all the high grass, and looked up to the blue sky and full clouds. The sun felt nice on such a cool day, and the small amount of heat that had absorbed into the rock warmed her body, and Hannah fell into a light sleep. Then, a few minutes later, she rose and walked back to her house where she noticed something out of the ordinary—the back door had been nailed shut with plywood, but not entirely. It was an illusion, a trick. She wasn't certain why she hadn't noticed it before, but she hadn't. The door had, at one point, been nailed shut. She ran her fingers over the nail holes in the corners, but now the plywood was a disguise, as it hung on a pivot-hinge that allowed the plywood to swing back and forth like an upside-down metronome. From a few feet away, the door looked like it was nailed tight; however, a slight push, and it moved to reveal the back doorknob. Let go of it, and it eased back into place, as if controlled by a hydraulic mechanism. The plywood was a snug fit, dovetailed so that anyone looking at it would be hard-pressed to notice the entryway. Hannah thought some homeless people had been sleeping in her house. Scared to go inside, she knocked, then pounded several times. When no one came rushing out the door or seemed to stir inside, she eased the doorknob until it clicked open then entered the house.

Hannah felt like Alice in Wonderland, and she might slide down a chute into some strange world. It was dark and cool with a moldy tinge in the air. The flashlight she brought beamed around the walls and floor into a small coatroom used as a holding place for her father's dirty boots and sweaty clothes. It was two steps into the kitchen to the middle, where her mother's wooden cutting table once stood, the one her father and Wendell made for her birthday. Years later, the legs became wobbly. Then, one day, the whole butcher block fell over and crushed their dog, Buster, breaking his back leg. Darnell had to take Buster behind the barn and shoot him. The kids buried Buster out in the woods and placed a creek stone on his grave. Her father was all set to fix the cutting block, but Lilith started arguing.

"I'm not using anything that was an agent of death," Lilith yelled at him when he turned the wooden block over to fix the legs. "It could have fallen on the children."

"I'll fix it even better."

"No, I've only asked fifty times. Forget it. I'll never use it if you do."

What about the kitchen table, Hannah thought. *True, it was an agent for birth, but the floor was also an agent of death. Better not walk on it.*

That evening, as the chill of fall settled, Darnell and Wendell built a bonfire and set the cutting block into the coals. Her father cut switches from a dogwood tree, and they stuck hot dogs and marshmallows on the switches and cooked them over the fire. Lilith would have nothing to do with it, repeating that it was an agent of death and the best thing for the butcher block was a slow cremation. Darnell even gave Wendell a few dollars to ride his bicycle to the 7-11 for more hotdogs and buns. The cutting block burned until the next morning, but by then the children had long fallen asleep. Lilith had taken them into the house where the sadness of their dog's death did not fade with such luxuries as roasted marshmallows, clean sheets, and a warm house.

Darnell stayed up with the fire until the next morning, which was just a faint glimmer by then. All that remained was a char of wood about the size of a softball. When the new day rose, the fire was not much warmer than sunbaked rocks. Darnell never built another cutting block, but instead made a fancy cutting board for the countertop, in the shape of a hog, which he called Wilbur. Lucas and Wendell helped him make it. With the cutting block gone, the kitchen looked big enough to dance in, but Hannah's mother and father never danced.

That was so many years ago, and as she stood in the doorway of her old house, Hannah felt as if it were someone else's life emanating from the walls, not hers. As she walked through the house, it was as quiet as a submarine waiting for a "ping" of sonar echoing or someone dropping a wrench on the metal floor, then sweating with fear that the enemy knew their position.

It's as quiet as cutting hair at the funeral home.

The house was old. No upgrades had been made since the mid-forties when Darnell's grandfather added a kitchen and a bathroom with plumbing. The wooden floors were never refinished because that would mean that they were at one time finished, which they weren't. The constant activities in the house kept them smooth. The floors required nothing more than sweeping.

Hannah's mother never splurged on anything in her entire life at the house, not because she didn't want to but because Darnell never allowed it. She always knew if Darnell ever kicked the bucket, she was going hog-wild. If Lilith bought a strand of yarn or a tube of lipstick, Darnell blew up and made her take it back to the store for a refund. The one thing Lilith bought without discussion was a yearly subscription to *Southern Living*, which she renewed at a reduced rate or waited for a special offer. Each month, she read her magazine, then sat at the kitchen table after Darnell had either gone to bed or had fallen asleep in his chair, sometimes from drinking too many beers, other times from being tired from having done nothing all day. She sat cutting out pictures of counter tops, marble floors, a dark wooden staircase, curtains, table arrangements, all the beautiful things they could not afford. These were dreams that never came true while living on the farm.

"Momma, how come you cut up your magazine?" Hannah asked.

"Sweetie, I'm just saving all the things I want in a house, an' maybe, someday we'll have a house with these things in it. I keep this in a folder in the drawer with the bills. Don't ever tell your daddy. He'll think it's nonsense and toss it out. He gets angry at me for thinking our life isn't that great."

"It ain't great. Anyone can see that."

"It upsets him to think I would like new hardwood floors or a non-stick pan instead of the cast iron pot that General Lee used for the troops. His idea is to buy me a case of floor wax and say, 'Get to work.' Someday when you and I are building a new house, we can pick out the prettiest things we like. It's all right here. I've been saving them for years."

Hannah sat for hours with her mother, year after year, looking through *Southern Living* and helping to keep her pictures in order.

The cupboards were dusty when Hannah opened them up, except for the lingering deep smell of her mother's spices, chives, and basil, which grew on the side of the house and dried in the cupboard. She shined the flashlight into the cupboards and found a few plastic cups from McDonald's and Burger King and some napkins that were a little chewed up by mice. The house looked larger than she remembered. In the living room, near the window, there was a large pile of candy wrappers and several *Popular Mechanics* magazines, the most recent being no more than a few months old. A board covering one window had a jagged hole the size of a baseball, like someone had jabbed it with a pocketknife. Hannah looked out the chink hole to see the locked gate guarding the driveway.

She was disappointed not to find more in the house.

What did I expect—a Thermador refrigerator and Viking range?

All that was left in the house was the history of whatever good, bad, or indifferent happened since her kin first began farming the land. No one got rich who ever lived in her house. No one living in her house graduated from college. Although her mother graduated from high school in Kentucky, Hannah was the sole person who ever grew up on the farm to graduate. No one who lived here became a professional. No one who ever lived here looked deep into the future and thought what they were doing would benefit their future kin or what they did would haunt the land like bad debt. Somewhere, there is a list of troubles that Hannah was certain could be traced back to Adam naming the animals and the way people treated other people on her farm. For such a long history, there were no great warriors in her past, and if the naming of the animals had been left to her family, it would have been "black dog," "white cat," "bird #1," "bird #2," and "big snake."

We're nothing but a clan of knuckle-dragging Neanderthals on a digging expedition, she concluded.

And out of the ground the LORD God formed every
beast of the field, and every fowl of the air; and
brought unto Adam to see what he would call them;
and whatever Adam called every living creature,
that was the name thereof.—Genesis 2:19

Standing in the living room and looking out such a narrow hole gnawed in the plywood, Hannah made the decision that once her baby was born, she would enroll at Georgia State University, maybe attend the satellite campus in Clarkston. She wasn't certain what she would study, maybe law, but Margaret said she would help her decide, and on nights she had class, Margaret would look after the baby.

In the dark kitchen, light emanated from her flashlight and one crack between the plywood and window, a sliver brightening a small part of the wall. She turned on the faucet and watched the water flow and swirl down the sink. The toilet flushed without issue. Hannah also stood for several minutes in her bedroom that she shared with Greta, thinking about the conversations they had before she ran off to California. As a little girl, she loved looking out the window, far across the backyard to the hill or down to the apple trees, to the field that led up to the woods then to Rapture Hall in all of its mystery and gloom. A few times during her childhood, while staring out the window, she swore that she saw the rapist men and that woman standing on the pond rock and staring at her house. She got so scared she jumped under the covers or slid into bed with Greta.

Looking out the window was not much different than looking at a map—there was a sense of possibility and adventure. Whether it was a drawn-out map or a list of directions, it lit the way to some worldly place. Out the back window always seemed the way to escape from her house to the rest of the world. Now, the window was boarded up and no light seeped through, as if the world did not want anyone leaving the farm.

As kids, they knew that traveling and moving on was not out the front door of her house. If escaping existed, it was through the backyard, late at night, on a moonless evening, through the darkened woods. Then, with fear pumping through the body, a person had to run as though they would be beaten if caught. Once they walked the empty streets of Rapture Hall, they could hitchhike from Goodman Road several miles to the Lay-Over Truck Stop, where they would find the next semi-truck going anywhere, and it didn't matter where that new place was as long as it was far from the farm.

Leaving wasn't as easy as eating an apple and being banished in shame. Many times, Hannah thought she could leave and never return, but some invisible hand always pulled her back. Unlike Greta, Hannah had never been able to cut the ropes. Greta found her freedom, even if to do so was to steal from the church, but when you're escaping and demanding your freedom, and when no one will give it to you, all means are in play. This is what Greta told Hannah, who felt the single way for her to leave was to die. Now, she realized, she could educate herself and find a job anywhere in the country cutting hair, perhaps one of the most portable jobs a person could have besides being a doctor or nurse. Greta, in her mind, planned and planned, never saying a word to anyone, and everyone thought she was the happiest young woman, and then one day, with nothing to her name and nothing to lose, she bolted to Cedar City, Niagara Falls, Philadelphia, Seattle, or Boston—letting her family think it was somewhere other than her true destination, some place no one would expect. Hannah never had the nerve to run away because the risk of returning home was too severe. A life-threatening whipping would be waiting at her father's hands.

Hannah placed her feet, one by one, on the rungs of the stairs as she climbed into the attic, balancing as she had done on the creek rocks. It was as she knew it would be—full of junk, boxes and boxes of nothing but old electric, water, and heating bills, since the dawn of time, fodder for some grand bonfire, because as her father used to say, "When I go to sell this house, the buyer's going to need to know what things cost. These old receipts will help sell this place."

Lilith took a beating from Darnell after she politely informed him that no one cared what the electric bill was from 1975. He had receipts dating back to the 1960s, not to mention that Memaw and Poppa Raymond also saved everything since the day the earth was formed. Hannah knew there must have been fifty boxes of old receipts, newspapers, farming magazines, and catalogs for everything imaginable. Ninety percent of the companies in those magazines were long out of business. Instead of going deep into the attic, Hannah stuck her head up like a ground hog, like Whac-A-Mole, shined the flashlight all around, turned around a few times on the stairs, then walked back down and closed the ceiling up. The musty smell threw her into a sneezing fit.

Outside, she opened the storm cellar that was about twenty feet from the back of the house. The hinges on the metal door screeched open, which reminded her of Eunice the cat screaming after being run over in Lilith's Kentucky driveway one Thanksgiving. Hannah turned on the flashlight and walked down the wooden stairs, which seemed to sag a little with her weight. At the bottom, the dirt floor was dry while the air was musty. Again, she fell into a sneezing fit and covered her nose and mouth with her shirt until she had fresher air. The cellar looked the same as it always looked, except she didn't remember her father having kept cans of kerosene and gasoline down there.

Must be for emergencies.

She counted more than a dozen one-gallon red plastic cans of kerosene and gas. Her mother and father always had a few extra blankets, water jugs, and Mason jars of food, all lined up on the wooden shelves for emergencies, "for the Apocalypse," Wendell said. There were also old, frayed decks of cards and kerosene lanterns on a shelf, organized, a testament to her mother being responsible. But those things were long gone. All that remained, besides the cans of fuel, were some jars with Lilith's handwriting, "Strawberry Jam. Blueberry Jam. Apple Jam. Green Beans. Okra. Candied Apples. Hot Rhubarb." Most wonderful for Hannah to find, apple preserve labels with red flowery circles. They were fading and peeling a little bit, but beyond that, they looked fine to Hannah.

In the corner, there were a few dozen opened jars with the contents gone, like someone had come down to the storm cellar and eaten whatever was inside. Hannah grabbed a bunch of full Mason jars and put them in a bushel basket then carried the basket up the stairs and into the gray overcast day. She knew they would keep for fifty years.

Margaret would love to have this jam with her toast.

She set the bushel basket on the ground and as she bent over, someone spoke, "What'a you doin' here?"

Hannah jumped and turned around to see Lucas sitting on the woodpile. He was unshaven and needed a haircut. His blue jeans were dirty, as if he had been working on a road crew and simply tossed them on the next morning. He wore a faded black t-shirt with a picture of Lucinda Williams playing guitar, which Hannah thought looked like Dwight Yoakam.

"What the hell, Lucas? You scared me!"

"What'cha doing, stealing Momma's preserves?"

"Not stealing. They belong to Momma and Memaw, an' I figure to me. Anyway, not to whoever owns the place now. Did you eat those in the cellar?"

"Not in one sitting."

"Are they still good?"

"The sealing wax is hard to crack but they're real tasty and reminded me of Memaw."

"Did you turn on the water?"

"Naw, it's never been turned off, if you can believe it. I don't use more than three gallons a month. Who on earth's going to notice that? Increments. You can steal a million dollars over a lifetime, and no one will notice, but if you did it all at once, you'd get caught. I've been thinking of buying the land back and starting me a cricket farm like O'Connell's. I mean, if that old hag can raise crickets, so can I. I even thought about stealing a hundred crickets a day and letting them loose in the barn. Then, after a year, I'd have enough to sell to bait stores."

"Not now."

"No, 'cause they're fixin' to tear the place down."

"What're you doing back in town?"

"Some men tracked me down and came to the job site while I was getting supplies one day. After they left, the foreman called saying they were bad dudes. I never went back. Just skipped town. I hitched a ride with a trucker to Branson. That's in Missouri. I did sheetrock for cash for a few weeks then caught a ride to Springfield. I thought that was where Abe Lincoln was from, but it's the wrong Springfield. I've just been bumming around working here and there."

"What about California?"

"Wasn't for me. There's gold, but you'll make more money selling supplies to folks than you will panning."

"Those men mean business," she told him, although she didn't tell Lucas that Hawkshaw Bales raped her.

"I ain't scared of Bales," he said. He lifted the front of his shirt to show her the pistol he'd won in a poker game. It was chrome-plated and big.

"I'm back in town 'cause I got business to tend to. Plus, it's Thanksgiving. I promised Momma I'd be home for the holiday. I've been back a half dozen times in the last three or four months. Most of the time I stay with Daddy. Sometimes, I stay here, but there's this girl I'm kinda seeing out in Waterton."

"When's the last time you had a haircut?"

"Months ago, maybe."

"Where'd you go?"

"One of the guys I work with cut it."

"It looks terrible."

"You got nothing to talk about. You're pregnant."

"Well, it happens. Look, if you want, stop by Margaret's house, and I'll give you a haircut."

Hannah sat on the log pile next to him, and for twenty minutes, they sat talking and laughing about the farm and growing up around the area. That's when Hannah realized nothing was ever going to be the same—Greta and Wendell were never coming home, and her parents were not reconciling. And, most important to Hannah, she realized she was never going to live on the farm again.

"Who's the baby daddy?"

"No one you know."

"You getting married to him?"

"I don't know what my plans are."

"You want me to put the fear of God into him?"

"No, I got things under control. Why're you so nosy about my business?"

"I hear about everything going on 'round here from Momma and Daddy. Daddy's worried about you and that Black girl hanging out together. Says she's a bad influence."

"He needn't worry about Margaret. She's real smart. Plus, it ain't his business."

"You want me to send some boys over to straighten him out, make the guy who did this marry you?"

"What makes you think I wanna get married?"

"I thought it'd be the thing to do for the baby."

"Like I said, I'm fine."

She then asked him to carry the bushel basket to her car because it was too heavy for her, and she was getting tired.

"What's your hurry?" he asked.

"It's fixin' to storm. You helping or not?" she asked.

From around the side of the house, Lucas pushed an oversized wheelbarrow—rusty. It had a good tire as he placed the bushel basket of Mason jars in the basin. Hannah helped Lucas carry the remaining jars from the cellar. Then, he pushed the wheelbarrow across the farm. Lucas told Hannah about how he'd been learning to play poker and traveling to Tunica and Biloxi to play in tournaments and how he'd won a stash of money.

"Not a ton, but a little. I'm saving it."

"You planning to use that money to buy the farm?" she asked.

"I was thinking about it, but they won't sell. Besides, I don't have enough. Don't matter now. This'll all be plowed under before you can fart the Lord's Prayer."

"That's a real nice thing to say."

"Some men cut down all the trees."

"Nobody has reverence for anything," she said.

"All I wanted was to prune the apple trees and harvest them. They've always been healthy with good apples. They just needed some TLC. I've been reading up on apple trees, and I know a right bunch about them. Daddy never did nothing with them. He could have cleared a good living from those trees if he'd put a little effort into it. I would have planted more each year down below where Poppa Charles had cotton and corn. Our fields just grew wild. I think I could have planted up to one hundred and fifty new trees down there. Raised crickets, too. It ain't glamorous, but a man can make a living with some effort. I could have made a go of it and stocked the pond and let folks fish for free as long as they tossed the fish back. That way they would come see me when they wanted apples, crickets, or anything else I was selling, maybe Christmas trees. They could bring their kids and sit on the big rock an' have a picnic."

Hannah realized his dream was like smoke rising in the wind, but also, it was not much different than what she'd been dreaming.

In the near background, lightning flashed, and the storm was headed their way. They smelled the rain rolling in. When they made it to the top of the hill, to the cracked streets of Rapture Hall, Hannah and Lucas were out of breath.

"Pushing this thing is hard work," he said.

"What about the golf course?" she gasped.

"It didn't come up, so I guess they never planned to build it. Maybe they lied. I don't know. I guess a golf course sounds better than a strip mall."

Lucas placed the bushel basket of Mason jars in Hannah's backseat. Then, he loaded the front of his truck with the other jars.

Hannah never said a word to Lucas about Hawkshaw Bales. She hugged him then hopped in her car, looking back through the rearview mirror to see him leaning against his truck before pushing the wheelbarrow back toward the farmhouse. Hannah sat in her car for a few minutes, watching the dark clouds roll in. About a mile down the road, it dawned on her—if Hawkshaw Bales' men were still trying to find Lucas, he still wanted his money. He had cheated her. He never forgave the debt.

"Dammit, dammit, dammit," she yelled and pounded on the steering wheel several times. "He never intended to forgive Lucas."

Even if the money had been paid, Bales would've beat up Lucas on principle.

She pulled the car off to the shoulder, then shook the steering wheel, strangling it. She lifted her head up and realized why the cans of gasoline and kerosene were in the cellar.

She returned to the farm and parked in the driveway and watched Lucas step out of the storm cellar with a red can of gasoline in each hand, which he carried behind the barn. A minute later, he stepped outside the hull of the barn with fuel streaming from the nozzle and ran a line away from the barn. Hannah eased down the asphalt a quarter mile away on Old Damascus Road, far enough that Lucas could not see her car, but she could see him returning to the storm cellar.

"Lucas cut down the apple trees," she whispered.

In those days Israel had no king, so the people did
whatever seemed right in their own eyes.
—Judges 21:25

Hannah knew why Lucas was there and wanted to stop him, and yet, knew he was doing the right thing. Even in her eyes, their farm, which was so beautiful at times, was an ugly place of malicious behavior. Hannah felt like a bird with one wing, injured, and spinning around in a circle as it tried lifting off the ground but lacked the ability to ascend.

Lightning flashed around the area, crackling varicose veins out of the sky, and dark clouds rolled overhead. Hannah wondered how long it would take Lucas to douse the house and property with gasoline. A half-hour? She knew kerosene burns hotter than gasoline, something she learned a few years ago when a man killed his pregnant girlfriend and burned her body using kerosene. It was the overriding factor the prosecution used in going for the death penalty, how callous and calculating he was in his efforts to conceal his crime.

Lucas had poured gasoline in the house and barn, on all the apple trees, and doused the chicken coops and dog pens, circled around the pond pouring a stream of gas, and back to the house. Then, he drew a straight line of gasoline from the house to the barn through the high grass to the first apple tree and then the others, connecting everything with a stream of fuel. Inside the barn, he had soaked the hay and ran a jet of gasoline into each stall, looping a string of fuel. With the other canisters of kerosene, he doused the trees in the woods until nothing could stop their burning except the hand of God. Lucas drew a straight line of gasoline from the barn to the creek where he stopped. He did not cross the creek. With a half canister of gasoline remaining, he walked back about thirty feet then poured the fuel on three fallen trees then set the canister atop in the middle of them. He walked to the creek's edge and stood in three inches of water. He bent over and struck a match on his zipper and tossed it a few feet into the dry weeds. He watched as the vapor above the grass expanded into one large ball of flame twenty feet wide. In a split second, the gasoline fumes exploded outward and then back to the grass. The stream of gasoline on the ground took off and followed its connection.

Lucas knelt down to watch the flames snake through the dried grass. It crackled in his ears like he had a mouthful of Pop Rocks. He stood and watched the red plastic container bulge and contract and a flame roar out the nozzle. The canister began to melt, and as it did, a new hole opened in the side and flames shot out and hissed before the canister twisted inward. Lucas ran back to his truck in Rapture Hall. As the grass caught in a wavering line, the flame followed like a string of dominos. From atop the hill, he watched the glow of grass rising, then a wave of white smoke hovering low along the ground, and soon he could not see through the wooded smoke to where he once lived. He knew the line of gasoline would catch and run through the pasture to the barn, the apple trees, and to the house.

Hannah was gone. She did not want to see the fire, the smoke, or be anywhere nearby. In an hour, everything would be gone, as if it had never existed. Maybe someday she would drive down her road and pass the strip mall and not even remember that generations of people had once lived their lives on that site.

From Rapture Hall, Lucas watched the plume of white smoke rise above the tree line in the distance. He skedaddled out of there, traveling in the opposite direction, occasionally looking in the rear-view mirror to see the smoke rising higher. He was hoping everything would burn before the fire department arrived.

Chapter 19

Delirious (with Pain)

The big story on the news last night was the fire at the farm. It was so huge, eleven fire trucks were sent to contain the perimeter of the property. The firemen allowed the farm and woods to burn unrestricted, but they contained it where needed, preventing it from spreading to neighboring land. One news crew stayed on site until this morning, and each time Hannah watched the news, her stomach knotted up, thinking someone had seen her and Lucas. When the morning paper arrived at the library, she read an account of the fire in the Metro Section, but it wasn't more than a few paragraphs. She also found the same article on the Internet reporting the cause was lightning.

Well, that's a big lie.

"Didn't those idiots find the canisters?" she asked herself, as she sat looking around the library, sticking her head up over the cubicle to see if anyone was suspecting of her. What irritated Hannah the most was the wrong information the newspaper reported, saying that fifty acres were burned, and the fire department used it as a practice exercise. They said it was an old, abandoned farm that had not been lived in since the late 1970s and that there had been no loss of valuables.

Fire Chief Kyle Whitehead was quoted as saying, "Nothing was burned that anyone was going to miss. My men did a great job and learned a lot on how to starve a wooded fire."

The article noted that the land was soon to be developed into low-income apartment housing and a shopping center, which Hannah did not like, thinking a golf course was still a better idea.

Maybe they'll find the slave graves, Hannah thought.

In the evening, when Margaret and Hannah returned home from dinner at LongHorn, they found a bushel of apples on the front porch. Margaret carried them into the house, placed a dozen in the refrigerator then took the rest down to the basement where it was cooler.

"Save the seeds to plant apple trees in the backyard. I want to preserve the past by growing something good from it," Hannah said.

"Maybe we can buy twenty acres and plant apple trees," Margaret said. "I bet we could make some money."

I will destroy this man-made temple and in three
days will build another, not made by man.
—Mark 14:58

§

On Thanksgiving Eve, at the funeral home, Hannah had two old men for haircuts, both for Saturday funerals, one in the morning, and the other in the afternoon. Mr. Fox gave her the choice of working on Wednesday night or Friday. She decided on Wednesday night, to get it over with, and by the time she finished, it was five minutes to nine. Before heading home, Margaret texted a list of things they needed for tomorrow's dinner, so she drove to Winn Dixie. She checked out, and as she was leaving the grocery store, Hawkshaw Bales was walking in, which stopped her in her tracks. She held her groceries to her chest, almost as protection.

"Well, if it ain't Miss Colorado."

"I got nothing to say to you."

"I disagree, Missy. Look at you, all plump-like. And look at your spunky, short haircut. You look like a tomboy."

Hannah turned away and walked toward her car. Bales jogged over to her and grabbed her shoulder to turn her around.

"Do not touch me. I'll call the cops!"

"Wait, wait. Is that my doing?" he asked, pointing to her paunch of a stomach. "See, this is what I'm fighting for, to help you through this ordeal. Stay right there. I don't want you going anywhere. I'm gonna call my guy and have him bring the paperwork."

Hannah turned and walked to her car. She told Bales that if he touched her or tried to stop her from leaving, she was going to scream like there was a murder in progress and run him over with her car.

"Go ahead. I know where you're going. We'll be over later to your little friend's house. I got years to wait on this. How about I wait until that kid's three years old, then I get custody an' take 'im from you?"

Hannah watched Bales walk away toward the entrance of the store. She wanted to drive her car through the front doors of Winn Dixie and slam Bales into the canned soups, trapping him between her bumper and hundreds of Campbell's *Chicken with Stars*.

Maybe Andy Warhol can get inspired by that, she mused.

Back at the house, she told Margaret what happened at the grocery store. All night, they kept the lights turned off. Nothing in the house was illuminated, save for the glow of the TV in the master bedroom.

Hannah and Margaret had invited Ilene and her boyfriend, Toby, her mother and father, and Ronnie Lee over for Thanksgiving dinner, as well as the two high school kids who worked part-time at the library, Amy and Jack. Her father texted Hannah, saying, "Can't make it. Going to Biloxi. Lucas showed me how to text."

Her mother accepted the invitation but said Ronnie Lee couldn't make it and Eddie Lee was fishing.

"Eddie Lee wasn't invited," she told her mother.

"We kind of figured he was invited as a courtesy."

"Nope. Not invited."

"Hannah, you shouldn't be like that. Jesus didn't tell anyone they could not worship."

"I ain't Jesus. He was a better person than me, so if you got an issue with Eddie Lee not getting an invite, take it up with Jesus."

Ilene also declined, telling Margaret at work that she was going home to Birmingham for the holiday.

On Thanksgiving, Hannah and her mother and brother, along with Margaret, sat around the kitchen table having dinner that Margaret prepared.

"You want a tour of the house?" Hannah asked.

"I seen it already," her mother quipped.

"I'll go," Lucas said.

While Margaret was in the kitchen sautéing onions and red peppers, and her mother was sitting on the sofa, Hannah gave Lucas a complete tour of the house, which he enjoyed. Hannah thought about telling Lucas that Bales might knock on the front door at any time in an attempt to serve her, but she decided not to. If the situation arose, Margaret said she would handle Bales.

"Which room is yours?" Lucas asked. She gave a tour of her room, the walk-in closet with all her clothes aligned in order. Then, he asked about Margaret's room.

"She's on the other side of the house."

Lucas's hair still needed cutting, but at least he shaved and wore clean jeans and a button-down shirt to dinner with New Balance tennis shoes, which she also liked wearing.

"This is the nicest house. If you ever go on vacation and need someone to stay here to watch the place, I'm your guy," Lucas said. "Momma wants to build a new house, maybe rent the other one out. Or sell it and build a few rental houses. I want a plot of land on a lake."

While Margaret was passing a plate of turkey to Lucas, he asked her, "What you got planned for the basement?"

"I'd like a game room, maybe," Margaret said.

"If you want it finished off, I can do it for ya. That's all I've been doing in Arkansas and Missouri, sheet-rocking basements. I can do it cheap."

Amy and Jack stopped by for apple pie. Lucas gave Amy some

fast eye, which made Jack testy with jealousy. Lucas liked how she dressed in prep clothes, but she wasn't interested in him, even when he told her stories of working at a real construction job in Arkansas and earning a good wage for a day's work.

Lilith and Lucas did not stay long after dessert was over, saying they had to be elsewhere. Hannah made plates of food for Ronnie Lee and Eddie Lee and gave them to her mother to deliver. She also gave Lucas several containers of food to take home. Jack took a piece of pie with him on a paper plate. Then, everyone left. Hannah and Margaret sat at the kitchen table, eating another piece of pie with coffee, relaxing, talking, and happy that everyone was nice to each other on the debut of their house.

Having no fights or arguments was a plus, Hannah mused.

The one misstep—Hannah forgot to buy *Cool Whip*, which bothered Lilith.

"You just can't have pie without *Cool Whip*. Everyone knows that," Lilith snipped.

§

When I was a little girl, Memaw and Momma asked Daddy to buy a turkey for Thanksgiving dinner, but he put it off and put it off, until finally the stores were out of turkeys, and we weren't having any holiday meat. On the morning before Thanksgiving, Daddy said he had a better idea.

"We're gonna have roasted pig this year."

Momma and Memaw knew not to say a word but understood what impending disaster was on the way. At first, I wondered where he was going to get a pig, because we didn't have any livestock on the farm except Wilbur, our pet.

Without shotgun shells or other bullets, and Daddy wasn't about to drive to town to buy any, he killed Wilbur the one way he could figure, by drowning him in the pond. Thinking back on it, he should have hit him over the head with a sledgehammer or a cinder block because drowning your family pet in the pond isn't as easy as it sounds. Daddy just figured he'd lead

Wilbur to the pond's edge, set his snout in the water, and bingo, we'd have ham for Thanksgiving. Lucas and me called him Wilbur after the pig in *Charlotte's Web.* When Daddy tied the rope around Wilbur's neck, I thought he was going to strangle him by hoisting him over a tree branch and lynching him, then bleed him out after slitting his neck. Wilbur wasn't a huge pig, but he was good size. Daddy said he didn't understand why he never grew to be a monster because he came from a long line of super pigs the size of cars.

"We once had a hog bigger than a VW Beetle," he said.

Daddy walked Wilbur to the pond like he was walking a dog in the park. Right off the bat, Wilbur knocked Daddy smack in the cold November water, and that surely pissed him off like bees provoked by a bear. Poppa Raymond was standing there with me and Lucas, and when Daddy went under, Poppa said, "I'll wager fifty dollars the pig wins this battle. You never wrestle with a pig because you'll get filthy dirty, and the pig will enjoy it." Then Poppa turned and walked back in the house.

It took Daddy the better part of an hour to get Wilbur back in the water, and the whole time I sat in the barn loft with Lucas watching and listening to Daddy cussing, and Wilbur squealing as Daddy held him under until he stopped. I figured it was over—Wilbur was dead—but then Wilbur popped right back up for air and squealed like he was yelling at Daddy, "What the hell are you doing? Where's that little girl who feeds me apples? She knows I'm a good pig. Stop trying to drown me, you asshole!"

Then it finally happened. Daddy took Wilbur underwater, and both were down for more than a minute. The surface of the water calmed, and I started thinking maybe Thanksgiving would be accompanied by a funeral. I wished for Wilbur to pop to the surface squealing and Daddy bobbing up, floating face down in the water and staring at the bottom like something down there was intriguing, like maybe he'd found Atlantis.

Daddy popped up and lugged Wilbur out of the pond, all dead and heavy, his lungs filled up with water. He dragged him across the field with the rope, flattening a line of high grass toward the barn where he slaughtered Wilbur right up. The wind was blowing, and Daddy was shivering cold but so pissed off his anger kept him going.

Daddy cut Wilbur open and gave his stomach to Wendell, who tied a rubber band around one end then blew it up and tied off the other end with another rubber band, and Wendell, Lucas, Greta, and me played football in the front yard with Wilbur's stomach until Wendell and Lucas fell on it and burst the side. That's when Wendell pinned Lucas down and put Wilbur's stomach on Lucas's head like a rubbery helmet.

Daddy was so tired he fell asleep after lunch and didn't wake up until the following morning on Thanksgiving Day. He was sicker than sick and completely missed Thanksgiving dinner and the apple pie. Memaw made the best. Poor Wilbur tasted pretty good, but it was hard not thinking that I was eating my pig friend. Daddy was in bed for two weeks with pneumonia, and the doctor came out a few times to check on him and bring medicine. Momma and Memaw lay a mustard pack on his chest. It was one of the few times when the house was quiet and jolly, and we laughed at the kitchen table all by ourselves with no fear of saying the wrong thing or getting smacked for making funny faces. One time when Memaw said something funny, Lucas laughed so hard milk sneezed out his nose. Momma cleaned it up with no more worry than if it was sprinkling outside on her petunias.

Whatever you do, do well. We should be industrious
and do the best work.—Ecclesiastes 9:10

Chapter 20

A Weird Girl from Heaven

While Hannah and Margaret were listening to a Sunday morning Christian radio broadcast and eating a healthy breakfast of smoked salmon, Greek yogurt, mango, and blackberries, as well as gluten-free bread, Hannah's mother called her phone and asked why she didn't call her back the other day.

"Momma, I got busy. Mr. Fox at the funeral home has entrusted me with a key and the door codes, so when I need to give some dead guy a haircut, I can go whenever I want. People've been dying like it's a two-for-one sale."

"Well, Eddie Lee's in the hospital, and he's in bad condition, laid up in traction with a body cast to prevent him from moving."

"Did he wreck his boat?"

"No, some men jumped him Friday night after he closed up The Diamond Eye. They beat the hell out of him, and now he's so wrapped up in plaster, he looks like a mummy."

"Did they rob the restaurant?"

"No, but they could have. All the receipts since Wednesday were still there, so it would have been a lot of money. When Eddie Lee didn't come home, Ronnie Lee and I drove over to the restaurant and found him unconscious, half in his car, half hanging out. We called the police, and they sent an ambulance. He came around and was alert in the hospital, but when the police asked, he said he didn't know, but he told Ronnie Lee he knew who beat'im up."

"The way he runs his mouth, I'm not surprised," Hannah said.

"The boy might exaggerate at times, but that doesn't give someone the right to kill him," Lilith said.

"Momma, he told you he was the daddy of my baby and said all that sex stuff about me. What do you think he says to other women? I'm sure he pissed off someone's husband or daddy."

"You ought to visit him in the hospital. Seeing family might cheer him up."

"He ain't family. How many times do I have to tell everyone that?"

"Regardless, he's banged up like he got hit by a Mack truck. They broke both legs and his right arm, knocked out some of his teeth, broke a bunch of ribs and fingers. He's got a concussion, so he's sleeping all the time."

"Fine, I'll try to visit him, but it won't be 'til later. I got stuff goin' on. And don't get mad at me if I can't make it. I got a life, you know."

"He's at Baptist Medical Center in Gainesville."

"I gotta drive all the way to Gainesville?"

"That's where they took him. The doctors there are real good."

"Come on, I got stuff to do."

Hannah complained about the distance and how she and Margaret had plans. Then, Lilith challenged her.

"I thought you rarely see each other."

"Today's one of the few times we're hanging out."

"Bring her along."

"What good will it do for me to visit if he's sleeping?"

"Naw, don't worry. He wakes up for everything."

Hannah felt a little guilty about the Eddie Lee situation because she was certain she knew who beat him up. She agreed to visit but said she wasn't bringing him any food or candy or flowers, and she was stopping by for a few minutes to say "hello."

"And that's all."

Margaret said she would go with.

It was all Hannah could do to get motivated to leave the house, procrastinating for hours, but finally, the two women hit the road to the hospital.

"You know, just hearing your voice will give Eddie Lee a boner. Beautiful women have that power over men, as well as dogs like Eddie Lee," Hannah said. "I'm serious when I say this, broken legs or not, that dog's gonna want to get naked and have us jump him."

"I done worse," Margaret said in a redneck voice.

"I'll caution you, I'm not sure how much Eddie Lee likes Black folks."

"Don't worry. I can handle him."

"I'm just saying."

When they walked into his room, Eddie Lee was asleep, which was perfect. Hannah didn't want to stay longer than the time it took to sign his guest book. When they looked at the names, there had been three visitors: Lilith, Ronnie Lee, and Marvella. Hannah remembered Marvella because she weighed about four hundred pounds and was the largest woman Hannah had ever met. Margaret signed her middle name—Anne—then told Hannah not to sign her name because Hawkshaw Bales would know she'd been there if he or his thugs visited. They both agreed. Hannah signed the visitor's book, Shelly Attenberg.

"Anything you can do to be a mystery gives you power," Margaret said.

"Maybe Marvella can help feed Eddie Lee. One piece of hot dog for you, two for me." Her laughing woke up Eddie Lee, which exasperated the women, since they hoped to sneak out without talking to him. The tubes and wires hooked up to the machines made him look like a medical experiment gone wrong. This made Hannah nervous. Over to the side, a few balloons were tied to a chair and floated up toward the ceiling.

"Hi, ladies," Eddie Lee said with a strained pain in his voice. "You ought to see the other guy."

They laughed. The sucking in of air from laughing caused his chest to rise and cause pain in his ribs, which made him cough.

Hannah introduced Margaret to Eddie Lee. They said "hi" to

each other, but they did not shake hands because he was as stiff as a board underneath the thick layer of plaster. Both of his legs were elevated several inches off the bed. Eddie Lee wiggled his pinky finger at her.

"Are you feeling okay?" Hannah asked.

"Never better," he said, then laughed but started coughing again. "I'm playing rugby tomorrow."

They all laughed again, and he coughed more, which led him to grimace. He raised the back of his bed a little with the hand-controller.

"The doctor said I ain't gonna die. The nurses are nice, but not one of them is good looking. Just a bunch of battle axes."

"Did Hawks do this to you?" Hannah asked.

"Yeah, that Black fella who says he's your baby daddy. Him and two other guys. I almost got my gun, an' had I, they'd all be dead, but I didn't see the fella who hit me with the baseball bat, the fourth guy."

They talked for a while about his prospects for getting out of the hospital, which Eddie Lee said would be about two weeks, possibly up to four.

"I got eight weeks of recovering at home."

He was proud of the fact that he had insurance and how the hospital would send a nurse over every day for a few weeks to help him recover, manage his affairs around the house, and drive him to the follow-up doctor's visits.

"Can you scratch my hand?" he asked. "There's a back scratcher on the table. It itches something awful."

Hannah took the back scratcher and stood as far from him as possible to scratch the top of his right hand.

"More pressure," he said.

She pressed down harder.

He instructed Hannah where to move the scratcher and how

fast or hard to scratch. She scratched other places on his arm he requested, and after she finished, he thanked her.

"Can you scratch my pecker? You don't have to use that plastic scratcher. You can use your hand."

"Gross," Hannah said.

"I'll do it," Margaret said.

Eddie Lee's eyes brightened up at the thought, and he tried lifting himself up in bed an inch, but he winced in pain and coughed.

Margaret walked over to him and pressed her thumb into his thigh muscle until he screamed in pain. Then, she poked him in the ribs with her knuckles. He started coughing. The pain was so intense it made his lungs ache and tears well up in his eyes.

He screamed again.

"What seems to be the problem?" Margaret asked. She released her knuckle from his ribs. Eddie Lee coughed some more, as his diaphragm contracted and released. Tears rolled down his cheeks.

"You didn't have to do that," he grunted.

"Let's go," Margaret said before jabbing her thumb into his ribs again. He screamed.

"What the hell. What's your problem, girl?"

"Next time you ask a woman to scratch your pecker, make sure you can stop her. She might do something worse."

"You ain't that tough," he groaned.

Margaret walked over to the sink and ran the faucet until the water steamed and rose up around her face. She filled a paper cup with scalding hot water and walked back over to Eddie Lee, who thought she was bringing him a drink of water. She squeezed the top of the cup into a funnel and poured the hot water down the back of his cast where it butted up to his neck. As he screamed, she covered his mouth with her hand. His eyes opened wide, and he thought she might kill him. The hot water rolled down the middle of his chest. It settled in the pockets and cracks the body has, like his navel, his sternum, all around, and down the side of his back. It burned but cooled within seconds. Through her hand, his muffled sounds were inaudible. She pulled her hand away.

"What the hell are you doing?" he wheezed. He started coughing uncontrollably, resulting in more and more pain in his ribs and lungs.

By the time Margaret tossed the paper cup in the trash, the water began to itch all over his skin. Some water then rolled into his crotch. Without saying a word, the women left him there, unable to find relief from the itching.

> If any man has sex relations with a servant-woman who has given her word to be married to a man, and has not been made free for a price or in any other way, the thing will be looked into; but they will not be put to death because she was not a free woman.
> —Leviticus 19:20

During the evening, while they were watching *The Campaign*, starring Will Ferrell, the doorbell rang. Hannah checked her phone. It was 7:12.

"That must be the Chinese food," Margaret said.

Hannah looked at the video monitor in the kitchen to see who was at the door.

"That's not the delivery guy. It's Bales and his friend," she said.

"Be quiet," Margaret whispered.

Hannah whispered back, "Do you think he'll just go away?"

"I doubt it."

"Lock the bedroom door and close the window blinds. Stay in there, and I'll get rid of him. Don't make a sound."

Hannah did as Margaret said and walked upstairs, quietly creeping around. She turned off the lights, then sat in the dark closet next to Margaret's Terrycloth bathrobe. She rubbed it against her cheek and took a deep breath. The smell of Margaret's perfume was like an elixir.

Margaret flipped on the porch light and opened the front door.

Between Margaret and the men was a new screen door with shatter-resistant security glass she had installed several days prior. Margaret lowered the glass one-quarter inch for the men to hear her. Hawkshaw Bales grabbed the door handle and tugged on it, but it was locked.

"Don't you see the sign? No Trespassing."

"That doesn't apply to us," the process server said. "As an agent of the court, I can ignore that."

"He can't," Margaret said, pointing to Bales.

"Call the cops," Bales said.

"I'm here to serve Hannah Gardner with these papers."

"She's not here."

"Yes, she is," Bales said. "I saw her pull into your garage an' I know she lives here."

"Even if she's here, that doesn't mean she lives here. She could be visiting, but, of course, she's not here, and I don't know where she is."

Bales tried the door again.

"If you open my door, I'll shoot you. See that camera? Self-defense."

Margaret pointed toward the porch light where a video camera was aimed at the men.

"We know she's here," the process server said. "I have video of her arriving. I can call the cops, and they can make her come to the door."

"Go ahead. To begin with, they cannot enter my house without a warrant or probable cause that a crime is being committed. Second, this is a civil matter, not criminal. They're not going to do anything except escort you off my property, and once I file a complaint and get a restraining order, they'll lock you up next time you bother me. Hannah doesn't live here, and I don't have anything to do with your issue."

"I'm about to run you out of town, Missy," Bales yelled. "When

I'm done with Hannah, I'll have custody of that baby! I'll have her deemed an unfit mother before that kid's born."

"You don't scare me."

Both men laughed at Margaret's feistiness. Bales grabbed the door handle one last time and tugged as hard as he could.

"I know you beat up Eddie Lee. You better watch your back. Those mountain boys don't fool around. Ain't you ever seen *Deliverance*?"

Bales laughed again while looking at the other man. He yanked on the door handle again.

"You step inside my house, it'll be your last."

"The way you're protecting her, you'd think she was your wife," Bales said.

Margaret did not say a word. She stood there staring at the men.

"How 'bout that," the process server mused aloud. "Are the two of you married?"

"What the hell, girlfriend!" Bales said. "Now this makes sense. You're thinking you're gonna be the father to that baby, ain't you? Or, at least, the second momma. Why the hell didn't I think of that before? You carpet muncher."

Both men looked at each other then back to Margaret, who stood behind the door saying not a word. Instead, she pulled her phone from her back pocket and dialed 911.

"Yes, can you send the police over to my house? Two strange men are on my front porch, and they keep yanking on the door trying to get in. I think one's a convicted criminal."

"I'm not done with you," Bales said, pointing his finger at her then pulling the trigger like he was shooting a pistol. The men walked back to the car and exited her property. It was a bluff. Margaret never hit call on her phone.

Upstairs, she found Hannah sitting in the darkness of the closet, leaning her head on a pile of clean clothes and bath towels. Margaret was upset, too, but did not want to let those men ruin her evening.

She and Hannah sat in the closet with the lights off talking about Bales until the Chinese food arrived.

"I can get a library job almost anywhere. We can live anywhere you want. We could move out west and you can go to college or open a salon."

They were laughing by the end of their talk, and Hannah felt good about the possibility of the future, that the women had options, and that they were not confined to live forever in Sundown. Like Sarah riding the bumpy, dusty trail from Pennsylvania to Utah, having set out on an adventure with no idea of what was ahead, Hannah realized their life could change.

The women sat in the dim candlelight at the dining room table with the stillness of the night locked away as they ate Mongolian beef and sautéed vegetables.

Once Margaret and Hannah had settled down for the night, Hannah felt as if she had caught her breath. She sat in bed with the MacBook and Sarah's diary.

Sarah wrote:

July 5

Ten weeks and I have grown tired of the wagon ride. They say three more. We lost time 'cause of weather. I wish to be back home slopping the hogs. We are down to thirty-two families. Along the way, folks dropped out, nearly half. One man died early on. He was alone and old. I spoke to him oncet. He said his wife and children had died of fever in '45. He had nothing left. They buried him in Vandalia at a cemetery. One of the men rode his team to town and sold off what was too much burden to travel with for money needed to pay for his coffin. His other things were auctioned off. John bought a cast iron pot for me. He paid two pennys. It is cured well. In my letter I told Susan not to travel here. I can not have that encumbrance upon my heart. There is talk that a railroad will be built across the country. A person can travel from New York City to the other ocean in no longer than two weeks. I cannot imagine such a ride through the country, quick like. I've never heard of such a thing. How do they travel over the mountains I have seen nearly reaching Heaven? God might think they are building another tower and then he will curse them with all tongues of speech. One learn-ed man said if you travel too fast your skin will fly off. He said it was proved by scientists. I once rid a horse real fast but that is all.

For some reason I just thought of this: one day last year a woman walked into The Cute Curl off the street for a haircut. She was nice, but so quiet. Finally, I got her talking a bit. She was about forty-five. In the middle of cutting her hair, she started crying. Her son who got messed up on drugs was killed that week. Heroin. She was getting a haircut before the funeral that Saturday. He's being buried in Watkinsville. When she wouldn't give him money for drugs, he stepped in front of a speeding train. I do not know how she continues on. I remember hearing about this on the news, and I'm sorry to say but I remember watching that story and saying to myself, "It sucks to be him." I'm feeling different about things now. Everybody hurts. Sorry to end on such a downer of a note.

Chapter 21

The Murderous Heart

Life was pretty good for Hannah and Margaret as winter settled without incident. The mornings were filled with cold air and deep blue skies, but by late afternoon on most days, the temperature rose to a comfortable fifty degrees. A few storms passed through the area since Halloween, but not many, so there were no complaints when it rained. Despite the rainy weather, Hannah and Margaret drove to Home Depot on Ponce de Leon Avenue for some potting soil, nursery potting cups for the apple seeds, and a hydroponic light for the basement.

Hannah was beginning to feel the deep effects of being pregnant—needing a nap every few hours, if only for ten minutes. As the days drew on, she became exhausted from any activity. Most of her pants and shorts were too tight, and she knew she'd have to buy new clothes soon. Beside losing sleep because her back hurt, she woke up four or five times a night to pee. Her imbalance was also an issue, as she bounced her shoulder into the walls and doorjambs negotiating back and forth through the house. She'd already purchased some clothes at Goodwill and a few other thrift stores, but she wanted some nice designer clothes for expecting mothers, like Laura Ashley.

I want to change who I am. I need a new image and I'm tired of being a Walmart and Old Navy girl.

She had seen a Laura Ashley dress online for $68 that was originally $140. Her goal was to fit into it after the baby was born. Hannah did not buy the dress because she could not predict her income or expenses with the baby.

She told Margaret, "Maybe I can buy a dozen sweat suits and wear those."

After pulling a cart around Home Depot, they stood in line to check out. A pretty, blonde woman walked up to them.

"Hi, Hannah," the woman said.

Hannah did not recognize her but said "hello," trying to be nice, and thinking maybe she had cut her hair once before.

"Hi, Margaret, I'm Sharona Newsome."

Margaret said "hello" back to her, as well.

Sharona handed an envelope to Hannah, which she took from the woman. She looked at the return address: Jones, Snelling, and Pitner, Attorneys at Law.

"Darling, I'm simply doing my job. These are legal papers for the legitimization of your baby."

Hannah looked at Margaret. They had let down their guard, and now she had to answer to Hawkshaw Bales and his attorney.

"Look," Sharona said, "I know this guy. He's a real piece of work, so you need to take care of this matter 'cause he's not going away. Get yourself a good family law attorney."

"I'm not gonna let him take my baby from me."

"Then you need to do whatever it takes," Sharona said. "Otherwise, he will own you and make your life miserable."

Sharona walked away, knowing that she was just doing her job but not feeling good about it. She almost wished she was waiting tables at IHOP. This was as bad as the time she had to serve a man in a coma. When she walked in the hospital room, his entire family was standing around his bed crying. Sharona laid the lawsuit on his chest then walked out.

Hannah watched her until she drove off in her pearl-colored Hyundai, thinking that Bales may be lurking around with her, but she never saw him.

As soon as they were home, Margaret and Hannah began researching their options and found three attorneys in the county who appeared to be good; however, there was nothing they could do until Monday morning. That did not make Hannah feel any better. In fact, it worried her even more. Margaret suggested that Hannah take a nap on the sofa, and while she did, Margaret filled the planting cups with potting soil and placed an apple seed in each one. She carried them to the basement and set them under the hydroponic lamp, making sure she was following all the instructions to the letter. At the end of the day, she was also exhausted. She stood over the potting cups and wondered what would come of everything.

After taking a hot shower, Hannah slipped into her pajamas and started reading a book Margaret was already reading, *Rosiebelle Lee Wildcat Tennessee* by Raymond Andrews. Hannah thought it sounded like a brand of whiskey.

Yes, sir, bartender, I'll have a double shot of Rosiebelle Lee Wildcat Tennessee.

Waking in the middle of the night from an uncomfortable sleep, Hannah realized that she no longer needed to hide from Hawkshaw Bales, and she would ask Wendy for her job back.

Outside the house, it was raining with the occasional flash of lightning and a rumble of thunder. Hannah conjured up in her mind the times when her family took shelter in the storm cellar if a tornado was bearing down. She was safe and unafraid underground and felt the same way at Margaret's house. In their storm cellar, everyone sat on benches or small rugs on the dirt floor and listened to her father spin a story or play his guitar, and it was one of the few times Darnell and Lilith tolerated one another, as though the possibility of death made any droplet of love they had for each other swirl into an ocean's helix of warmth and compassion. They almost remembered that they were a family when danger reared itself. That emotion never transcended up the stairs and back into their house, but for those moments when the family was in the underground storm shelter, it was the best her family would ever be.

"If you ever get bored with your life, risk it," her father would say.

Hannah decided that after her baby is born, she will join Margaret's church and have her baby baptized.

§

Wendy had not rented Hannah's chair at The Cute Curl, so she welcomed her back. It was like being on a long vacation. After cutting a few men and a couple young kids in the morning, Dave Edwards entered the salon at eleven o'clock, almost on the hour, the same time he always arrived. Feeling that the truth was nothing to be ashamed of, and having always felt comfortable with him, Hannah told Edwards her entire story of Hawkshaw Bales and how she had been served with legal papers the other day. As Edwards sat listening, he said little to Hannah other than asking a few personal questions before becoming quiet again and allowing Hannah to saunter on in conversation, as though they'd been best friends for years.

"I'll be back in a little while," Wendy told Hannah. "I've got to run to the bank. Do you want lunch? I'm going to Zaxby's."

"It's tempting, but no. I brought carrots, sliced green peppers, and three peanut butter sandwiches. Plus, I keep eating ice cream like they've stopped making it."

As she cut Edwards' hair, Hannah detailed the rest of the events regarding Lucas and Bales and how the family garbage wound up on her front door, her rape, her father's tires being slashed, Lucas's trailer burning up, and Eddie Lee's beating.

"They beat up Eddie Lee, and he didn't do nothing. After all he promised me, Bales is still hunting for Lucas."

Hannah then told Edwards that prior to Hawkshaw Bales, she had never had sex with anyone.

"See this?" She turned sideways and lifted her shirt up to reveal her baby bulge. Edwards looked at her stomach. "This is his fault."

"Were you dating him?"

"Oh my God, no. I don't even like the guy. He blackmailed me into rape."

"He raped you, and you were a virgin?" he asked.

Hannah, tearing up, nodded her head. She blew her nose and wiped away her tears.

"Karma always evens out the score," he told Hannah. Then, he didn't say anything more.

Margaret and Hannah contacted several attorneys over the course of several days and chose the least expensive one, Alice Bookman.

When they walked into Alice's office on Wednesday to meet for the first time, Hannah recognized her from the funeral she attended last month. Hannah had cut her grandmother's hair and given her highlights, and being so taken with the dead woman, she attended the funeral. Hannah did not mention this to the attorney, how she sang to her grandmother and asked her questions about her life while giving her a haircut.

Both Hannah and Margaret were not pleased with the news the attorney had and what was in store for her from "Mr. Bales," as Bookman referred to him. Hannah had ninety days to respond to his demands, which included everything from a list of Hannah's past sexual partners and potential fathers to her finances and a complete background of information detailing every aspect of her life. Hannah was angry and said she did not feel compelled to supply him with all this information

Bookman warned, "He has you over a barrel. The judge will be angry if you don't comply.

"I'm the victim here, but I feel like the criminal. It's like being raped again."

"If you need a private investigator, I got the best one around, Troy Breathnach," Bookman said.

On the car ride home, when she wasn't crying, Hannah told Margaret she was not going to comply and was not going to do one thing to help Bales. Margaret did not say a word. In the quiet of the car ride home, she grabbed Hannah's hand and squeezed it.

Did Sarah ever shut down and not want to talk to her husband or to anyone on the trail? Sometimes a body just needs nothing.

For three days we have been unable to travel. Mud! Tempers jump quickly. Women snap at men and children and men snap at women and now women snap at the other women. There was a brawl between five 'er six men the other night. Nothing too bad 'cept for a few bloody noses and a cut lip. All of them but one were younger men and not married. It might have been 'cause of a woman. Most of the men are out hunting, some for leisure, some for food. I reckon they just need a reason to leave camp for a time. One man got shot in the arm two weeks back when a young boy thunk he was a deer. There is no doctor here but some folks fixed him up right well until we found a town along the trail with a doctor or even a blacksmith. I don't remember the name of the town as I did not leave the trail. He ran a small fever but his wife who was asking everyone for some sulfur said he was suffering less. Some men went fishing and there is a lot of food to go around and people are sharing some. That is keeping tempers down but not entirely. That seems to be the one sign of hospitality. I wish the mud would firm up so the wagon wheels can find a foothold. No use in cleaning up. Mud is every wheres and you cannot rid yourself of it. Like lice. At least today it is warm and sunny for time to write some. The boys are chasing after the girls, some times with a frog or snake. One boy had a dead rattlesnake until his father re'lized what was going on. He put an end to every thing. Livestock got mud in their ears it's so bad. They say there is a good size river three days from here that can be crossed. Maybe we should all be baptized when we wash the mud from our bodies. Some souls need it mighty. There's a lot of carrying on around here that I do not approve of. There is a business man who is going to set up a general store at the end of our journey. He has two wagons of supplies, like I told John we should do, but he is asking more than the normal cost in Meadville. He has a young man to drive his other wagon. But mostly I disapprove that he brought four pretty girls not his daughters or relations. James told me that he saw one bathing in the creek last week. I asked if he turned away and gave her some privacy. He said he did after ten minutes of watching. I said to tell his father but James said his father was with him.

What a dizzying evening. It is Sunday, midnight. Thank goodness I do not have to work tomorrow. Mr. Fox took everyone out to dinner for the Christmas holidays. He invited me and a guest, so I brought Margaret. Mr. Fox reserved a private room at Conestoga Steakhouse, which neither of us had ever been to before—it's kind of pricey. There's an entire history of the restaurant in the lobby. I took pictures with my phone. It's the oldest steakhouse in Georgia and opened on September 22, 1877, the same day Rutherford B. Hayes, the President, visited Atlanta. On the third day of his visit, they rode in buggies to Avondale Estates to have dinner at the restaurant. Hayes was trying to mend relations years after the Civil War ended. He was quoted in the *Atlanta Constitution*, "This is one of the finest establishments I have ever dined in. The best steak I have eaten in my lifetime."

Margaret counted eighteen people at dinner—Mr. Fox and his family, all of us at the funeral home, and everyone's wife or husband. We had three waiters. M and I had a filet, which Mr. Fox recommended. He had one, too.

"Hey, if you want the best steak in the world, this is the place," he said.

He toasted each of the employees and said something nice. He said that I was the spunkiest and brightest star shining in the county, and he's so glad I'm working at the funeral home. He also said that I never complain. Then he looked at Shelleena, and everyone laughed because all she does is complain. He said some nice things about her, too.

Mr. Fox doesn't know this yet, but for Christmas I bought him an old Miles Davis record, *The New Sounds*, which I found on eBay. It wasn't cheap. That's the kind of music Mr. Fox likes, old-school jazz on old vinyl records. The record I bought was made in the 1950s. I cannot imagine what life was like back then. I don't know much about his music, but I like Nat King Cole. Natalie Cole is really wonderful, as well. That's kind of the same.

Chapter 22

All Who Are in Rome

OMG EMERGENCY! EMERGENCY!

HAWKSHAW BALES HAS BEEN MURDERED – four days after Christmas! Holy S---. I'm so scared I can barely type. My hands are shaking like a jackhammer. I'm sitting in a study cubicle with M's MacBook, so damn scared I forgot my password. I'm so scared I need to pee every three minutes. M keeps coming back to see me, asking for new information. I keep checking the Internet, but there's no update. OMG, WTH is going on?

It's Monday, and I was working this morning, thinking how I spent too much money on Christmas, having bought Margaret a new big screen TV—a 75-inch 4K Vizio—when around eleven-thirty the radio announcer came on with the news. This isn't nice, but I was thinking that if more people died, I could make some extra money to pay for Christmas.

I did not expect this. I had just finished cutting a man's hair and was sweeping up when I heard the news on the radio: "Hawkshaw Bales was shot and killed last night."

"Wendy, did you hear that?"

"I wasn't paying attention. What'd it say?"

I told her then dropped everything.

"I'll be right back. If anyone comes in, will you cut their hair?"

I did not wait for her to answer. I dashed out the door.

Margaret and I got on the Internet for the story but found nothing more than six lines of info, and each story concluded with the statement that they will post more details as the police continue their investigation.

The library is swarming with people, so M can't hang out with me. I'm listening to the Internet radio with an earbud, but I've heard nothing more than the crime squad is investigating. That's all for now.

§

It's later, almost seven o'clock at night. I had to go back to work and was there all day trying to find some details between cutting hair.

Wendy and I were busy but kept the radio on WSB to hear the news every quarter hour. I tried concentrating on my work, but all day I thought I was going to throw up. I had to stop and breathe, deep breaths throughout the day to settle my stomach. Wendy bought me a ginger ale from the fountain shop.

For now, the police said he was killed last night, which would have been Sunday, but one report said it was this morning. Both reports said he was shot with a rifle, dead in his driveway, right through the chest when he got out of his BMF Lexus. Of course, they didn't mention BMF (Bad MoFo), but I knew.

The radio station reported he was dead before hitting the ground. One shot. The police found no spent shells. No tire tracks. No foot tracks. No evidence. No one in the neighborhood heard a shot. One report said it was a head shot. The police determined the angle where the shot was fired, but they couldn't determine the exact foot location. Not yet, but they will. They estimated it came from one to two hundred yards away down the road. The shot knocked him back into the driver's seat where he was slumped over the center console. So far, they have not found anyone in the area who heard the shot or witnessed anything, so they think the shooter used a silencer. That's James Bond stuff and it scares me.

§

I decided not to spend Christmas with my family, but instead told them I was vacationing in Daytona Beach.

"Are you going with Margaret?" Momma asked.

"No. I'm going by myself to clear my head and figure out what I'm going to do with my life."

"What's she doing for Christmas?"

"She has friends and family in North Carolina. I think she's visiting them."

Momma didn't say much more than that, never harped on me or questioned my decision to visit Daytona Beach. It is, after all, the Redneck Garden of Eden.

§

I missed everyone, but in truth, since leaving the farm, Christmas has been a pain in the butt. I go to Daddy's first because he always asks about Momma, so this way I can say I don't have any news. If I went to her place first, I'd have to tell him everything that was said and who got what for a gift. I also did not want to see Eddie Lee or Ronnie Lee or answer questions about Hawkshaw Bales and the baby and everything. This was better.

M and I spent Christmas together here at the house, because we had so many expenses this year with buying the house and attorney fees, we decided not to buy any gifts but make them instead. Regardless, I bought Margaret a TV, which is really for the house. I gave her a scrapbook with photos of us and places we've been to (a lot of selfies together), pictures of movies we've seen, drawings, and Bible verses that pertain to her and us, verses to be uplifting. I had to sneak off to Rite Aid to have pictures made. I had never done that before, and the man there showed me how to crop the digital photo and correct the color, so they turned out nice. When he asked me what I was making, I told him. He showed me how I did not need to have photos made, that I could make an entire scrapbook with digital pictures.

"You can go to our website and make a photobook up to fifty pages. If you want one bigger than that, you might consider Butterfly Books. They do a good job."

I scrapped (sorry for the bad pun) my scrapbook photos and opened a Butterfly account and made M's book online because my book is nearly seventy pages. I did all the work in secret on her MacBook. I even hid my online history, so she'd have no clue.

The cover of the scrapbook is us standing at the overlook at Tallulah Falls. The centerpiece was at Stone Mountain, where we like to hike and have picnics. One night, late enough that the park was closing, we were still out hiking and coming down the mountain when we stopped under a picnic pavilion and kissed. That was all we did. It was nice. Margaret said she was "fuzzy."

"What's that mean?" I asked.

"It's a nice way of saying horny."

That made me laugh.

I also made a scrapbook of photos for Momma and Daddy, one for each, from all those photos I've been scanning into the computer at the library. M knew about those scrapbooks but not the one I made for her. I uploaded my family photos to Butterfly, where I constructed the Christmas books from a lot of old dead relatives, good times for Momma and Daddy to remember. Everything went into a picture book. The front cover was different for each book, an old picture of the farm from the 1940s for Daddy, and a picture of us kids at Graceland for Momma. I crammed the entire history of our family into it. I included Momma's family in her book, and Daddy's family in his. I overlapped some of that stuff.

Christmas morning, after I gave Margaret the TV, as we were drinking tea, she slid an envelope along the table. She moved it in front of me, being coyish. I opened it.

"Are you serious?" I screamed.

"All you have to do is call her."

M is incredible. She located an address and telephone number for Melanie Carlisle, my Daddy's first wife.

"Have you spoken to her?"

"Last Monday. She's very nice and wants to meet you."

"No, she doesn't."

"Sure does. She wanted me to answer a bunch of questions about your daddy, but I told her I've never met him. And here's the thing, they were married and she's Black."

§

A week after New Year's Day, Margaret called Hannah's phone and said the police investigators wanted to speak with her and had just left the library. They were on the way over to The Cute Curl. In less than three minutes, two police detectives entered the salon, both dressed in brown suits and sporting fedora hats, which made Hannah think they were from the 1950s, like Dick Tracy or guys in a B-movie gangster film. Before they could say a word, she spoke first.

"I know you fellas want to talk to me, which is fine after I'm done cutting Peter's hair. It'll take about ten minutes. If you want a soda, the fountain shop next door can set you up. Otherwise, have a seat and I'll be with you."

Both men stepped back outside and stood on the sidewalk talking and looking in the salon every few seconds to make certain Hannah did not slip out the back door.

"What's that all about?" Wendy asked.

"They're investigating the murder, so they need to ask me some questions since I kind of knew Bales. They were just at the library talking to Margaret. That's who called."

"Don't bring any publicity to the salon."

After Hannah finished cutting Peter's hair, he held the door open for her and thanked her for a nice haircut. Then, he walked down the sidewalk to his car. Hannah stepped outside The Cute Curl to talk with the investigators.

"You mind if I sit down?" she asked, pointing to the bench.

"Go ahead," one investigator replied. They introduced themselves as Mike Burris and Ray Merritt, both with an attitude that Hannah did not like. One man placed his foot on the bench, which looked as if he was trying to keep a pregnant woman from running away.

"Do you mind moving your leg?"

He eased his leg away slowly, as he didn't like being told what to do.

"Why have you been avoiding us?" Burris asked.

"How am I avoiding you?" she asked. "I didn't know you wanted to talk to me."

"You certainly made it difficult to track you down."

"In comparison to what? I'm here most of the time cutting hair. I mean, the police station's across the street. I couldn't have made it any easier if I'd walked in with my hands up."

"Why are you being defensive?"

"I'm not defensive. I'm explaining that I've been fifty feet from your front door. A blind dog with no nose could have done a better job finding me."

"You should have come forward," the short, white investigator said, "being that Hawkshaw Bales is the father of your baby."

"That's what he says. I say different."

"Still, you made it difficult for us."

"I didn't make it difficult for anyone. I've been hanging around this redneck excuse of a town all the time."

"You're just a little too confrontational."

"What I am is a woman who doesn't like incompetence. I cut hair here and at Grattan's. That doesn't sound like someone hiding. You probably walk right by my window three times a day. If you weren't such lousy cops, maybe you would have done your job better."

"It's odd, strange almost, that the father of your child was murdered, and you don't step forward for any reason," Mike said as he pushed his glasses back up his nose.

"Mike," Ray Merritt said, "I don't think we should accuse her of hiding or avoiding us."

"I got this," Mike said.

"If you have something you want to ask me, let's get to it. Otherwise, I have to work."

"You don't have to get testy," Mike said.

"Again, I'm not testy. I'm pointing out the obvious. Let's get something straight. Hawkshaw Bales is not the father of my baby."

The men looked at each other, irritated that she wasn't rolling over and being scared of them. Ray took out his notepad and began to jot down what Hannah said.

"Who's the father?"

"Ain't none of your beeswax, Mister."

"You sure are cocky," Mike said.

"Why'd you tell the apartment manager you moved to Chicago?" Ray asked.

"It wasn't Chicago. It was Colorado. They tried making me pay for damages to the apartment that I didn't do. My apartment was already a dump. When I said I didn't have the money for any repairs, Tony What's-his-Name said we could take care of it another way. I knew what he meant. The carpet and kitchen floor were torn up when I moved in, and I wasn't paying a dime. He said there was pet damage. I never had a pet. I lied to Beth Johnson about where I was moving because I wasn't paying for squat."

"How'd you hear about the murder?"

"On the radio."

"Did it bother you?" Ray asked.

"It scared me more than anything else. I've never known anyone who was murdered."

"What do you know about Hawkshaw Bales' murder?" Mike asked.

"Nothing. I met the guy two or three times, so I don't know him or the people he associated with. I know he was a bad guy and figured someone was mad enough to kill him."

"Where were you the night he was shot, the night of the twenty-eighth and the next morning?"

"I was home the entire weekend, except when I was here working. The rest of the time, watching TV at home with Margaret."

"Do you live together?"

"I rent a room from her. She owns the house."

"Tell us about your relationship with Hawkshaw Bales," Mike

said.

"Weren't you listening?" she asked. "I met him earlier in the year by happenstance. Then recently, I ran into him outside the CVS with a young woman, a Black girl. He said she was his niece."

"Did you ever say you'd kill him?"

"Do I look like a girl who could kill someone?"

"I asked if you said it."

"No."

"Who might have wanted to kill him?" Ray asked.

"Despite what you think, I don't know him. I heard he was a real mean guy who beat up a lot of people, some guy in Flowery Branch or somewhere near there. Beat him with a baseball bat. That's what I heard."

"How long did you know him?"

"I didn't have any relationship with him if that's what you want to know. He was just a guy who started talking to me. Then, I ran into him a few other times around town, all by accident. I didn't want anything to do with him."

"What was your sexual relationship?"

"He raped me. Is that what you want to know?"

"Did you report it to the police?"

"No."

"Why not? That's a violent act."

"It was my fault, and you don't call the cops on a guy like Hawkshaw Bales. He knows people. There's not much to say. I made a mistake, and he raped me. One day we sat around talking, drinking coffee at a hotel, and he invited me to his room where he grabbed me and forced me onto the bed and raped me."

"Ray, that sounds like the perfect motive to kill someone," Mike said.

"I agree," Ray replied. "Revenge."

"Except I didn't do it. I don't even own a gun."

"How do you know he was shot?" Mike questioned.

"They said so on the radio."

"I can't believe you didn't report the rape." Mike said.

"Well, I didn't. If he raped you, would you report it?" she asked Mike, which made Ray laugh.

"The police could've arrested him," Ray said.

"If Hawkshaw Bales raped you, a *Deliverance* kind of rape, would you report it? Would you take it to trial, so the entire world knew he raped you? You wouldn't."

They looked at each other before lecturing Hannah about how much motive she had, what she would gain from Bales' murder, and that it appeared she had more motive than most people. She argued back that he was such a rotten person and a criminal that there were dozens of people who might have killed him.

"I guess you don't have to worry about responding to the legitimization papers now," Ray said.

"I guess not. I'll have to ask my attorney."

"You may not have heard, but his family in Louisiana, according to Bales' attorney, may continue on with the lawsuit to gain custody of the child, or at least legitimation so they can secure visitation rights."

Hannah did not say a word, but inside she felt her heart shrink and her stomach tighten, to think that she would have to share her baby with strangers, that even after he was dead, Hawkshaw Bales was controlling her life. She wondered what right any grandparent would have to a child, especially if the parents didn't like them and didn't want to associate with the next of kin.

"Does that bother you?"

"It's the first I've heard of it. I guess I'll have to ask my attorney about the options. I don't know these people an' never met them. I cannot imagine any judge would take a woman's baby away to give to strangers, even if just for the weekend or Christmas."

"If you didn't kill him, someone did you a huge favor."

Hannah paused for a few seconds to think about that. They

were right. Someone did her a huge favor. They asked if she owned a rifle. She replied, as before, by telling them, "No," that she had never shot a gun in her life. They asked if she knew anyone who might own a .223 rifle.

"I don't even know what that is."

Her father owned some guns, but she did not tell the investigators. She thought that Lucas might also own a rifle, but she did not say a word to the investigators.

"Did you know Margaret was in the Army?"

"Yes, but I didn't know her back then, and she's never talked about it much."

"Did you know she's an expert marksman?"

"What's that mean?"

"It means she can shoot a fly at a hundred yards."

"I didn't know that."

"Yeah, she used to train soldiers how to shoot," Ray said.

"What did you and Margaret watch on TV that night?" Mike asked.

"We channel surfed, so it was a variety of shows. I read some of the newspaper, read a book, so did Margaret. We both like the Sudoku puzzle so we alternate."

"If I ask her the same questions, will she tell me the same thing?"

"I would think so. But didn't you already talk to her? I mean, she's at the library right over there, fifty yards away. Or don't you remember being there fifteen minutes ago?"

"I can't believe you don't remember one show you watched," Mike declared.

"I can't believe you don't remember talking to Margaret. If you get a blind dog, he'll help find the library for you."

"You said you can't remember," Mike argued.

"I never said I couldn't remember. I said I channel surfed. We watched *Parks and Rec* and *The Office*, you know, reruns. I remember watching *The Colbert Report* for a few minutes. I also read some. I talked to Margaret. I had some tea. Boring stuff."

Hannah knew Margaret did not leave the house because they always slept together, arms and legs wrapped around each other, wrought like ornamental iron, but she'd never admit this to these men in this narrow-minded town. She didn't need this personal business circulating around.

"How would you know if Margaret was home all night?" Ray asked.

"Did she leave the house?" Mike asked.

"How'd you know if she had not left?" Ray continued.

"Do you know for sure" Mike said, "if not, then you don't know where she was or if she was home between two and four in the morning."

"Do you know for certain that Margaret was home?" Ray questioned again.

"Yes, I do."

All the questions came so quickly they were confusing Hannah, which is what the men wanted.

"How?" Ray asked.

"I would have heard the security system indicating a door had been opened. I'm a light sleeper an' wake up for anything that squeaks."

Hannah was not going to confess to these men that she and Margaret sleep together. Maybe Margaret had told them already, but she was not going to let the genie out of the bottle in Hebron. The detectives finished questioning her, so Hannah returned to her workstation in the salon to sweep the floor and regain her composure.

"Are you fine?" Wendy asked.

Hannah nodded and watched the detectives walk across the street and enter the police station. She sat in the chair and sent a text to Margaret:

spoke to po-po buttholes
no big deal work n til 7
will b over after work
I was a snot to them
should of been nicer
but they were jerks

Chapter 23

Let the Hairpin Drop

I remember everything, each time Daddy slapped Momma, each time my clothes didn't fit and there was no money for anything new, every Sunday dinner being delicious and the house warm and toasty, those times when I thought our lives were normal. I just wanted Daddy to have a job, and Momma to be home when we stepped off the school bus, and dinner would be on the table at six o'clock like the Cosby kids. After dinner, Daddy would help us with our homework, and Momma would have hot chocolate for us before bed, and Greta and Wendell would read to me and Lucas, and we would sleep in clean sheets and have a thick Chenille comforter, and we would fall asleep listening to Chopin or Mozart or some easy-listening music. Momma and Daddy would be in the den watching the news or reading the newspaper by the fireplace, and maybe Daddy would smoke a pipe and our dog would sit at his feet, and laughter would fill the air, and of course, they would not be fighting, and Daddy wouldn't be drinking a whole six-pack of PBR, and Wilbur the pig wouldn't be getting into the house with muddy hooves. Greta wouldn't get caught having sex with Billy Gilson in the barn, and Wendell wouldn't get caught stealing a Christmas tree from Big JoJo's lot, and Momma would never have to take a job cleaning other folks' houses because the farm wasn't making any money. Then, one of the houses wouldn't be Cindy Faber's house and the next day after Momma had cleaned her rat's nest, Cindy wouldn't tell everyone in school what Momma forgot to clean or didn't clean well.

"The only reason my mother keeps your snotty old lady on is out of pity for you kids," Cindy said.

She just had to say that so everyone at the lunch table heard it.

"Your mother needs to learn to fold my clothes the way I

like'em folded, just like in a department store. She also can't clean a toilet bowl to save her life."

I once saw Cindy Faber working as a carhop at the Sonic near the Buford Dam. She didn't wait on me. She attended college for a semester at Lanier Tech. Last I heard, she got pregnant by her Sonic manager who already had a family and wouldn't marry her or leave his wife, just like Beth's mother in *The Queen's Gambit.* Happens to the best of us, I suppose. I don't know what became of her after that.

Maybe my momma was like Sarah, sad because of her situation. The way the men are in my family, Daddy most likely grabbed Momma by the hair and dragged her caveman-style along the wooded trail from Kentucky to Georgia.

"You wanna marry me? Good. I got a nice farm with apple trees. Hey, if you didn't want me dragging you back to Sundown by your hair, you shouldn't a grow'd it so damn long."

I think Daddy and Sarah's husband, John, have a lot in common.

> We have crossed many rivers creeks hills and mountains venturing through towns and places with barely a tent flapping in the wind. When the weather was nice life was wonderful but it turned some days so fierce it was likely to kill a newborn. It was the most wretched existence I have known, riding in the hot dust of the wagon train or having rain smac you like a switch. Last night when Charles couldent fall asleep he asked me about his brother James and I cried and he put his arm around my shoulder. I held him tight-ly. He is such a wonderful boy, always helping with tasks that are too big for him but he tries to show me he can do them, to be my helper. I slept with my children beside me this last night and it was the best I have slept in many weeks.
>
> The other evening two nights back a pipe of wine was opened and most of the men got drunk. It was a sorry spetakle. No work was done the following day. They chased many of the women around and for aught I know some let

thems be caught in the snare. One man chased down his elbow relations. John came home stinking of some sour drink and was grabbing at me. He was weak with liquor so I pushed him out of the wagon and he fell hard to the ground. I was a bit scared that this time I killed him but not entirely so. He did not move for a long time but later woke and was in the bushes bent over moaning. This is the second time fer him to act this way on our jurnee.

Today is beautiful sunny but no travelin made the day long as any storm day. I packed up a sack of food and while John slept in the wagon under cover from the sun the children and I walked for a ways and had a pic nic. They chased butter flies and picked wild flowers and brought them to me. We picked sweet unyons which grow by the creek. I will use them for soup. Charles brung me some pretty stones and said he wanted to start a holiday called Igneous Rock Day and celebrat by having a pic nic with his mother. Today is August #1. I declared the day to be Igneous Rock Day from here on. I did not tell John. It is a secret 'tween my children and me.

There is a real smart man here from Ireland named Thomas Ward. He, along with his young wife, Annemarie, are travelin as far west as they can to teach school children. When there has been a delay, he gathers the children around a fire and tells them stories about our country, the Revolution War, the 1812 War, the bible and what the Constitwoshun means. The children sit with no attension going elses where. His voice, the wonderful accent, captures them. I have sat in and listened when I had time. He is like a magician with unexpected stories and tales. He also makes jokes with words and plays games with the children. I mention this because I had to ask him how to spell Igneous. It is not a word I know. Charles looks to Mr Ward for worldlee nowledge. I can see it in his eyes. He gave Charles a book to read to borrow for a spell. John is jealous because Mr Ward is smart and I can read. I read aloud some of his book to my children.

The other day, Preacher Towns came into the salon looking scrawny. He has cancer. It's bad, but he's fighting it. I couldn't help thinking about the last haircut I'll be giving him. He was upbeat about the prognosis. We had a wonderful conversation about life, God, and faith, and I felt so much better about everything, just like when I actually attended church, but then he paid without leaving a tip. I did a wonderful job and was rewarded with zilch. What a cheap old fart. I cannot pull myself up to lift a finger toward getting to church or giving a damn. I am a sinner. I am a misfit.

I am definitely joining Margaret's church to have my baby baptized.

Jonathan made a special vow to be David's friend.
—I Samuel 18:3

I have now cut more than fifty dead people's hair. It's not a bad gig because Mr. Fox pays cash, which I don't report. I pay enough taxes already. There's something comforting in the work I do at the funeral home, as if I'm the last person tending to the needs of those who cannot help themselves. I feel good about myself. It's a warm feeling inside for doing something that maybe no one else can do to help the body move into the spirit world, as if I'm closer to God because from my hand to His, the dead are handed off. I'm hopeful these men and women are there with me at the funeral home, watching in spirit, as I honor them with excellence, and talk and sing to them. I think if their spirits spoke, I would not be startled. I have hope for the spirit. Is it Heaven? Is God there? If they spoke, it would answer my question about the future. I could then tell everyone my story, even go on the *Today Show* with this revelation.

It's been six weeks now since Hawkshaw Bales was murdered. We are well into the new year. Tomorrow is Groundhog Day.

§

Melanie Walters lived in Columbia, South Carolina, which is why it took some effort for Margaret to coordinate a get-together between Melanie and Hannah. Because Melanie was already scheduled to be in Atlanta on Thursday, February 13th, they met that afternoon at the Alibi Café across from Emory University: Hannah, Margaret, Melanie Walters, and one of her sons, Marshall Walters. They greeted Melanie and her son inside but then sat outside in the sun, because even though there was a slight chill in the air, it wasn't too bad in the direct sunlight. There was no wind either, so it was a pleasant day.

"It was a shock hearing from you, Margaret," Melanie said. "Not a day goes by that I don't think about Darnell. See, Marshall's his son!" She pointed to him. "I had him in 1982."

Hannah and Margaret looked at him, both focusing to see the resemblance, which was apparent except that Marshall had skin darker than Darnell's. He had Darnell's smile and nose.

"Hannah, your father has denied it all these years. I took him to court for support and won, but he told me he'd never work a day in his life if it meant paying me any money. He was compelled by the court to pay child support until Marshall was twenty-one, but he never paid a cent. Not one penny."

Melanie explained how Darnell claimed he couldn't work because of a war injury, which the judge accepted at face value.

"He wasn't injured. It was all a lie. He gets money from the government, but the judge said I can't touch that. I had a judgment that I renewed every seven years, but I let it lapse after a while. I tried garnishing his wages, but he never had a job."

She continued to describe how she worked in several free clinics helping poor people, which did not pay much, but for several years, it was the one job she could land, until she was offered a good job at the Army Health Clinic. Even though it was third shift, it was a good job.

"After a few years, I got on with Dr. Larson."

"How do you know my daddy's Marshall's father?"

"Just look at him. They look alike, don't they?"

"I think so," Margaret said.

She's right, Hannah thought, *except Marshall's Black.*

Hannah saw how a man could be fooled by Melanie's light skin into thinking she was white, or at least not Black. She looked like she'd been on vacation at the beach for a few weeks. Hannah also thought Melanie was pretty and carried herself with an air of dignity and confidence. Her nose was thin, and her eyes were dark brown almonds, big and round, like a China doll. Her hair, although Hannah didn't know what it looked like years ago, was straight, almost like Mary Tyler Moore's but with a lot of gray streaking throughout. Hannah wanted to tell Melanie she could knock it out with a dye job. Hannah also noticed that Melanie had full, puffy lips. Marshall, on the other hand, had Darnell's high cheekbones and was about the same size and build. His head was shaped like her father's, with a receding hairline in the front beginning to appear.

"Did you ever visit my daddy?" Hannah asked.

"In court. Right here, down the street in DeKalb County. Other than that, I never saw him," Melanie replied.

"Wait, why here?" Margaret questioned.

"I tried suing him in all three courts in the Tri-County area, but the judge tossed it out each time because there was no proof Darnell was living in Sundown, Hebron, or Antioch. Well, I knew he was. I hired an investigator to track him down and get proof of where he was living. He found proof that Darnell lived in DeKalb County, with Mavis Sterns, who was his cousin or aunt or something."

Melanie told the women that things are different now in the courts. Women have more rights, and the judges give them credence with their claims, but back in the day, she fought an uphill battle, even after serving Darnell with papers and proving in court that he was living in the county.

"The investigator swore in court to the evidence, but the judge was not sympathetic toward me. He allowed for the lawsuit to proceed, and I won, but there was no blood in that stone. I did your father wrong back then, I know it, but we could've made it work. He never forgave me. When Marshall was eight, I married Conley Carlisle, had another boy and a girl, and Conley adopted Marshall."

"Marshall, have you ever met my father?"

"Nope," he said. "I keep thinking I ought to, but in truth, Conley's my father. I've known him since I was three, and he's always been in my life. Darnell Gardner was just the donor. I don't hold a grudge, but a man needs to step up and meet his obligations, his responsibilities. My mother did. Conley did. I have. I have a wife and a little girl, and somehow it all works out. I go to all her school affairs. I never miss them. Conley did the same when I was younger. Even before he was my legal parent, I told all the kids he was my father. He went to my baseball games, my Scout meetings, my school productions, everything. He was there, and he was my father. That's hard to understand or even appreciate when you're a child, but now that I have a daughter, I see the importance of it."

"I guess that makes us brother and sister, doesn't it?"

"It does," Melanie said.

Marshall smiled at the idea and fist-bumped Hannah.

Everyone talked for more than an hour about both families, drank several cups of coffee, ate bagels, and got to know each other, but when Melanie began to explain the past forty years she said, "I lived through so much, without Darnell, without his child support, without any reassurance of his love, and I somehow survived. The past is what it is, dead and buried. If you dig it up, it stinks. We got divorced. Annulled, technically. The judge ruled in my favor, but there was no enforcement of the order. So, I did what I had to do—I moved on. Life did not turn out as I'd dreamed, but it still turned out good. If your father and I had stayed married, I wouldn't have my other children, and now my three grandchildren. My daughter has two boys. Would I change any of it? Absolutely not. Knowing what I have now, how could I? I came here today to see the daughter of the man I loved years ago, not to see him, not to ask for money, not to yell at him, not to rant to you, but to see the daughter of the man I once loved, to see if his daughter is as wonderful as my children and grandchildren are. I so much want his life to have turned out beautiful and happy."

Knowing the story, Hannah looked at Margaret.

"What?" Melanie asked. "Is he doing okay?"

They didn't say anything, but turned toward each other, and then Melanie asked again, prodding for an answer. Feeling compelled, Hannah told her all about her father. Melanie shook her head in disbelief, saddened things had not turned out better for Darnell. Melanie teared up, and then Marshall hugged her and handed her a napkin.

"Things should have been better, but my daddy never lifted a finger," Hannah confessed. "He has some sort of rage in his heart."

Melanie went on about what Darnell was like in the early days, a description Hannah seldom saw in her life, save for when danger reared itself and they were in the storm cellar, or sometimes late at night on the front porch when he played his guitar.

"I hope I've helped you," Melanie said, "to move on with your life. From what Margaret has told me, you're having trouble moving forward."

"Kind of," Hannah said as she sipped her decaf tea. "I'm stuck between wanting to have a different life and being on the old farm, connected with my family and trying to hold it all together. Margaret and I have talked about it a lot."

Melanie reached over and grabbed Hannah's hand and then Margaret's hand and squeezed them, reassuring her that the world is a wonderful place with all sorts of opportunities, and they both need to move on to what will be best for them in their lives.

"I'm sorry, but I figured you'd be resentful for the way he treated you," Hannah said.

Margaret nodded her head, thinking the same thing.

"I was filled with rage. For years I wanted to shoot him, but where does that get you? I conquered my rage by jogging, burning it off. Many years ago, I used to drive to Birmingham a lot, and I'd go out of my way to drive by Darnell's farmhouse, but I never stopped. Once, about two in the morning, I pulled into the driveway and stopped my car, but I turned around."

"I've always wondered what he was like when he was young, before my momma knew him."

"He was funny. He could make a joke out of anything. The first time I met him was at The Steak House when I was a hostess. He shoved two cigars up under his upper lip like walrus tusks, and he tried talking to me about the cuts of beef we served and if there was much blubber on them. He said he liked blubber but couldn't find a big fatty cut to his liking."

Margaret watched Melanie, admiring her relaxed, confident demeanor, and how she could not tell Hannah about her father without laughing and getting silly, her eyes lighting up, which is what Margaret liked about Hannah, how silly and funny she could be about most anything.

"I'll tell you what's funny," Marshall said, "the story about the racist who married a Black woman without knowing it."

Melanie just laughed then said, "Marshall, that's not nice. You promised."

"It's true," he interrupted.

Melanie shook her finger at Marshall because he had agreed not to get ugly.

"After our marriage was annulled, your father went off to Germany, but before that, he lived in Texas for a few months training soldiers at Lackland. I'm from Yemassee, South Carolina and all my family is as black as wet walnuts, everyone except me. My momma said I was darker when I was born but that my skin lightened up. My father used to say my daddy was the postman. Look at me, my skin is light, almost as if I'd been in the sun for a few days. Where'd that come from? Who knows? It is what it is. Maybe it's a gene in the family history, and somewhere along the line, there was a white father. No one knows. All I can tell you, Hannah, is that your daddy fell in love with me, but because my family was Black, it never worked out."

"What happened?" Hannah asked. "That's something no one in my family knows, not even my momma."

"Honestly, all I know is that people change. The man I sued in court wasn't the same man I fell in love with. There was a lot of indignation in him that wasn't there before. But that's too simple of an explanation. You'll have to ask him."

They had more coffee and pastries and continued talking about Melanie's life with Darnell, for the six months they were married. Then, she asked, "What's your story, Margaret? How do you fit in this picture?"

"We're roommates. I have a house in Sundown, and Hannah rents from me. I'm a librarian. I haven't been promoted yet to assistant librarian even though I have all the responsibilities for that job and a master's degree."

That was the story, but Hannah knew it was a half-truth. Without reason that she understood, Hannah felt like a liar and was disappointed in herself because Melanie had been so forthright.

"That's not quite accurate," Hannah confessed.

Because of the seriousness of Hannah's voice, Melanie and Marshall turned their attention toward her and studied her face. Margaret looked at her as if she couldn't believe what she knew was coming. She looked at Margaret and then to Melanie and Marshall. And then Hannah said it.

"We're together."

"A couple?" Marshall asked.

Hannah looked at Margaret, and tears began to run down her face. Margaret scooted her chair closer to Hannah and hugged her.

"We haven't told anyone," Margaret said.

"You haven't come out?" Melanie asked.

"Ha! This is going to be great," Marshall laughed.

"Stop that, Marshall," Melanie quipped at him, "this is serious business."

Marshall was laughing and smiling. His mother reached over to pinch him on the leg. He scooted away from the table and almost fell over onto the sidewalk, while in the background, a cement truck roared by and turned onto the Emory campus.

"I gotta write a novel 'bout that," Marshall said.

Melanie glared at him as she reached across the table to grab Hannah's hands, cupping them in support. She ran her fingers over Hannah's hand.

"Never mind him, Sweetie. We're the first people you've told?"

Hannah nodded. Margaret said, "Yes."

"We haven't said a word to anyone. In fact, I write in my journal almost every day and I have never even hinted about this because if it ever gets in the wrong hands, Lord knows what trouble that could cause. It happened by accident."

"Your old man's going to have a conniption fit," Marshall said.

"Marshall, shut up!" Melanie yelled at him.

Chapter 24

This Bird Has Flown

"You never told Momma or Poppa Raymond or Memaw about Melanie Carlisle," Hannah yelled at her father. She leaned against his kitchen counter and waited for him to admit he was married.

"Who the hell is Melanie Carlisle?" her father asked.

"Melanie Walters."

"Oh. What do you want me to say? That was a long time ago, an entire lifetime, so long ago, it's not even part of the past."

"No one knows you have a Black son, by a Black woman who looks white. Aunt Mavis told me all of this. She was right."

"She was crazy."

"She said you killed Foster Williams."

"I didn't kill him. He was my best friend."

"Don't you see the problem, Daddy? You fell in love with Melanie despite her race. You hated her once you found out her family was Black."

"First off, you don't know anything. You don't know the whole story, Hannah. I thought she was a white girl. She looked white. She never said otherwise. She was a deceiver, like Satan. You oughta stop snooping around in other people's lives."

"Daddy, you were wrong not supporting them."

"Look'ere, you and me are a lot alike," he tried convincing her.

"No, we're not, Daddy. You have been wrong about so many things for so long, and you just don't understand that I'm not like that. I have my life now, and I want it all to change for the better so my children can grow up in a loving and peaceful world. My baby's going to college. I'm going back to college."

When her father stepped away from the kitchen sink and toward her, she thought he was going to smack her across the face, but she was ready. She would toss her glass of water at him and run out the door or hit him in the forehead with the glass. She asked how he could be so cruel to Melanie, but also cruel to his family by refusing to work so he wouldn't have to pay child support.

"We had nothing while I was growing up. Hardly food or clothes."

"I did the best I could."

"At keeping secrets."

"If it hadn't worked out as it did, you wouldn't ever been born!" he yelled. "You ever think of that?"

"You acted this way so no one would know you had a Black son."

His rebuttal fell on Hannah's deaf ears as he tried convincing her not to say a word about this to anyone. When Hannah wouldn't agree, Darnell yelled at her again for digging up his past.

"Let the departed stay buried," he said. "Concentrate on the good things with our family."

"What, like Christmas in the eighth grade? Do you remember that? Momma bought you a new television, and you were drinking, then you got into an argument, and you threw a beer bottle through the screen of your new color TV. Then Momma ran outside, and you chased her down the road to Mr. Sanders' front yard and beat her with your belt. That was a wonderful Christmas for everyone. We stood in his front yard crying while Mr. Sanders and his family watched you smack Momma until the police arrested you."

"Those charges were dropped. It doesn't count."

"The memory counts," she reminded him.

"I don't have to listen to this!"

"You don't have to like it, but it's the truth. The past always is the truth, no matter how you remember it."

"This ain't my Judgment Day," he yelled.

"You've forgotten how you behaved. Well, now there's no one here for you to yell at or beat with an axe handle. You're all alone in this house."

"Your mother's coming back, just wait and see."

"Momma's never coming back. Don't you realize that? Neither is Wendell or Greta. Neither am I."

That stopped the conversation dead cold. For several minutes the two of them sat at the table in silence. Hannah stared off toward the rose-colored wallpaper with small paisleys, and Darnell stared at the thin gold circle designs on the kitchen table.

"I was good to your mother," he said.

Although she wanted to scream at her father, Hannah did not, but said, "She should have pressed charges when you smacked her around. How about the number of times you were drunk and passed out on the floor? How about when you smacked me on the back of the legs with a golf club? Why'd you do that, Daddy? All I wanted to do was be with you, and you didn't want me talking while you hit some stupid little ball from the front yard into the pond. Remember when we went on vacation to Gulf Breeze, and we weren't there two days before you and Momma were fighting, and then you beat up Wendell because he tried to stop you from hitting Momma? We got kicked out of the hotel and had to come home. That's what I remember. I will not tolerate this in my life from anyone."

"You don't know the all of it," he told her.

When all at once, there in their synagogue, a man
under the power of a foul spirit screamed
out.—Mark 1:23

On the drive back to the house, Hannah received a telephone call from Mr. Fox at the funeral home, saying he had two people who needed haircuts this evening.

"I got one feller here who's being flown to Baton Rouge tomorrow afternoon. He needs a haircut before they transport him to

Hartsfield Airport for the flight."

Hannah did not know they would fly a body home in a casket, but then she thought, *Why not, you have to get home somehow.*

The other haircut was for a woman whose funeral was in three days, but the family was having a viewing tomorrow night. Hannah told Mr. Fox she would be right over.

Instead of going home to change her clothes, Hannah drove to the funeral home, figuring a quiet atmosphere and a cup of Earl Gray tea would calm her down after her father's antagonistic disposition. Mr. Fox was in a talkative mood with Hannah, making suggestions to her about all sorts of things in life, and regaling her with stories of his mistakes and how to avoid doing what he did wrong in his life.

Before she began working, she made her tea and turned on the television in the back room where she cut everyone's hair, turning the dial to easy listening on Music Choice, which always soothed her, and she enjoyed the variations of popular music by conductors and arrangers because she could sing along or hum. Every night when Hannah cut a dead person's hair, it seemed a song played that was not appropriate for the occasion, as it was with "Tonight's the Night," which Hannah found funny singing to a dead woman, as well as "Do You Know the Way to San Jose."

"You're not going there anytime soon," she sang, then laughed.

Hannah finished the haircut on the woman and then gave her a quick manicure and polish, nothing extravagant, just a quick once-over with a nail file and light pink polish so her nails were not dark underneath.

"That's caused by a fungus under the nails," Mr. Fox had told her.

She buffed the woman's nails to add shine. When Hannah rolled the gurney from the cold storage bin and pulled the sheet back, she stood dumbfounded. Who she stared at paralyzed her. She didn't want to touch the body or the gurney, or breathe the same air, frightened the man would sit up and speak to her or rape her again.

She took several steps backwards, away from Hawkshaw Bales, and sat down in a chair. She wanted to run out of the funeral home and keep running down the road until she was in Colorado. Hannah immediately rifled through Bales' file sitting on Mr. Fox's prep table. Bales had been at the county morgue since December 29th, the day he was murdered. The county coroner had conducted an autopsy, but then the body remained at the coroner's, unclaimed.

Mr. Fox had driven over to the coroner's office in Decatur this morning to pick up Bales' body. To Hannah, Bales was gone, out of her life, and if he had stayed on his side of town, it would have all been the same to her.

"Mr. Fox, this is Hannah," she said calling his phone. "I've got Hawkshaw Bales right here. Am I supposed to give him a haircut?"

"Yes. His family's been slow as molasses about shipping him back home to Baton Rouge 'cause no one wanted to pay the cost, but someone came through with the money."

She asked if it was okay to keep a body that long. He laughed and told her not to worry about it.

"I can keep him on ice forever."

She could not believe this was happening. She stood on the other side of the room in the corner as far away from Bales as possible, talking to Mr. Fox on the phone and staring at the father of her baby. She sat in a chair then stood up, looked at Bales, and sat back down. She shook with fear.

"Hannah, do you want me to come back up there?"

"No, sir. I'm fine."

"Why don't you stop what you're doing and go out to dinner with me and my family? We're going to the Triangle. Join us. I'll take care of Mr. Bales tomorrow."

"Thanks, but I'm fine. Really, I am. I've got this."

Being in the same room with Bales frightened Hannah. She wanted a gun in the event a body might rise up and chase her around the building and into the parking lot and down the street like in *The Walking Dead*. She knew Bales was the kind of dead person who would do that, if just out of spite. She wondered, if tomorrow was Groundhog Day, could Hawkshaw Bales crawl out of his cave trying to find his shadow, ring her doorbell, and pull on the door handle. She didn't want to wake up like Bill Murray, morning after morning, experiencing the same nightmare.

For more than an hour, Hannah sat across the room from Bales until Margaret called to see what time she was coming home. Hannah told her about the situation. Margaret wanted to come over and see his body, but Hannah wouldn't allow it.

"I'm gonna cut off his balls and shove'em down his throat," she told Hannah, laughing but still quite serious.

"That's what I'm afraid of."

Hannah put on a new pair of latex gloves and stood over Bales' body with her electric clippers. She knew she had to cut his hair because he wasn't going away. In the background, "Do That to Me One More Time" played with violins and piano. Hannah turned off the music. She wanted complete silence to hear any creak or flutter of a feather hitting the floor. If there was any strange noise, she had mapped out an escape route to her car.

It was her job, and she knew this would be the last time she would ever have to deal with Hawkshaw Bales and all the pain he caused in her life. She stepped back and said a prayer, and much like Margaret forgiving her father for raping her and knowing he was in Hell, Hannah tried as best she could to do the same thing; however, she kept returning to the idea of revenge and wanting to do something to hurt Bales. But there was nothing she could do to physically harm him, although many ideas came to mind. That's when it dawned on her: *Honor Him with excellence*. She knew God would find a way to dole out a just punishment for Bales, but for Hannah, by giving Bales the finest haircut she could, she was honoring God and herself, while also showing Bales that she was stronger than him. She was not honoring Bales. She was honoring herself and God by being the best stylist she could.

All God asks is that I honor Him with excellence, she thought. *I can forgive sin, but I cannot forgive evil.*

So, whether you eat or drink, or whatever you do, do all to the glory of God.—I Corinthians 10:31

She did not sing. She did not talk to him. She was curt and stood over him doing her work. He was just a faceless, lifeless, soulless man who needed one last haircut as well as a shave. She did not like shaving men, but she did it on a regular basis. But this time, she kept imagining Celie in *The Color Purple* ready to cut Mister's throat until Shug Avery stopped her.

But at last my people will confess their sins and the sins of their ancestors for betraying me.... Leviticus 26:40

I've decided to tell my momma this weekend. Then Daddy. I want to marry Margaret. But I got something else to discuss with my momma, and even if we don't discuss it, I will let her know what's on my mind.

I cannot imagine what it was like for men and women twenty or thirty years ago, or longer, when they were in love and could not express themselves without fear for what might happen. I feel that now. I guess the world is more understanding than during the days of Stonewall, which I did not know about until Margaret explained it. I feel caged in by how others may judge us. Maybe she and I need to move away from Sundown to a place where we're strangers and can be who we need to be. Just M, me, and the baby.

Margaret and I sleep together but we have never had sex. Our bodies touch because in bed we hold each other and we have taken many showers and baths together, yet we still have not had sex. We have decided to wait until we are married in Memphis. And, once the baby's born, we'd like to begin a relationship that's healthy. It sounds silly to think about that when I write it and read my words, but we are trying to re-establish our virginity and present it to one another as a gift. This may not work for some people, people who think we are immoral or whatever they think (that's their problem). We are charting out the future, carefully planning how we wish to love each other, which is no one's business but ours.

The other day we sat down and decided on names. If it's a girl, Jessica Michelle. If it's a boy, Theodore Austin.

I hope things are different when people read my *Document of Life* in one hundred years. The world is much different than Sarah's world, so I have hope for women.

Late this afternoon, I called Antioch Bank to ask how to rent a safe deposit box for the next one hundred years. They hung up on me. I wanted to know how much it'll cost and if I have to pay it all at once or monthly. I called Wells Fargo and was told I could rent a safe deposit box, annual or semi-annual, and renew it annually. The customer service lady did not know how I could go about securing a box for one hundred years after I'm dead, but suggested I get the safe deposit box first then state in my will that I want my box paid for after I'm dead. I thought that was a good idea.

What did Sarah do with her accumulation of pages after she ended her journey? Did she hide it under the house in a wooden box wrapped in buffalo hide?

Christmas: We've been living in Salt Lake City since arrivin a few weeks b'fore the end of summer after a stop in Denver for a spell then Fort Collins but John did not like either. He's talking about the rewards of San Francisco. John found a cabin un lived in so we took it for the fall and now into winter. Three days later snow fell like a blanket of sifted flour over the trees fence posts railings paths. The children played for a few hours in the snow until tired. A dog not belongin to us showed up and run around. I brung him inside to be warm. The children fed him a biskit piece by piece and he did tricks for them so's I know he belonged to a person who taught him those things. When John came home he yelled that a dog is another mouth to feed. He tossed him outside. The snow was beautiful but the next day it was froze up so if you fell it might break a bone. When Caroline stepped on to the porch to toss the pot she found the little dog curled up like a stone. The children may never forgive John. Charles and Antom brave the chill and dug a hole barlee deep enough to bury him. It was the best they could manage.

Thank the Lord we are going no wheres 'til spring. Maybe by then John will have found work. We are in a big valley sirrounded by mountins. Although I wear extra socks my feet are always cold. John says we will leave for San Francisco at the first sight of a snow melt. I do not respond. I have never been so cold and we have little fire wood for heat. The children walk in the fields and woods looking for stiks to burn. We try to keep a low fire all the time. The walls are thin and a draft brushes across the floor like someone is tick'ling my ankles with ice. When we can we make mud to fill the cracks. This helps limit the draft.

We have no money and I have taken in the laundree which burns with cold this time of year. I cannot get a new cast iron pot or fire wood even but John can drink when the notion sirrounds him. He has been with another woman. He goes into town now and does not come back for days and when he does he smells like her. He says he is off lookin for work or huntin but no deer ever smelled this nice. I won't let him touch me. The laundree earns not much more than a few pennys each week. I work hard to keep John happy. I teach the children what I know about reading and addin up figurs. I'm better than John at both, but he's a man and a man has advantages.

John found my diary and tore some pages from it and burned them. I begged him not to throw it in the fire. He threw it and hit me in the face scrapin my cheek bone under my right eye. Some of the pages scattered out. He slammed the door then his horse clumped away. The children were without words as I knelt on the floor ruflin the pages together. Charles rescued my diary from the fire but a few pages were burned complete. Charles helped me gather the pages then Caroline and Antom sat at the table with me and placed the pages together not in any order. I am going to hide my diary in the rafters until it is safe to write about life here or in San Francisco where ever we are in the spring or by summer.

That is how Sarah's diary ended. What else can I do except speculate about the rest of her life? We don't know her name, when she died, or where she lived afterward. Margaret and I have a plan to travel to Salt Lake City to research anyone named Antom from back in those days since it's the least common of the names in Sarah's family. Maybe this'll lead us to Sarah and what happened. Margaret also suggested traveling to Meadville, to check the birth records for any Antom born in a ten-year period, from 1840 through 1850. Margaret said we could research the churches during that time, checking records for any marriage for a man named John who got married. Without her real name, I cannot even search for her in Meadville. M said during that time, there were about 1,300 people living in Meadville, maybe more if she included the folks living in the county. Still, it isn't many.

I was thinking the other day, maybe Sarah and John and the children left one day, and she forgot her diary in the rafters or maybe John came home that night and beat her to death, and no one found the diary for one hundred and fifty years. I hope she had a good life, and her children grew up to make her proud. Maybe, even if she was old, she was able to ride the train back to Meadville, to her old life, to see her momma's grave and her sister, Susan. Maybe when she arrived, the town had a coming home party for her or a parade. I pray she had closure and a good life.

All this time I have been calling her Sarah, and I hope that's her real name, but it's unlikely. I love that name. It's what my momma whispered into my ear when my baby sister was born long ago when I was six years old. I have been scared all my life, but I remember every detail in the kitchen, but not much in the woods.

Margaret and I have decided that from now on, we will celebrate August 1st as Igneous Rock Day, and have a picnic somewhere, and enjoy our life together, and celebrate Sarah, whoever she was. Also, and most importantly, March 2nd is the day we've chosen to get married.

Margaret and I are going away together, traveling in M's car to Memphis, for a few days to visit her friends from college and get married there. We are leaving after work on Wednesday, March 1st. We'll already be packed and in the car by eight o'clock. We will have Thursday and Friday off from work, and we will drive back on Sunday, March 5th, returning to work on the 6th, married and happy. We are getting married Thursday evening at Lafayette's Music Room. Margaret's college friend lives near there with her husband and their young children. They teach at Memphis State University. Margaret wants to visit Graceland, Beale Street, and Stax Records.

People who cover their sins will not
prosper....—Proverbs 28:13

§

It's Sunday afternoon and I'm on the back porch with Margaret's MacBook, typing everything you're reading right here. It is 56 degrees outside, but there's no wind, so it's comfortable in the sun. I'm drinking a cup of coffee M made for me. She's reading the newspaper, doing the Sudoku, and sitting across from me. We are wrapped up in blankets, but it feels nice outside. From this vantage point, we cannot see our neighbors, and they cannot see us. I can see our backyard, the creek, and the line of trees into the wetland area. I feel as if the rest of the world does not exist.

I told M that I had an idea but wasn't sure if I could do it without getting arrested. In the spring when it warms up, I want to go back to the farm and sleep all night on the big rock, in a pile of sleeping bags and blankets. I want to be under the stars one last time. M liked the idea.

This is how we have decided to live our lives. I called Momma earlier yesterday and woke her up at eleven o'clock.

"Momma, I'm getting married."

"Sweetheart, you're not even dating anyone. Who's the boy? Do I know his parents?"

"No, Momma, I'm going to marry Margaret."

"Who the hell's Margaret?"

"You know, we've been living together for several months."

"The Black girl?"

"Yes, Momma."

"There's something wrong with that girl," she said. "You just hold on. Me and your daddy'll be over there to straighten everything out for you. You can't marry no Black girl."

"Momma, I'm getting married to Margaret, and you can't stop me."

Click. The phone slammed down in my ear. I did not have an opportunity to discuss Sarah, her baby girl. Maybe it was for the better. I know the truth—but that does not mean I need to air out our dirty laundry. It's momma's secret, and as I have my own, I will allow her secret to remain buried. If some day it bubbles to the surface, so be it. Not on my watch. I've given myself over to what the future has in store.

I called Daddy two minutes later. He did not get angry with me, which was a surprise.

"That's fine, Darling," Daddy said. "You got to live the life God dealt to you. I'll tell Lucas but don't go expecting any of us to show up for the wedding."

I told my daddy that I loved him, then said good-bye and hung up. Without hesitation, I blocked the phone numbers for everyone in my family.

And that was that.

Chapter 25

Unexpected Angels

On March 1st, in Baton Rouge, Dave Edwards sat in a beige wicker chair on the porch of an old white clapboard house. Across from him sat Dottie Bales, the mother of Hawkshaw Bales. Edwards had introduced himself as Rick Forbes, an attorney from New Orleans who was visiting on the behalf of his client, Hannah Gardner. He had business cards and looked like an established southern attorney in his seersucker suit, blue bowtie, a pair of Tom Ford Austin Oxford shoes he bought at Neiman Marcus, a Buccio Bergamo leather briefcase, and a Versace Sport Tech Chronograph watch. He looked every bit the part of the successful southern lawyer, including the rented Jaguar XJ that was as deep blue as the ocean.

Edwards looked around at the comfortable house. It was clean and orderly, white with black shutters. The porch wrapped around to one side with a small set of stairs leading to a gravel driveway. As with the other houses in the neighborhood, none of the property lots were large enough for a garage on either side, as this neighborhood was built years before the advent of cars. The houses were divided by a strip of land, sixteen feet wide, which between the 1920s and the 1940s, became a narrow driveway for every house. If a person had a garage, it was small and built years ago in the backyard, large enough for one car. It was not a big house—two bedrooms, one bath, but it was clean and nice.

Edwards had parked his rented Jaguar on the street.

Every morning, Dottie Bales swept the leaves and dusted off the porch before sitting down to read the newspaper and have her coffee. After a few months of grieving for her son, the pain had not subsided, and she had failed to find any pleasure in most anything she did. She always knew something like this would happen to Hawkshaw. He was a man with a desire that made him fight hard to lift himself up from the life she struggled to provide. She realized he had to be tough to succeed, but with toughness comes an opposite force.

Dave Edwards heard *The Price Is Right* emanating from inside the house, along with several children playing and giggling. They were her grandchildren from her two daughters.

Dottie asked Edwards if he would like a sweet tea or water, but he declined.

"No, ma'am. Ms. Bales, as I mentioned, I represent Hannah Gardner, who is pregnant. Reportedly, your son, Hawkshaw, is the father."

"I know that, and I know he wanted his child to live with me and all these gran'chil'en. He was plannin' on movin' back here to be a father."

"Yes, ma'am, be that as it may, I don't believe that was going to happen because settling down wasn't in his nature, and he had too many interests in Atlanta. There are two issues I would like to discuss. One is your son's estate. You're the beneficiary of everything he owned. Did you know that?"

"He told me once."

"As such, any person who is a blood relative can place a claim against those assets, such as his unborn child. Hannah Gardner has the right to sue your son's estate for as much of its value as she feels necessary to raise her child, just as Mr. Bales was trying to sue her to claim his paternity. The child's interest supersedes your rights to a claim of any of his wealth."

"Mr. Forbes, she wants my money?"

"Yes, ma'am, but not entirely. What Ms. Gardner would like is to allow you to keep all the money and assets your son has in his estate, including this house, but in return, you must waive all claims to her unborn child now and forever."

"What on earth do I want with her child? I got five I'm taking care of now. One mother's in prison and the other ran off to God-knows-where with some fella from Fort Worth."

"Your son, before his murder, was trying to take her baby away. I'm here to guarantee that does not happen and that you do not want or try to request any rights to see her child. In exchange, you keep your son's entire estate. You get to keep everything. Ms. Gardner will not lay claim to any of it. If not, she plans to sue the estate and take everything, all in the name of the child, who, by law, is the rightful heir. The fact that your son was attempting to prove his paternity should indicate a legal right for the child to inherit everything, including this house, which is in your son's name. His estate owns it. There isn't a judge around, either here in Louisiana or in Georgia willing to rule in your favor over the child. Ms. Gardner's unborn child will be deemed the sole beneficiary of everything, and you will not receive a single penny. I'm not here to strong-arm you, but I guarantee the child will inherit everything."

"And leave me with nothing?" she asked.

"Yes, ma'am. The best thing for everyone involved would be to forget the child exists, to go on with your life, and use the money to help raise the children you have."

Edwards handed Mrs. Bales a six-page legal document detailing the agreement. Then, he explained that signing the document relinquishes her rights to the child. Edwards reiterated to her that Hannah understood that he was here on her behalf. However, what he did not tell Dottie Bales, was that everything he had told her was a lie.

"I am acting in her interests as a mediator to help resolve any issues, and to allow her to move forward with her life, but also to allow you the economic security your son wanted."

"I guess I'll need an attorney to look this over and explain it to me," she said to Edwards.

"No, ma'am. This is a one-time opportunity. You need to read it now, understand the document, and sign it. I'll be more than happy to explain something. If you sign it now, I'll have it notarized, and you'll receive all of your son's assets. If not, within the next seven business days, Ms. Gardner will proceed to lay claim against your son's estate in the name of her unborn child, including this house, which, as I said, is in your son's name."

"This house ain't in my name?"

"No, ma'am."

"I thought I owned it."

"Legally, your son owns it, which means it belongs to his estate. He bought it when you moved here from Stone Mountain. Ms. Gardner will win and take the house. The child is going to own everything. You won't get a penny, and you'll be on the street. I promise, if you give up your rights as a grandparent, it will benefit everyone involved. You will never see or hear from any of them. I promise you'll never see me again the rest of your life."

Dottie Bales read the first page then flipped through the documents, skimming along. She looked up at Dave Edwards. He held out his Meisterstück Le Petit pen. She reached for it as if she were reaching for a hat that blew off her head into a pond full of alligators.

"Isn't that a nice pen?" he said.

"It certainly is."

"When I made partner, that was a gift to myself. I paid one thousand dollars for that," he lied.

"A thousand dollars. For a pen?" she said looking at the craftsmanship of the gold, the fine etchings carved in the cap.

"Where do I sign?"

Edwards showed her. She signed her name with a slow, graceful artistic flow as her wrist moved up and down. Edwards placed the cap on the pen then handed it back to her.

"Ma'am, you keep it."

"I cannot keep this pen. It means a lot to you."

"Yes, it does, but it'll mean more if you keep it."

It looked like an authentic Meisterstück Le Petit pen, but it was a twenty-five dollar knock-off. Edwards pulled a handkerchief from his pocket and wiped the pen down, removing his fingerprints. He handed it to Mrs. Bales, and she reached out for it. He placed the documents in a manila folder, then into his briefcase, stood up, shook her hand, and walked away.

"Do I get a copy?"

"I'll have my secretary mail you a copy as soon as I return to my office."

"Mr. Forbes, my son wasn't a bad boy. He just had to fight hard for what he wanted."

Edwards wanted to tell her how horrible Hawkshaw Bales was, the number of lives he destroyed, but he refrained because he saw in her eyes the grief of outliving her child.

"I'm sorry about your loss, ma'am. My prayers are with you and your family."

Edwards knew this document would never see the light of day unless Dottie Bales tried suing Hannah Gardner for legitimization at some later date. Then, it would surface. Scared she would lose everything, he knew Dottie Bales would want nothing to do with Hannah's child and risk being kicked to the street. He placed his briefcase in the trunk of the Jaguar, next to a FN Scar 20S rifle with a Trijicon scope and was ready to enjoy the drive on the backroads and blue highways to New Orleans. He would return the Jaguar back to the rental agency then fly to Atlanta and return home to Sundown to see what else might be shaking.

§

Late at night, while Margaret and Hannah drove up Interstate 22 to Memphis in Margaret's Camry, the song "Girl Crush" blared from the speakers while the two women laughed and sang. A few minutes later, Janis Joplin sang, *"Oh Lord, won't you buy me a Mercedes-Benz? My friends all drive Porsches, I must make amends."*

"I love this song," Hannah said, "but truthfully, I don't want a Mercedes-Benz. I did at one time, but if God wants me to have one, he'll give me one."

"What if He gave you one?" Margaret asked.

"I suppose I'd drive it, but that's not what brings happiness. This right here, with you driving down the road to Memphis, singing songs on the radio, an' being free from all the rotten stuff in other people's lives that we're supposed to deal with. I don't need that. Most of all, knowing that God and Jesus love me makes me happy."

"You know what makes me happy?" Margaret asked.

"Neapolitan ice cream?"

"Very funny. Just 'cause I ate the entire quart the other night doesn't mean it makes me happy. In fact, it made me sick. What makes me happy is seeing you happy after all you've been through with Hawkshaw Bales. When I look out the windshield, I see all the lights way off in the distance. To me, that's God's steady light bringing us home."

Hannah fussed around in the glove compartment for a piece of paper and pen, as a few ideas came to her, an idea for a story even though she never thought about writing something made up. She remembered a short story from high school about a family that was shot and killed by a misfit man and how the grandmother was an irritating person. Hannah couldn't remember the title but thought how the family was out for a Sunday drive, kind of like she and Margaret. If they had only had a gun, she figured, they could have defended themselves.

Danger lurks everywhere, she thought. *It's in the cracks of a tea cup.*

In the tenth grade, she read a short story for Mrs. Brown's English class, "An Occurrence at Owl Creek Bridge," and just like the man about to be hung, she escaped the situation and ran back to the family farm only to be pulled out of the dream at the very second when her hand touched the doorknob. Hannah often felt this would happen to her and Margaret, that somewhere in the shadowy background of the world, someone was pulling the strings to yank her into all the horrible situations she had endured. When she told Margaret this, Margaret assured Hannah that they had a clean slate ahead of themselves and that she would not allow anyone to do that to her.

In the glove compartment, she found an envelope with Margaret's vehicle registration and a half-chewed pencil. She took the registration papers out, straightened a few creases, and placed them in the envelope and then into the vehicle service book. Then, she stared out the window at the vast terrain of land and thought how the world was comprised by how far a person elected to see. Sometimes the tree line held their eyes in check, and they couldn't see beyond the swaying limbs and glittering pine needles. For thirty minutes, Hannah and Margaret listened to an '80s station, as Hannah gazed out the window, unable to remember any Bible verse that was appropriate for her life right now, as if the entire slate had been wiped clean. Nothing came to her.

As Margaret's Camry passed a farm, she read aloud what was painted in whitewash on the side of a barn and illuminated with lights, "Will you enter the Kingdom of GOD?" It sparked a thought. Hannah pulled the registration envelope from the service book and jotted down a Bible verse in pencil:

> Don't you know that those who do wrong will have
> no share in the Kingdom of God?—I Corinthians 6:9

Hannah folded the envelope in half, and then in half again, turned it sideways, and slid it into the front pocket of her jacket. Looking out the window, there was no moon, only stars, and a sky so black, a person could run away and be lost in the white ruins of the world. She rolled down the window and stuck her head out, feeling the cold rush of air push her hair back and dry her lips to a shiver. She sucked the cold air in through her teeth. The ocean of air froze her ears, and the noise drowned out the stereo and Margaret singing "Open Arms."

I wonder if this is what Mary felt like when she and Joseph traipsed along with a donkey in search of a place of comfort?

Hannah looked up into the deep pitch of the sky at all the stars, steppingstones to the map of life, she thought, God's beacon for me—the light from billions of years ago guiding her travels as she ran off into the future. She was following the night flares to some new place she had not known existed. Where she was going could be anywhere, and she welcomed the mystery and adventure, because she knew she was not making the journey alone.

She scribbled on Margaret's registration papers: My Document of Life II

I have told you these things so that in Me you may have peace. You will have suffering in this world. Be courageous! I have conquered the world.—John 16:33